Mortals All

---

*Zach was just looking for a novel
one-night stand.*

*Mary was searching for her
place in the world.*

They found each other.

*In a future world, where the creation of artificial
humans has led to a caste of "non-people," the fight
for civil rights takes on new meaning.*

*A loner who's an expert on lust but a novice when
it comes to love, falls for a naive but beautiful
androne. He teaches her what it means to be
human, but can't give her what she really wants--
her freedom.*

Praise for *Mortals All*

*"Steeped in the ambience of classic 1950's Galaxy magazine...
social satire, irreverent anti-establishmentarianism, and pseudo-
hardboiled narration...Golden writes with zest and good pacing...
a certain flippancy of characterization and delivery..."*
Asimov's Science Fiction

*"A sexy, sometimes satirical take on a unique and forbidden
relationship...a wry look at the human condition in the tradition of
Heinlein and Asimov...science fiction with heart, and a book
destined to leave a lasting impression."*
Speculative Fiction Reader

Other Books by Bruce Golden

Better Than Chocolate
Evergreen
Dancing with the Velvet Lizard
Red Sky, Blue Moon *(upcoming)*

To Robert A. Heinlein for creating characters
I wanted to be and be with.
To Samuel L. Clemens for making me laugh
and making me think.
To Robert E. Howard for forging worlds of wonder
I wanted to run away to.
To James D. Morrison for the timbre and hue
of his images.

Mortals All 2nd Edition 2012

ISBN-13:
978-1481021012

ISBN-10:
148102101X

Shaman Press

Mortals All

Bruce Golden

1

ZACHARIAH STARR

I was just a writer of over-hyped, testosterone-driven space operas when she walked into my life. I should have known better. I should have paid attention to that tingling I always get along the nape of my neck when trouble's headed my way.

She was drop-dead gorgeous, a real riser. That should have been my first clue to stay clear. But women, especially beautiful ones, were like an itch I had to scratch. It didn't matter that I often ended up opening a vein and watching my heart bleed out onto the pavement. I had to have them.

I didn't let the fact that I wasn't graced with good looks stop me either. Hey, let's face it, I was downright homely. Not actually grotesque, I mean I didn't have a hump or anything. But the real finelines gave me a wide berth, unless they were selling and I could pay for it--which I did. You pay for it with most women one way or the other anyway. So it didn't really bother me--and it meant I got to spend the night with some of the most attractive, sexually gregarious women on the planet. Or at least my little corner of it.

The night she walked into my neighborhood hangsite I had long passed boredom and was working on comatose. So I started feeding my "what have you got to lose" attitude and looked to see where she was going to sit.

It was an establishment of some ill repute--never too crowded, and dimly lit so a guy could be anonymous if he so desired. You could get anything you wanted there--black-market booze from Mars, sex/death vids, mood enhancers, body parts, or a body of divine perfection. That's what she had. But she wasn't selling it. She had on this simple, dark green work outfit. Not the kind of thing you put on to advertise your wares. However, as a connoisseur of the feminine form, I saw right through the getup, so-to-speak.

She seemed to be looking for someone, someone in particular. When she failed to recognize anyone, she picked a table located in a strategic corner facing the door.

In less time than it takes to swallow your pride and spit it back out again, I pieced together my patchwork courage and made my way to her table. She was so busy watching the door, she didn't notice me coming. So I quickly wrote myself an opening line.

"Sister, you've got a chassis that would make any Detroit foreman proud."

Well, I didn't say I was a *good* writer.

Anyway, the look she gave me was as cold as titanium. However, I rebounded, and I think I caught her off guard.

"May I join you?"

"Join me?"

"Thanks, don't mind if I do."

I sat down before she could twitch. She gave me this puzzled look, then turned to check the door once more.

"I haven't seen you in here before have I?"

Oh yeah, I had the charm sputtering away on all cylinders.

"No. You have not."

"I didn't think so. I would have remembered a dish like you."

"A dish?"

"My name's Zachariah, Zachariah Starr. But you can call me Zach."

"If your name is Zachariah Starr, why should I call you Zach?" she asked, turning her attention from the door to me.

"Well, it's easier to remember."

"I have an excellent memory."

She was as stiff as a priest's collar. I was going to have to bring my A-game to bear if I was going to loosen this one up.

"My family name is Sturzinski. Starr is my pen name. I'm a writer." I always tried to ease that into the conversation. Some babes were actually impressed, but not this one.

"Why do you find it necessary to have so many names? Are they symbols of
your social stature?"

"No, I don't think any amount of monikers is going to help me there. Let's make it simple. I'd prefer it if you'd just call me Zach. Okay?"

"All right...Zach."

Then she turned again to watch the door, as if I wasn't even there. Now I don't mind getting the brush-off, but I refuse to be ignored.

"So, what's *your* name?"

"My name?"

"Yeah. The polite thing to do when someone introduces himself is to introduce *yourself*."

"Excuse me. I have not had any training in the social amenities."

I was beginning to think she wasn't all there. You know, like she wasn't totally online. She was a little slow to find the right words, like someone speaking a foreign language. Maybe that was it. Funny though, I didn't hear any kind of accent.

Then she turned her attention from the door and looked right at me. I was drawn into those incredible blue eyes of hers and, for the moment, I didn't care if she had an I.Q. of 80 or 800.

"My name is Mary."

I shook myself loose of her mesmerizing stare and held out my hand. "Nice to meet you, Mary."

She seemed unsure of what to do, but then took my hand. I gave her a gentle squeeze and let go. She withdrew her hand gingerly, as if analyzing a new sensation.

"So, where are you from, Mary. What do you do?" I didn't think she was a pro, she didn't have that smell. In fact she wasn't wearing any fragrance I could detect.

"What do I do?"

"Yeah. Are you a model, an actress?"

"I am a fully-trained domestic facilitator."

"You're a maid?"

"I also play the piano and related keyboard instruments."

"I get it. I had to work a lot of odd jobs until my writing started to pay. I was a pump jockey down at the space yards one rather lean summer. Where you working now?"

"I...I am not currently employed."

"Been there done that. Don't worry, a looker like you shouldn't have any trouble getting some kind of work. You can always waitress till something else comes along. The tips alone should keep you in sugar."

"Sugar?"

"You know, jolly joints, vids, vibromassage, whatever your personal poison is."

"Poison?"

"You don't get out much do you?"

"No. My previous...position did not allow me to go out much."

Now I've run into some strange babes in my time, but this one was beginning to creep me out just a little. There was something about her, something I couldn't quite put my finger on. I was that thinking maybe she had been born off-planet when I saw it.

She had turned to watch the door again, and several strands of her hair shifted out of place. When she ran her fingers through her hair to pull it back, I saw it. Every drone had one. Most had more than one. This particular implant was a tiny one, no bigger around than my thumb and conveniently hidden under her long, dark blonde tresses.

It made sense now. She was an androne, or to use the more socially-correct term, "artificial human." But she sure didn't look like she'd been grown in a breeding facility, even if they did use human genes as templates. They were just about everywhere nowadays, but I never paid them much attention. Supposedly, they were completely human, except of course for the cybernetic implants that enhanced them at the genetic level to give them better eyesight, stronger hearts, more efficient nervous systems, etcetera, etcetera.

Essentially, she was a clone, fitted with bionic implants that could be tapped into as a way of downloading information. Of course, that wasn't what I had been thinking of downloading myself.

"You've got a beautiful head of hair, if I may say so."

"Why do you ask permission when you have already made the statement?"

"I uhhh...I wasn't really asking permission. It's just a figure of speech."

"Yes, of course," she said as she turned her attention once more to the entrance. Staring at her, I found I could no longer think of her only as a body-to-die-for, a tempting receptacle for my lust. She was somehow more...and less. Let's say her being a dronette confused the issue. Lately, it seemed, just the mention of andrones would stir up trouble. Were they people or things? Was the continued production of drones morally right? Economically viable? Was it the best thing for society, or were andrones a growing danger?

Me? I could see both sides of most issues if I tried hard enough. Mostly, I didn't get involved in politics or issues of great philosophical debate. It was all I could do just to write a couple of cheap-thrill adventures and get myself in the fur every so often. Of course, if I had spent as much time writing as I did trying to get online with some fineline, I might have become more than a hack for hire.   Speaking of which, I had never done it with a dronette before. Not that it was unheard of, if you had the money. We're talking mega-credit here. Though it wasn't highly publicized, everyone knew about the pleasure drones the ultra-wealthy could buy. Flesh and blood playthings, genetically sterile like all drones, programmed to do any and everything you could imagine and then some.

Mary wasn't one of those, but with her looks she could have been hatched from the same tank.

"Can I buy you a drink?"

"No thank you. I am not in need of fluids at this time."

"You know, you'd better learn to speak the local drool. You won't be able to disguise the fact you're a drone if you keep talking like that."

That seemed to make her uneasy. She shifted her gaze from the door to me. "I *am* an androne. Why should I want to disguise it?"

"I don't know. You tell me. I guess it doesn't matter, if you're here on legitimate business. If you're just waiting for your steward to come through that door then you've got nothing to worry about. However, if you're a rogue, you'd better learn to blend in."

It hadn't occurred to me up until that moment that she might actually be on the run. I was playing with her, seeing what kind of reaction I could provoke. You know, trying to light a fire under her chilly disposition. But when she heard the word "rogue" I could sense all her systems going on alert. It was a subtle change in her manner, nothing overt. Still, I knew a cornered rabbit when I saw one. I'd been in that corner a few times myself.

"I assure you, there is no cause for alarm," she said after taking only a second to compose herself. I admired her self-control. I didn't know drones could lie so well. "Tell me," she continued, "if I were trying to 'blend in' as you say, what would you suggest?"

"Well, you certainly look the part. Not that a babe with a bod like yours could ever go unnoticed. But if you keep that implant on your scalp covered, no one could tell just by looking. However, your vocabulary needs some massaging, and you need to start using contractions."

"Contractions?"

"You know, like don't instead of do not, I'm instead of I am. Look, being as I'm a writer, this is kind of my field. I'd be glad to help you out. I'm sure, with my expertise, I could have you drooling like a gutter rat in no time."

"Drooling like a gutter rat?"

"That's slang. You know, street talk. See what I mean. You've got a lot to learn. Why don't you go back to my cradle with me? We'll crack open a bottle and begin your first lesson."

"Is the bottle a necessary teaching tool?"

"No, but it couldn't hurt."

"I do not believe you desire to improve my speech patterns. It is more likely you seek a...a sexual encounter. You are not the first. Several men have requested my cooperation, but I am not that kind of drone."

I couldn't help myself. I burst out laughing at that, and she stared at me like I was a rabid dog.

"Why do you laugh?"

"It's just what you said," I managed in between a few fading chuckles, "that you're 'not that kind of drone.' It's funny. It's a joke. It's, well that's a whole other language lesson."

"It was not meant to be a joke. I do not have the necessary programming for sexual pursuits and my secondary commands forbid such functions."

"Like it forbids going rogue? It's my understanding that androns are as capable of adapting to new situations and learning new behavior as humans."

"That is correct."

"Well, you may not have the necessary programming, but you've got all the right equipment. And from where I'm sitting, it looks like it's in excellent condition. All you need is the right teacher. Someone to show you the ins and outs of unending ecstasy, the seething, heaving passion, the insatiable desires that lie deep within the--"

"I have observed," she said, interrupting me, "sexual imagery and innuendo such as you have been using, in all facets of human communication. It seems mankind cannot eat, drink, sleep, or select a mode of transportation without invoking words or pictures designed to remind them of what is essentially a primitive means of reproduction. This obsession led to the rampant overpopulation that plagued Earth in the latter part of the last century."

"I guess you could say that had a lot to do with it."

"What is this fascination humans have with sex?"

"Give me a couple of hours and I'll show you."

"Hours? Is that much time necessary?"

"It is if you do it right."

She didn't seem impressed or even slightly titillated. It was apparent I didn't have a snowball's chance in hell of getting this delicious looking dronette to come home with me. She wasn't programmed for witty repartee. Her idea of a good time was probably oiling her implants. Still, there was one more gambit I could try.

"You know, if you need a place to--"I shut up, because I noticed she wasn't paying attention to me anymore. She had seen something, or someone, that had set off a warning signal inside her. Not that she was beeping or anything, but I could tell she had suddenly shifted into "red alert" mode.

I turned toward the entrance to see what she was looking at. There was nothing especially threatening. It was pretty much the usual dregs of the earth which frequented that particular establishment. I did see this one butch-looking tabby who appeared to be scanning the scene rather judiciously. At least I thought she was a she. After another glance, I wasn't so sure. She, or he, had this leather and chain androgynous thing going on. Then I noticed chains weren't the only metal she was wearing. She had more than the usual number of implants showing and it looked like she might be packing heat.

"May we go to your home?"

That about knocked me out of my chair. I looked around to make sure it was Mary who actually had said it.

"Are you saying you want to go back to my cradle with me?"

"Yes, your 'cradle'."

"I don't know. I don't want you to think I'm easy or any--"

"We must leave now." She got up, grabbed me by the wrist, and began pulling me towards the rear exit. Now I would have liked to have thought it was my charm that swayed her, but, by the way she kept looking back over her shoulder, I figured it was more likely she had spotted someone she wanted to avoid. My money was on the drone with the heavy metal.

When we reached the exit, she let loose of me, not knowing which way to go. She faced me with a look that was almost desperate.

"It's that way," I told her. "Near 54th and Holly."

She took off, not waiting for me to show her the way. She wasn't exactly running, but she was walking at a pace I found uncomfortably close to a real workout. Not that I was against physical fitness you understand. I just preferred to get my cardio-vascular exercise in a prone position.

"Hey, where's the fire? You don't want to wear me out before we get there do you?"

She pretty much ignored me, and while I was scrambling to keep up, she continued to look behind us.

She kept to the back streets and alleys--not the shortest route home, but I didn't have the oxygen to argue. After a few minutes she slowed a little, which was fortunate for me, because all those years of sitting on my butt behind a comdat were beginning to show.

I was breathing pretty heavily by the time I got close enough to grab her arm and stop her.

"Wait a minute...wait a minute. Are you going...to tell me...who you're running from?"

"I am not certain."

"You're not certain? Look, if--"I heard a loud *bang*, like something very large and very metallic being tossed around. That was followed by a grinding *screech* and another *bang*.

Mary didn't hesitate. She was off and running, turning a corner and moving like a frightened deer. I threw it into overdrive and followed her.

***

She still had that wild animal look when we reached my cradle. "Open says me, one, two, three." I recited my code, the HC switched off security, and the door slid open. "Lights, lock up." I noticed the v-mail digicon was flashing on my comdat screen. I wasn't expecting anything important so I ignored it. Probably my publisher calling to nag.

I could see the caution in her eyes as they swept the place. She wasn't looking at it the way most women do. She wasn't measuring me by the disarray or the cheap furniture. She was sniffing out traps, looking for signs of treachery. I knew the first thing I was going to have to do was calm her down.

"I know it's not much, but make yourself at home. Can I get you something to drink? I bet after that forced march you need to replenish your fluids. I know I do."

"Yes. You may give me something to drink."

"What'll it be? What would you like?"

"Whatever you are drinking."

"Okay, two Scotch-rocks."

"Rocks?"

"Yeah. Here, I'll show you." I proceeded to throw a few cubes in the two clean glasses I found and added the whiskey. "See. Scotch-rocks, or Scotch on the rocks. Rocks being slang for ice. There, you got your first language lesson.

"Sit down," I said as I made a place for her. She was still walking around, getting the lay of the land. She picked up the book I was using for a paperweight and looked at its cover.

"'*Guns For Ganymede* by Zachariah Starr.' You wrote this?"

"Yeah, years ago though, before the first man ever set foot on Ganymede. It's a bit dated now."

"The books I have read were all on the Net or in disc form."

"Well that's a real one. Most copies are sold on disc, but my publisher indulges me with some hardbound editions. Believe it or not, there are plenty of collectors out there who want the real thing and are willing to pay for it, so she makes money on it."

"What is the story about?"

"Oh, it's about how the colonists of Ganymede fight for independence when they rebel against the control of politicians on Earth."

"It is about a fight for freedom then?"

"Yeah. That's the catalyst for all the action anyway."

"I would like to read it sometime."

"Sure, be my guest. It's not one of my best books, but it sold a few thousand copies outside the Net."

"Where do you...how do you get your ideas for stories?"

"That's the hard part, especially when just about every storyline has already been done to death."

I decided if she wasn't going to come sit by me, I was going to her. I got up and handed her the drink. "I get my inspiration here and there. Mostly I recycle."

"Recycle?"

When I got close enough to hand her the drink, she walked away and sat down. I didn't know if she was playing coy or just doing that drone thing.

"Recycling is taking a tried-and-true plot and dressing it up with new characters, new settings, maybe a different kind of alien nemesis. The ingredients may be stale, but the recipe works forever."

"And you earn credit for these stories?"

"Hey, I don't write them for the exercise. As you can see, I'm not swimming in silk and diamonds, but it pays the bills."

Jekyll chose that moment to make his presence known. He leaped up next to her, startling her a bit I think. He held his tail high in challenge as he looked her over. She recovered from her surprise and stared right back at him.

You have to understand, Jekyll was more human than feline. When he spoke he wasn't just meowing, he was talking to you. And you'd better pay attention. He didn't just look at things, he studied them. He even liked to watch the Net, if the right program was on.

"*Mrrrouw*," he said, still looking at Mary.

"What does it want?"

"*It* is a *he*, and *he* has a name. His name is Jekyll, and he wants you to touch him."

Didn't we both.

She reached out tentatively, unsure of how to go about it. Meanwhile, Jekyll held his ground.

"Haven't you ever petted a cat before?"

"There were no cats in the household in which I was employed. Only a small, blue canine that matched the furnishings."

"A designer doggie huh?"

"Is your Jekyll designed for specific genetic traits?"

"No, he's just mongrel alley cat, a stray that followed me home one day. But he's a glutton for attention." I walked over and sat down next to her. "Here, let me show you." I stroked his solid black fur a couple of times so she could get the gist of it and then gave him a good scratch between the ears like he liked. All the time, he kept his green eyes fastened on her.

"Go ahead, you try."

She reached out tentatively once more and carefully touched Jek's back. "Good living to you, Jekyll," she said as she began to stroke him. When he kicked his purr into full gear I think she actually smiled, though it was so quick I couldn't tell for sure.

"There. Now you have a friend for life."

"He is very soft, and the sound he makes...."

"That means he's happy."

"I am glad I can make him happy."

She may have had the body of a woman, but the impression she left was childlike. Of course, drones aren't even harvested from their tanks until they pass into adolescence. I've read when they do come out, their exposure to the outside is limited as they are given the necessary education and training for their designations. Mary had probably only been in the real world for a few years, though it didn't seem polite to ask for an exact number.

She decided to take a sip of her drink, then got this cute little quizzical expression on her face. "This is an unusually bitter tasting beverage."

"You've never had Scotch before?"

"I do not think so."

"It's an acquired taste. You'll get used to it. It'll do wonders for your disposition."

She took another drink.

"Music up," I told the HC, and some soft tunes drifted up around us.

"What about you, Mary, are you really a maid?"

"I am a fully-trained domestic facilitator."

"Who do you facilitate domestically for?"

She hesitated before answering. I could see the gears clicking away in her
head, so-to-speak. "I am currently in transition. My former steward died and no legitimate claim has yet been approved. I am awaiting the outcome of various
. . . legal proceedings."

Yeah, and I was a green Martian monkey who plays poker and sings opera. I knew she was lying, and I decided to go for the haymaker while I had her on the ropes. "You've gone rogue, haven't you?"

Once again she got that jittery, apprehensive look about her, and began scanning the room for I-don't-know-what. If I had said "boo!" she would have set a new high jump record from a sitting position.

"Don't worry. There's nobody here but us, no hidden cameras or microphones, and I certainly don't care if you're a rogue. In fact, I think it's kind of sexy. Of course, I think anklets and floppy hats are sexy too."

I was trying to make her feel at ease, but she didn't get it. She just sat there staring at me. I guess she was trying to decide if she could trust me. After a few moments, and another sip of her drink, she let it out. "Yes, I am what you would call a rogue."

"What do you call it?"

"We call it wanting to be free," she said, staring straight at me. The wild animal look in her eyes had been replaced by one that warned she would fight if necessary. That was a look I had learned not to mess with.

"What do you mean, 'we'?"

"There are others, others who desire the freedom to make their own choices, to determine for themselves how they shall live. They want the same rights all humans have, nothing more."

They were nice words, but it sounded more like a recitation than something she truly believed in. However, I decided to give her the benefit of the doubt.

"Equal rights for drones? It's a radical concept, I'll grant you that. However, it kind of defeats the purpose you were created for in the first place. It would play hell with the economy, I can tell you that."

I don't think she cared much for that comment. She gave me a look that could have frozen fire.

"Is it wrong not to want to be a slave?"

"Hell, we're all slaves to something--professional pride, religious beliefs, fantasy, love, mind-altering substances, our tastebuds...you name it." She turned her head then, not really looking around but just thinking. As she did, I couldn't help but notice the smooth white slope of her neck and the swell of her breasts as they yearned to be free from the v-neck of her outfit. What can I say? I was easily distracted.

"You know, being free isn't always what it's cracked-up to be. What would you do with your life if you *were* free?"

She turned back to me, looking determined as ever. "I do not know what I would do. I only know I want to be free. Perhaps when I am free to choose what I want, I will know."

"Well I know what I want."

"What do you want?"

"I want you." That caught her off guard, and surprised me a bit too. I didn't usually blurt it out like that. But let's face it, the usual moves weren't going to work on a drone who hadn't a clue. "I want to make love to you."

"You are referring to sexual intercourse?"

"That's a pretty clinical way to put it. Actually, this is a time when slang expressions could be useful."

"Which slang expressions?"

"Well, there's actually quite a few of them. Let's see, there's screw, bang, ball, bop, bone, get down, get online, input the output, knock boots, go net, go sheet dancing, hide the salami, do the wild thing, the horizontal mambo, make the beast with two backs, and the ever-popular, plain ol' fuck."

"So," she said with more seriousness than I could have mustered at that moment, "when you say you want to 'make love' to me, you could also mean you want to 'bang' me. Is that correct?"

"Yeah, I mean...well sure, yeah."

"Why do you want to 'bang' me?"

She said it with such dead seriousness, it took all the self-control I had not to laugh. "You know, at this stage of our relationship, I'm not really comfortable with that particular expression. What do you say we go back to 'making love'?"

"If you prefer. Why do you want to 'make love' to me?"

"Because you're beautiful, and...well, you've got a great body and--"

"So your desire to 'make love' to me is based upon my physical appearance?"

"I...uh, yeah, I guess that's right. I guess I'm also turned on by the idea that you're a drone. I've never done it with a drone before. Are you...I mean are you built for...?"

"Unlike neutral androne, my anatomy is fully functional."

"Have you ever done it? Have you ever made love with anyone before?"

"No. As I told you, sexual contact is forbidden by my secondary commands."

"Doesn't the first step towards being free come with overriding those commands? Don't you have to start making your own decisions? Didn't you override those commands when you decided to go rogue?"

"Yes."

"Then you're no longer a slave to those commands, you're free to make up your own mind."

"Yes."

"Then, if you wanted to make love with me, you could choose to do so."

"Yes. However, I do not have the necessary programming for such sexual pursuits."

"Don't worry about that. Half the fun is in the learning."

I could tell she was thinking about it. But too much thinking usually resulted in the big "NO" with most women. With a dronette I wasn't sure, but I wasn't taking any chances. I stood up and walked over to my desk like I had lost interest.

"You know, we probably shouldn't. I mean, you're right. You're not programmed for it and you probably can't do it right. It's nothing to be ashamed of." Jekyll gave me that "Oh, *please*" look and decided he'd had enough. He jumped off the couch in search of something more interesting to do, but I didn't let him interrupt my flow. "Of course you *would* be missing out on one of the more pleasurable experiences in life. I'm sure, though, you compensate for it in other areas. Just because most women enjoy it doesn't mean you would. After all, you--"

"I want you to make love to me," she said as straightforward as could be.

You could have knocked me over with a lunar pleasure feather. I mean I was giving it the old school try, but I never expected her to actually fall for the reverse psychology gambit. Maybe she just wanted to shut me up.

She stood up as if she were ready to go for it. "Should I remove my clothing?"

"Whoa, don't rush it. Sit down and finish your drink. Let's talk some more first."

She sat back down, her confusion apparent. "Is talk necessary?"

"No, but I'd like to know more about you. Despite my lustful inclinations, I'm not a complete animal. It would be nice if you'd call me Zach occasionally too."

"All right, Zach."

"What's your last name, Mary?"

"I am Mary 79."

"Right, you get your names from model types and batch unit numbers. You
know, you should give yourself a last name. It could be the first act of liberation to christen your emancipation. Let's see, it should be something that says you. What about Freeman? Or Freebird? No? How about we get some alliteration going? What about Mary Mantle or Mary Michaels?"

"I do not know."

"Yeah, sure. A name is something you're stuck with for a long time, so you don't want to rush into it."

"How did Jekyll get his name?"

"He got that because of his split personality--because he acts like he's half animal, half human. You know, like the story of Dr. Jekyll and Mr. Hyde?"

"I have not read it, but I have heard the reference. What about your 'pen name,' how did you select Starr?'"

"Since I write stories about outer space, I'm thinking planets, moons, stars, then I remember this drummer from a group I like from way back when, and I came up with Starr with the double R."

"I think I understand. Yes, I will have to give some consideration to an appropriate name."

"I'm curious," I said, scooting a little closer to her, "what was it that first made you think of going rogue? I mean, at what point did you realize you weren't satisfied with being someone's drone?"

"At first it wasn't...." She paused, took another drink of her Scotch, and seemed to be reconsidering her answer. "It is, as you would say, a long story."

"Well then, give me the abridged version."

"Very well. I can just say that when the time came, I was ready. I watched the Net, read books, and listened to what I heard other andrones saying. I came to believe my existence was without substantial meaning."

"I know you didn't get anything that serious out of one of my books. What books have you read?"

I suddenly realized how off track I was getting. Did I actually ask her if she'd read any good books lately?

"Charles Darwin's *The Origin of the Species*, John Stuart Mill's *Liberty*, William Shakespeare's *Romeo and Juliet*, Chad Affleck's *Development of the Androne*. Also John Steinbeck's *The Grapes of Wrath*, Jacqueline Susan's *Valley of the Dolls*--"

"I see you've covered a variety of genres."

The conversation was proving to be less than stimulating, so I scooted closer to her.

"What about music? You said you play music. What kind do you like to listen to?"

"I listen to all forms of music," she said as I leaned slowly over, brushed her hair aside, and kissed her neck. "I try to absorb and interpret what I hear."

"You must have some favorite kinds of music," I said, raising my lips from her neck just long enough to speak. "Aren't there any specific bands or certain songs that you like?"

"I am familiar with certain pieces. I can read music and have performed many songs. However, I have no special feeling for any particular melody."

"You play music...but you don't...care about it?" I said, punctuating my speech with more soft kisses down the slope of her neck. "That seems...counterproductive."

"It is not that I...." She paused momentarily, seemingly distracted by my attentions. "It is not that I do not like music, or am not capable of liking it. It is only that I have not been able to devote much time to the appreciation of it."

She turned to look at me with an expression that would have shriveled a mere mortal makeout artist. But I was expecting the unusual from her--being a dronette who'd never done it before. She looked at me as if to ask "What in the hell I was doing," then she did ask, in her own drone way.

"Is this touching of my neck with your lips part of your...foreplay?"

"I uh, yeah. You must have seen it on a Net video or something."

Yes, I have both observed and read about such things. However, I have never had them performed on me. It is quite different than just watching."

"Yes, it is. Do you like it? Does it feel good?"

"It feels...unusual. I do notice a heightened sense of awareness along certain nerve endings."

"A uh, heightened sense of awareness, that's good. It's a start. Maybe it's time for a little music appreciation." I got up and went to my comdat, opening my personal music file. I began looking for something that might break on through her icy exterior to the passionate soul I was hoping was inside. I decided on something primitive, figuring that might be the quickest way to penetrate those human genes of hers. "We'll see if you like this. It's very old. Kind of a high-tech take on Native American tribal rhythms. An artist by the name of Cusco."

The music began with the heavy beat of drums, eventually intertwined with mesmerizing flutes. Mary seemed very absorbed by it. Almost as if she felt obligated to enjoy it. "Lights dim," I told the HC, and sat beside her, hoping to alter her focus until the rhythms became only a distant but moving backdrop to her inner music.

As she listened intently I stroked her hair. When she finally turned to look at me, I kissed her. It was, well, a blank. There was nothing there. I would have gotten more response out of a houseplant. But it would take more than that to discourage me. I was on a mission. I was either going to come back *with* my shield, or *on* it. I kissed her again. This time there was an inkling, a hint of a reaction on her part. At least she was trying. I knew, though, that it was up to me to make it happen.

When I kissed her again, I held it and even took hold of her lower lip for a moment. She responded in kind, and before I knew it, our tongues were playing tag. When I paused and pulled back to look at her, I could tell she was acquiring a taste for it.

"This act of kissing results in some very interesting sensations. I think I am beginning to understand some of the fascination you have with it."

"Hopefully, it's only the first of many interesting sensations I can introduce you to." I kissed her again and as I did I reached out and lightly touched one of her breasts. Her body actually shuddered at the touch, and she momentarily pulled back from my lips. The look on her face was one of surprise, with maybe a touch of fear. But just as quickly she was back in my arms. Her kisses grew more fervent.

I began to undress her, caressing her flesh as it was revealed to me. My own detachment, thinking of her as just a sexual oddity, was deserting me. I was getting caught up in the moment. It wasn't until I ran my tongue down her stomach and saw the implant where her belly button should have been that I was reminded this wasn't just another woman. Below the implant was a sequence of lines and spaces, thick and thin, tattooed onto her skin. She noticed my hesitation and seemed almost embarrassed by this reminder that she wasn't completely human.

"It is my embryonic tube."

"Yeah, I can see that."

"Is it a hindrance?" She started to sit up from the reclining position I had maneuvered her into, but I wasn't about to let an ersatz piece of body art and a barcode tattoo dampen the mood.

"No," I said, moving so she couldn't get up. "Doesn't bother me at all. Actually, I think it's kind of kinky." I began sliding my tongue all around the implant, and then worked my way back up to her incredibly beautiful breasts. When I fastened my mouth gently around a nipple, her body quivered again. She was beginning to lose that drone self-control, and that was just what I wanted.

2

MARY 79

I was no longer sure what it was I wanted. The events of the previous night had left me confused. That human, that Zachariah Star--Zach—had done something to me. It was not only the sexual act. That had proven a source of overwhelming physical pleasure. Even so, it had felt incomplete. Like something was missing. Some element I did not have access to.

It was peculiar how the method utilized to extract the bodily fluids necessary for procreation would also result in such intense sensations. So intense, I seemed to lose contact with some of my higher functions for the period of the encounter. When Zach first entered me it was a feeling that was both unusual and highly stimulating. At that juncture it felt as if each epidermal contact led to another wave of arousal. Of course, practically speaking, the exercise would prove unsuccessful. Androne were not designed to procreate.

However, there was something else. Something besides the physical sensations that were new to me. Emotional responses I was unfamiliar with, and, apparently, unprepared to assimilate. Yet, some part of me yearned to repeat the experience. It was this part which was the source of my confusion. I knew I should not let anything distract me, not while I was exposed to public scrutiny.

It must have begun to rain after I went to Zach's home, because the streets were wet and large droplets still fell from overhanging structures. The people I saw were scurrying to and fro, like busy insects. It was strange how humans seemed more timid after a rainstorm, as if nature's elemental fury had somehow tamed them.

It was a substantial distance for me to walk, however, I had to reach the secondary rendezvous point. Either Patrick 221 had been delayed on his way to the initial meeting place the previous night or...I did not want to think about the alternative. He was my only contact with the group. I knew if a tracer had expired him, I was alone.

I had been fortunate. While sitting with Zach I had seen the tracer before it had identified me. It was not a human tracer, I had seen its implants. It was an androne, one programmed to expire...no, not "expire," that was the human term. It was an androne programmed to *kill* other androns. Though I was not positive, it looked to be a neutral, an early genetic design, neither male nor female. It did not matter though. Male, female, neutral, or human, if it tracked me down it would mean the end of my existence.

I reached up to make sure my hair was in place as I passed a small group of people exiting an eatery. I realized the gesture to make certain my cranial implant remained hidden was becoming habitual. I continued down the street, looking ahead, avoiding others when I could. I tried to think only of my meeting with Patrick 221, and what it might mean.

My thoughts were interrupted then by a voice. My first inclination was to look behind me. No one was there. Then I heard it again. It was inside my head, though I heard only a single word, *"Submit."* Then again, a minute later, it repeated, *"Submit."* I tried to cover my ears, but I could still hear it. *"Submit."*

When I saw a pair of women walking towards me I became self-conscious and lowered my hands from my ears. I hesitated, pretending to look through a store window. I was suddenly overcome by a strange emotion. I reasoned it was fear, fear of the humans passing by me. Even though they appeared disinterested in my presence, I was afraid to move. Perhaps it was the thought of how close that tracer had come to finding me. Perhaps since I had gone rogue I had become more aware of my surroundings. Or perhaps it wasn't only fear I was experiencing, but paranoia.

I continued looking into the window, waiting to see if the voice returned. A mannequin dressed in a yellow silk blouse and a long, narrow black skirt stared back at me. I wondered what it thought of the people who passed by. Did it want to leave its glass-framed world and join them? Or was it content with the security and serenity that lifelessness offered? I did not know whether to pity it, or envy it.

I continued on, trying not to see danger in every face I passed. It was not easy, but after a time I began to relax. Even if they recognized me as an androne they would have no reason to react. They had no way of knowing I was a rogue, and many, like Zach, would not care. The thought helped, though it did not eliminate my apprehension.

The voice inside my head had gone silent, but I heard something else. It was ahead of me and sounded like shouting. I saw a large gathering of people on a corner plaza I remembered was usually populated with pigeons. The shouting came from a man who stood atop one of the concrete columns surrounding a fountain. I was unsure of how to proceed. He seemed to hold the crowd's attention, so I decided to make my way slowly through it. I eased unnoticed into the throng and acted as if I was interested in what the man was saying.

"...for the future. They tell you it is for the good of mankind. They tell you technology will be our salvation. Well, brothers and sisters, I'm here to tell you that technology will be our damnation. Better brains though computer implants, more beautiful faces via surgery, less work and more leisure time with the use of artificial lifeforms. These are the things that make us less human. These are the evils that plague our society."

He continued to expound upon his theme as I made my way leisurely through the crowd. I noticed some of the people were intently listening while others appeared more amused than engrossed. The speaker's compatriots were passing out printed material, and, like those around me, I accepted one. I only glanced quickly at its cover. On it was the photograph of a man I had seen somewhere before. The caption read "Give God Your Vote. Reverend Jackson Roberts For Senator."

"Do you want a world where birth and death are controlled by bureaucrats? Where the weather never changes and everyone looks the same? Who will be beautiful when we all look alike? Do you want a world where machines do everything? A world where men and women are no longer necessary? You there, Brother," he said pointing down at a man in the crowd. "Do you want to lose your place in society to a drone, a genetically engineered mutant-thing with no family to feed?" The fellow shook his head. "You, Sister, do you want to lose your man to some high-tech harlot?" I froze then, because I saw he was pointing at me. I knew a response was called for, however, I had only vaguely heard his question.

"I do not...." Fear overcame me. I did not want anyone in that crowd to know who--what I was. I thought about something Zach had said about "blending in." Then I responded, "I don't know."

"You don't know? How can you not know, Sister?" He looked right at me as he asked the question, then turned his attention to the rest of the crowd. "How can you not know what it is that you want out of life? Do you want the machines to decide for you? Should we all be implanted and programmed from birth like drones?"

He was no longer looking at me. I realized it was unlikely he ever really *looked* at me. I was another face in the crowd.

"Man wasn't meant to build dams and change the course of God's great rivers. He wasn't meant to leave this beautiful world that God created for some secular existence on another planet. This is where the Lord put you, and this is where he wants you. Praise God, praise Nature."

I kept moving, and as I passed through the opposite side of the gathering and continued on my way, I could still hear his prophecies of hellfire and technological damnation.

3

JERI 08

As I sat there waiting, that peculiar sensation came over me once again. There was no logical reason for it I could discern. The only time I ever noticed it was when I was summoned to see Mr. Satchmeyer. It was an unusual physiological response. As if my neurological outputs had cross-circuited with my digestive tract.

Mr. Satchmeyer did have a tendency towards emotional outbursts. Possibly the sensation was simply a conditioned response, a reflex action. There was an obvious connection, but even that realization made no difference. The complexity of it was disconcerting. I was not trained to solve complex physiological problems. I was trained to trace, disarm, and take into custody suspected and convicted criminals. It was a task I excelled in.

The majority of my assignments involved tracing rogues, though, on occasion I have been assigned human criminals. I preferred assignments involving andro?es. They were much more predictable than humans. And, once located, there was a complex set of guidelines involved in taking a human into custody. Rules involving when and when not to use deadly force, proper procedures in a medical emergency, explanation of legal rights and responsibilities. With rogues it was a simply matter of expiration. As Mr. Satchmeyer would say, "No muss, no fuss."

I had never been able to comprehend the motivation to turn rogue. I had heard talk concerning such vague concepts such as "free will" and "self determination." I found the ideas unsettling. What would I do without my steward to give me assignments? If Mr. Satchmeyer decided he no longer needed my services, what would become of me? Freedom seemed to me chaos, and self-determination could only be defined as a lack of direction. Surely those of my kind who had gone rogue suffered from defective cranial implants or some other disorder.

Mr. Satchmeyer's secretary walked back into the room and I activated my mobile comdat to refamiliarize myself with the current fugitive list. She sat down and gave me a look I could only describe as disapproving. She had never appeared comfortable in my presence, though I did not know why. So I kept my eyes on my screen.

Peter 26, transportation specialist, normal coloration, height, and weight specifications for a Peter unit, last known location sector 1253a on 12/30. Linda 251, administrative assistant, altered hair coloration to blonde, otherwise normal specifications, last known location dated, no new information. Mary 79, domestic facilitator, normal coloration, height, and weight specifications for a Mary unit, implant signal traced to sector 1169a less than 24 hours ago, signal lost. Eric 07, food preparation specialist--

A tone sounded from the secretary's comdat, interrupting my review. She activated her digiscreen, though the angle was too severe for me to see to whom she was speaking.

"Good living, Bonds and Bounties."

"Let me talk to Satch."

"I'm sorry, Mr. G, he's in a meeting right now. Can I take a message?"

"It's urgent, hon, be a doll and wire me through."

"I'm sorry, Mr. Satchmeyer can't be interrupted right now. You may try back later if you wish."

She made no other response, so I determined the caller had ceased transmission. Before she could turn her attention elsewhere, another sound demanded recognition. I noticed she was prompt and attentive in responding. In all likelihood, that signified Mr. Satchmeyer would be ready for my report. That peculiar sensation in my abdominal region, that had begun to dissipate, returned in full.

"Daisey, send through my v-mail and get Bill Franks on the line for me, and don't take 'no' for an answer." Mr. Satchmeyer's voice blared from her comdat. "Then send me the new fugitives list."

"Yes, Mr. Satchmeyer. Uh, you remember *it's* still out here waiting for you."

"What?"

"You know, 'Butch' is out here," she said, giggling. I did not understand her reference to "butch."

"Who?" replied Mr. Satchmeyer, sounding somewhat irritated.

"Hey, you," she said looking at me. "What's your designation?"

"Jeri Zero Eight."

"Jeri Zero Eight, Mr. Satchmeyer. Remember, you wanted him...er her...you know, *it* to meet with you this afternoon."

"Right, right. Okay, send it in."

She switched-off, but didn't bother to look up at me. "He wants you in his office *now*."

I considering offering her the typical "thank you" response, but decided, based on her tone of voice, that it was not appropriate. Instead, I walked into Mr. Satchmeyer's office and quietly sat down. He was engaged in conversation and made no attempt to acknowledge my presence, so I remained silent. I was optimistic the time I would spend in Mr. Satchmeyer's presence would be limited. I hoped to be able to return to my dwelling in conjunction with the commencement of the evening's scheduled gauntlet match.

"Dammit, Bill, if I don't get those exclusive contracts I'm screwed. I've already had to sell-off half my tracers just to keep my doors open." He was extremely agitated, but that was not unusual. He was a large man, "rotund" I believe would be the proper word, and he sweated quite profusely. A glandular imbalance no doubt.

He was wearing a headset and had the sound on his comdat turned off, so I was unable to hear the other portion of the conversation.

"I know, I know we haven't fulfilled our last contracts yet....I know, Bill. Hey, this is Saul you're talking to. Remember me? I'm the guy who got you started. Don't tell...don't tell me what I already know. Look, you owe me.

. . . What?...That's goo!...If I have to, I'll take my business to Aaron.

. . . Hey, I will if I have to....Yeah, well, just see what you can do."

He angrily pulled off the headset and turned his eyes to me. I do not believe my abdominal fluctuations had ever been more severe.

"What have *you* got for me?"

"My report, sir. I have--"

"I don't want your goddamned report, I want to know how many rogues you've bagged this week."

"Sir, my investigations have not resulted in any expirations over the last seven days, however--"

"However nothing! Listen, genetically-engineered-shit-for-brains, I'm going
down here, and if I go I'm taking you and the rest of your metalhead friends with me." His use of the term "friends" was incorrect. Though he still employed, to my knowledge, the services of two other androne tracers to whom I was acquainted,

we were not friends. "I need those bounties. You savvy? If you don't score by week's end, I'm going to sell your sorry cybernetic ass to waste disposal. You won't like it very much when the only thing you're tracing is a plugged-up sewer line."

As I said, he was usually quite agitated, though I had no memory of his ever before threatening to dispense with my services. He then abruptly changed his tone. "Is your trace sensor functioning properly?"

"Yes, sir, I believe so. Only last night I locked in on the designated frequency of rogue unit Mary 79. I traced her to an establishment known as *Satan's Alley*, however, the signal began to move before I located her. It then wavered and I lost it to interference."

"*Satan's Alley* huh? I know the place. A Mary unit is quite a looker isn't she?"

"A 'looker,' sir?"

"You know, a babe, a riser, a...oh, I almost forgot you neutrals don't recognize the finer aspects of gender."

"I am familiar with the physiological differences between males and females."

"Maybe, but you don't really appreciate those differences, do you? Your investigative training doesn't tell you that if this Mary unit was actually in *Satan's Alley* she probably left with some dude."

"A dude?"

"Yeah, some guy took one look at her, got her drunk, and took her to his place for a plug and a poke. Didn't that ever occur to your keen investigative mind?"

I recognized his sarcasm, though I did not believe it was warranted. "I do not perceive why such a deduction would influence my actions. As I reported, the rogue unit's frequency was dissipated by unknown interference and--"

"Delete it. I don't want excuses, I want results. Now get out of here and get on the trail. And don't be shooting no innocent civilians and sending my liability premiums through the roof."

Without another word, I got up and made my way out of the building. I did not believe there was any justification for his tirade. I had performed in complete compliance with my training. I saw no logic in his reference to gender or some theoretical sexual encounter. I considered his assumption erratic. A speculation based on insufficient data, and another example of humankind's preoccupation with sex.

4
ZACH

By the time I managed to wake up, she was gone. Not so much as a goodbye kiss or a thank you note. Of course, I was so dead-to-the-world I wouldn't have been revived with the sexiest goodbye kiss ever.

I couldn't remember ever being more exhausted, or sore, from my ankles to my eyelashes. When I accepted that first hint of consciousness, I tried to recall what or who had hit me, and how many of them there were. That's when I remembered and opened my eyes to look for her.

I didn't have to get out of bed to deduce she'd fled the scene. I couldn't have at that moment even if I'd wanted to. Her clothes were gone and she wasn't in the cleanser, but I could still smell her. It wasn't the smell of cheap perfume-- she wasn't wearing any. It was the scent of raw woman, one of my favorite things in the whole world.

She'd apparently flown the coop without so much as a how-do-you-do or by-your-leave. Well, drones weren't known for their social niceties. Still, it had been an incredible night.

Her frosty demeanor had thawed considerably once she got into the spirit of the thing. I could still see the innocent look of wonder in her eyes when she first put her hand between my legs. Of course, soon after that I showed her what she could do with it, or at least some of the things. After all, it was only one night, even if it did seem like forever before she got tired.

Okay, so that's not completely accurate. The truth is, she never did get tired, she just took pity on me when it was obvious I was only seconds away from a severe heart attack. Either I was getting older, or they weren't making women like they used to.

I guess, in this case, both were true.

I figured I'd never see her again, and did what any red-blooded male would do in a similar situation. I activated the Net and tried to drown my sorrow in another zany but revealing episode of *The Harvey Wallbanger Show*. Today's episode was titled "Modern Serial Killers and Their Pets." That Wallbanger was one maniacal personality. I watched until the part about a boa constrictor that swallowed live piglets, then I lost interest and began thinking about Mary again.   I selected "scan" and discovered such current fare as *Net Court, The Transsexual Game,* some kind of drone wrestling, and the *Star Trek Channel.* I stopped when I hit the news. I decided to drag myself out of bed and let the latest natural disasters and civil disorders keep me company.

> *"...murder rate on the North American*
> *continent continues to fall—down eight percent from*
> *last year. In contrast, the suicide rate for the region*
> *has increased by eleven percent over the same*
> *time period."*

That's what boredom will do to you.

> *"Not a single suicide has been reported from*
> *the Ganymede colony, where work on the New*
> *Phoenix biosphere is reported to be proceeding*
> *ahead of schedule. Colonists have actually begun*
> *planting crops in hothouses using native soil. No*
> *word yet on what a Ganymedian grapefruit would*
> *look like."*
> *"Ganymedian grapefruit, huh? That's a good*
> *one, Gloria."*

Yeah, Gloria, you're a real wag.

> *"Moving on to the Pacific West Region senatorial*
> *race--Reverend Jackson Roberts, once considered*
> *a token candidate, has seen his status elevated to*
> *that of a dark horse. A recent poll revealed his*
> *popularity has nearly doubled, with 19 percent*
> *now favoring Roberts. That's compared to 26 percent*
> *for Victor Longley and 43 percent for the*
> *incumbent, Senator Juan Vargas. Senator Vargas*
> *isn't relying on the polls. While on the campaign trail,*
> *he declared yesterday's gun battle between police and*
> *an unknown number of rogue androngs to be a*
> *non-issue. The senator stated the problem of rogues*
> *was limited to a handful of malcontents, and not*
> *worthy of debate. Reverend Roberts, however, took*
> *the opportunity to advance his anti-androne*

campaign, calling the violence another example
of technology run amuck."

Sure, next thing you know, convection ovens will be taking over the world.

Drones weren't just pieces of tech, they were educated, programmed in a sense, for specialized tasks. Occasionally, of course, the programming would crash, or whatever the technical term was, and the drone would go serkers. It used to be thought that those who misfired could be "corrected." Nowadays they didn't bother much with that. It had proved too expensive and the results dubious, to say the least. Instead, they just shut them down. "Expired" they called it. It was a messy business that had become even messier of late.

"In a related story, Androtech has completed its
rumored merger with General Electric. Details of
the merger were not released, but news of the deal
led to a flurry of activity on Wall Street. Meanwhile,
members of the radical fringe group LEDA
continued their protests outside the local
corporate offices of Androtech, lead by their
president, Dr. Patricia Henry. They were joined
by others from a new faction known as PETA, or
People for the Ethical Treatment of Androves.
Police report no arrests at the rather sedate
demonstration."

Equality and ethical treatment for androves wasn't playing well in the world's boardrooms, but they should have seen it coming.

The technology used to create drones had been around quite a while, it was the politics that had changed. I was certainly no expert on social and cultural dynamics, but it doesn't take a genius to figure out how it all got started. After the world was united under one government, the concept of national defense became obsolete. Not that there wasn't still conflict. Religious and ethnic hatred was deep-rooted in some areas. Regional police forces did what they could, but the problem was as old as all mankind.

However, the trillions previously spent on military might were used to fight poverty and disease, and even to colonize some of

Earth's neighbors. It was the infamous "Debacle of New Dakota" that opened the philosophical door for drones. Up until that entire Mars expedition was wiped out, the moral purists held the high ground when it came to the artificial creation of human life. Eventually, their shouts of "sacrilege" were drowned out by the logic that androne were the best tools for the risky business of terraforming other worlds. Of course, once the initial dangers were overcome and the foundations laid, the drones became mere workers for the human colonists that arrived.

On Earth, plummeting sperm counts attributed to environmental pollutants, along with lavish government incentives for birth control, did a great job of reducing the population, despite biotechnical advances that increased the average lifespan. Not that everyone wanted to live to see their hundredth birthday.

With under a billion people, the standard of living rose substantially. Individual wealth eventually increased to the point where many people could be very selective about what kind of work they wanted to do and how many hours they were willing to do it. Many chose not to work at all. Professions were selected more for pride than paycheck. The more menial tasks had few takers.

That's when some bright boy came up with the idea of creating androne for what they called a "financially expeditious labor force." There were those who objected to the idea on moral grounds. They ranted and raved, and a few demagogues still do. But not one of them wanted to clean toilets or seal toxic waste containers. That's Mary's job now...her and those like her.

> "...the fluctuating price of rice due to
> anticipated shortages has led to another day of
> rioting on the Pacific East peninsula of
> Malaysia. Though there is no shortage of
> other foodstuffs, there is a strong cultural preference
> for rice dishes in the region. Authorities report
> more than 200 people have been killed and
> thousands injured since the riots began four days ago.
> In France, farmers continue to do battle with an
> invasion of South American fire ants. Reports
> of decimated grape orchards have led to the
> widespread hoarding of French wines."

Just keep those ants away from the Scotch orchards and we won't have a problem.

> *"There's one man who won't have to worry about*
> *the price of wine."*
> *"That's right, Gary. Zambie Mu...Mubutu, if*
> *I pronounced that right...anyway, the South*
> *African cab driver is one billion dollars richer*
> *today. Last night he won the World Lotto Jackpot."*
> *"Mu...bu...well, let's just call him Zambie*
> *. . . Zambie says he'll use the money to buy his own*
> *cab company."*
> *"Oh come on, Zambie, use your imagination.*
> *What would you do with all that money, Gloria?"*
> *"Oh, how about a very slow cruise around the world*
> *with the Pac West Ironmen?"*
> *"You'd like that, wouldn't you? Just you and a*
> *dozen genetically enhanced super athletes. Speaking*
> *of the Ironmen, sports is up next. But since we*
> *here at CNCNet didn't win the lotto, we're going to*
> *have take a commercial break first to pay some bills."*
> *"We'll be right back."*

Ah, nothing like a little mindless talking-head chit-chat to get your blood circulating in the morning, even if it was the same old violence in the streets, posturing politicians, and environmental maladies. Just another day in paradise. At least you could always count on the commercials for a laugh.

> *"...so make your move to Mars now, before all*
> *the prime lots are taken. Because the three*
> *most important words in colonization are*
> *'location, location, location'."*

> *"Tired of all that laundry? Sick of wearing the*
> *same outfits week after week? Then you should try*
> *new Disposadress. Dress for less, dress for success.*
> *All you...."*

My attention span being what it was, wandered from the

digiscreen to the kitchen. A little food was what I needed to take my mind off the world. Of course it wasn't really the world I was concerned with. It was her. I flashed on a memory that was only hours old, and the image that came to me gave rise to a hardy reflex I wasn't prepared to deal with right then. I wondered where she was, and whether I'd ever see her again. Stupid me.

5

MARY

It was midday when I reached the agreed upon location--an electronics outlet teeming with consumers. If Patrick 221 were still alive, and able, he would be here. If he was not, I did not know what I would do. I was not accustomed to making so many decisions. It seemed as if one decision led to another and so on without end.

I walked inside and tried to look around as if I was interested in making a purchase. I made my way down an aisle, pausing occasionally to pretend I was examining one item or another. Instead, I took each opportunity to try and locate Patrick 221. As I turned to try another aisle, I noticed something odd. It was my reflection--no, it was me. My face had suddenly appeared on a wall hung with dozens of digiscreens.

For a moment, I was fascinated. I was everywhere. There were dozens of me. I looked around and located the camera that was recording my image. It was a tiny thing, no larger than a pen. Then my fascination gave way to panic. I realized I was exposing myself to the scrutiny of dozens of people, so I moved out of the camera's range and continued to feign an interest in the variety of goods for sale.

It was not long before Patrick 221 approached me. He said simply, "Mary 79." I turned and he pointed towards the far corner of the store. "We should go look down there." I nodded my head in agreement and followed him back to where there were fewer people.

I had seen Patrick 221 twice before, and spoken with him once. I did not know him well. I guessed he was one of the leaders of the group I now wished to join. At that first clandestine meeting I had attended, he spoke of such things as slavery and freedom and self-determination. I had been skeptical and unsure. However, the ideas intrigued me. When I had the chance, I read about human history and human laws. I thought about how I lived, how all andrones lived, and wondered if I was content with my life. All of this was on my mind when it began. When I realized someone was trying to kill me, taking that first step was easy.

"Do you still desire to join our group?" Patrick 221 asked after we reached a quiet corner of the store.

"Yes, I must. I have already left my household."

"Good. First our leader will want to meet you, speak with you."

"I thought you--"

"I will arrange for you to meet him at this location." He handed me a card that read "Techno Head."

"The time and date of the rendezvous are on the reverse side. If you cannot be there, or if no one meets you, try again at the same time the next day."

"I have no place to go. Can I not go with you?"

"No. Not until you are part of the group. We must be careful. One spy could mean dozens of expirations.

"I am not a spy."

"That is not a judgment I can make. You must be patient. Patience is the key now to all of our plans. You must find a place to conceal yourself until you are permitted to join us."

I nodded my head slightly in agreement. My true feelings were not agreeable. I thought only of my own predicament, my own danger. And then I felt it. At least I think it was what I felt. The hint of another new emotion. I believe I was feeling ashamed.

Patrick 221 started to leave and then turned and said, "Good luck, Mary 79."

6

JON 155

I laced the ties through their loops and fastened the cords as I had a thousand times before. Once in place, I slapped each piece of pad-armor, testing its strength and placement. I securely buckled each boot and stood to check the traction as I pulled on my gloves and strapped them tight. Then came the familiar black and blue jersey, emblazoned with the numbers one-five-five. Unlike the other gear, it served no purpose, other than a standard that millions rallied around with their cheers, their applause, and, on occasion, their hisses of disapproval. I reached for the helmet-mask and pulled it firmly onto my head, knowing, no matter what happened, I would be wearing it for the last time.

"Hey, Jon. Where the hell are you?" Coach entered my cubicle in his usual brusque manner. He had a name, like other humans, but we had been instructed to refer to him only as "Coach."

"The rest of the team is already suited-up. Are you gonna join us, or do you need a special invite?"

"I am ready."

"Then get your butt out here with the rest of these jockheads. And don't be giving me none of that prima donna superstar goo. We've got an important match tonight."

"Are not all of our matches important?"

"Damn right they are, but this one's against the Dynamos. You know how I hate them."

"Hate is not a strategically sound approach to a match against a formidable opponent."

Coach looked at me as though he did not know how to respond. The look was one of either anger or disdain. I could not be sure which.

"You've got 60 seconds to get out here," he said as he departed.

I took one last look around my cubicle. It was only a symbol of my confinement, my prison within a prison, despite the victory trophies and awards of honor that adorned its walls. Yet part of me, a part I seemed to have no control over, insisted this was *home*. To leave it and never return was, in some strange way, frightening. This sensation, this *fear* was new to me. I had never experienced it before.

There would soon be many new experiences, many new sensations. This fear would not slow me or keep me from my goal. I would overcome it as I had all my opponents. It was time to quit brooding and join my teammates for one last match. The opportunity for reflection would come later. I would commemorate the moment in verse on another occasion.

As I made my way I noticed how peculiar it was that everyday things began to look different. My cubicle, the hallway I had traversed a thousand times on my way to the main locker-room, even Bill 02, the locker-room attendant, appeared to manifest a new appearance.

"Have a good run, Jon 155," said the old androne as he traditionally did before a match.

"I will, Bill 02," I replied as I passed by him. I had never devoted any thoughts to Bill 02, however, on this occasion I stopped and turned to him. "Bill, are you content?" I asked without using his numerical designation--my first overt act of defiance.

"Content?" He ceased his janitorial work and looked at me as if the word had no place in his vocabulary.

"Do you ever wish your life was...different?"

"Different? How would it be different, Jon 155?"

"Do you not ever yearn to be free?"

"Free? Free for what?"

I realized then the concept was beyond his capacity to reason. His programming and exposure to the Net had been limited. It was humans who were responsible for his limitations, just as they had attempted to limit me. But they had failed.

"Disregard the question, Bill. Continue with your work."

"Have a good run, Jon 155."

"I will, Bill, I will."

My perceptions were still tainted by a heightened sense of awareness when I joined my teammates. I noticed for the first time how exhausted they looked, how battered and scarred. My presence appeared to invigorate them to some small degree, but that only led to another unsettling sensation.

They respected me, depended upon me. When the match was on the line, I was the one they handed the buckler to. I was the one who could, as Coach said, "snatch victory from the jaws of defeat." And now I was going to desert them.

"All right, you jockheads, gather around." Everyone moved into place, knowing the sooner Coach began his talk, the sooner he would be silent. "I don't have to tell you guys I hate these Dynamos from my bald spot to my ugly ingrown toenail. I despise their coach, I loathe their uniforms, I can't even stand their cheerleaders. And what really galls me is that we're looking up at them in the standings. There's no way we should be three games behind these eastern lunkheads. Now let's see some drive out there, some determination. You have to *want* to win. You have to want it more than anything else in the world. Now get out there and show them what the Ironmen are made of."

Coach was right. To win, you had to want it more than anything else. However, that's not what I wanted anymore.

7

ZACH

I didn't pay a lot of attention to *The Gauntlet*, even though it was one of the highest rated shows on the Net. I mean I didn't watch the standings or study the statistics, but if there was a match on and I wasn't doing anything else, I might catch a few runs. That night there was a real clash-and-bash going on. The legendary Jon 155 and our Pac West Ironmen were taking on the undefeated Dynamos from the east.

When I tuned in, the score was tied and they were in sudden-death overtime. Now, no one usually actually died running the gauntlet, but there had been instances. Jon 155 once even delivered a fatal blow to a defenseman--the only time I ever heard of that happening. Usually it was only the runners who got hurt bad. There were always some maimings, and your usual assortment of broken bones and lacerations. You know, a nice clean blood sport for people with no more wars to root for.

> *"...so the Ironmen will now go on offense. Normally, in a situation like this, you could bet home and hearth that Jon 155 would get the buckler. But he was pummeled pretty badly during his last run."*
> *"That's right, Don. After he fell he was getting beat so bad, the coach had to forfeit the run with a timeout. So I think, instead, we're going to see--"*
> *"Well, look at this, Joe. Jon 155 has the buckler in his hand and he's coming out."*
> *"What a player, what a competitor--undoubtedly the greatest gauntlet runner of all time."*
> *"He's taking his mark on the starting line. He looks pretty battered, but I bet those defenders would prefer to be facing just about anyone else in this situation."*

The announcers weren't anything if they weren't the overlords of the obvious. *Of course* the defenders would rather see any uniform number but 155 coming at them right now.

"The buzzer sounds and there he goes. What a move!
Did you see that, Don?"

I don't know if Don saw it, but I did. It was poetry in motion. With an uncanny burst of speed, Jon 155 was past the first defender before he could lift his staff, and sidestepped the next guy with a move that would have shamed the Russian ballet. He got hit pretty hard by the next guy, but managed to keep his balance and avoid crossing the foul line. Then he brought the buckler to bear and showed off the sheer brute force he was famous for. It didn't matter if the defender was using a bludgeon or a staff, Jon 155 countered every blow, danced over every attempt to trip him up. I knew I'd be seeing this run on highlights for years to come.

"...he scores! The Ironmen win 9-8, dealing
the Dynamos their first loss of the season!"
"What an incredible run, Joe. That he was able
to demonstrate such power and agility this late in
the match is phenomenal. The Dynamos defenders
were just overmatched."
"It's like he's in a league of his own, Don."
"The Ironmen have gathered for the post-match
victory run, but I don't see Jon 155. That's strange.
He didn't seem badly injured."

It was a little unusual, though I didn't give it much thought at the time. Normally, Jon 155's teammates would be crowded around him, delivering the traditional hearty head-butting and backslapping, but the star of the game was nowhere to be seen. You could tell even the other players were looking around, wondering what had happened to him. I didn't have time to give it much thought, because just then my sexy doornag sang out.
"Zach darling, you have company."
I threw on some pants and asked my HC for a looksee. "Door view." My digiscreen switched to security view mode and I saw Mary leaning on the doorhail.
"Zach darling, you have company. Zach darling,
you have company."
"All right already. Door open."
She stood there, windblown and bedraggled, like a lost puppy

come home with its tail between its legs. Only her tail was much prettier. She didn't say anything, so I offered, "I was hoping I'd see you again. I wasn't sure what happened to you."

"I had to go somewhere." She didn't make a move to come in, and looked like she didn't know what else to say. I figured if she wanted to tell me where she'd been, she would...eventually.

"I'm glad you came back."

"I had nowhere else to go."

"Don't just stand there, come on in. I don't want my neighbors thinking I keep gorgeous women waiting in the hallway. What would they think of me?"

"I do not know," she replied seriously as she walked in.

"Lock up," I told the HC. "Sit down, sit down. Make yourself at home. Mi casa, su casa."

"*Yo no sabia que hablabas espanol.*"

"Say what? What was that you said?"

"I said I did not know that you spoke Spanish."

"I don't. That was a figure of speech. You know, another example of slang."

"Oh yes, slang. Like 'do the wild thing.' I remember."

"That's right."

She looked right at me then with those dead-serious blue eyes of hers. "I enjoyed doing the wild thing with you last night, Zach."

That caught me off guard. I didn't know quite how to respond. "It was my pleasure, believe me."

"Perhaps we can do it again sometime, that is if you would like to."

"Sure, why not." This dronette was making all my moves *for* me--kind of taking all the fun out of it. Okay, not all the fun. The way she said it, so serious and all, was just too damn cute. "So, are you hungry?"

She thought about it for a moment. "Yes, I am very hungry."

"Still having trouble with the contractions, huh?"

"I did remember what you told me, Zach. Today I used a contraction when I spoke. I said 'I don't know.'"

"Hey, it's a beginning. Pretty soon we'll have you slinging slang and using gutter grammar like real human trash. We should celebrate your giant leap for dronekind. How about I take you out to dinner?"

"I do not know, Zach."

"*Don't*--I *don't* know, remember?"

"Yes. It is a difficult habit to master. I *don't* know, Zach. I would rather not go out. Can we stay here and eat?"

"Even better. Why don't you go get cleaned up while I order out. Do you like Chinese?" She gave me that quizzical look again. "Never mind, you'll love it."

I don't know what got into me. Something that made me feel like a kid again, I guess. After I ordered the food I turned on some music, lit some candles, and even tried to clean up a little. I should have known that wasn't a good sign. But I felt good, better than I had in a long time, and I wasn't in the mood to question it.

I heard her turn on the cleanser and caught myself wondering if her implants were waterproof. Up until that moment, I guess I had forgotten. I had become oblivious to the fact she wasn't human. But she was human, dammit, just a different kind of human. I realized I didn't care if she was a drone. Viva la difference!

I heard the cleanser go off and a minute later the door opened. She stood there, towel in hand but otherwise naked from top to bottom. Her hair was still wet and drops of water glistened off the contours of her well-rounded flesh. It was an incredibly lovely sight, not to mention stimulating.

"My clothes are quite dirty. Do you have something else I can wear?"

"Uh, sure, just a minute." I forced myself to turn away and found a shirt and some comfortable old lounge pants. "Here," I said, handing them to her and forcing myself to look only at her eyes. "You'd better close the door while you put these on."

"Why?"

"Because you're an extremely beautiful woman, Mary. And because I have only so much self-control. Actually, I have very *little* self-control, and it's about all used up."

"You are...attracted to me, but are worried you cannot control yourself?"

"You got it."

"The sight of my body without clothing makes you want to sheet dance with me?"

"Yes, yes, very good use of slang. Now get dressed," I said, pushing her gently back and grabbing the door. The touch of her silky skin gave me pause, but I remained disciplined. "Hurry up now, the food will be here soon."

"All right, Zach."

I closed the door and then, of course, regretted it. I guess a little spontaneous sheet dancing wouldn't have hurt either of us. Next time.

"Zach darling, you have company."

I expected to see the same pimply-faced kid who always showed up with the deliveries. Instead, it was this ancient-looking geezer--white hair, wrinkles, bent like he carried the weight of the world on his shoulders.

"Door open."

When he handed me the food I noticed his implants. He was pretty beat-up. Obviously one of the early models. For all I knew, he might once have built comdat parts or worked as an air traffic controller. Now, way past his prime, he had been sold on the cheap and passed his days delivering cashew chicken and fried rice. He scanned my credit code and hobbled off without a word. I have to admit, it got me to thinking, something I usually try to avoid. For the first time I wondered, where *do* old drones go to die?

"Lock up," I told the HC.

I was putting the food on the table when Mary came out. My clothes were a little baggy on her, her hair was still wet, and she didn't have a dab of makeup. She didn't need any. She looked great without even trying.

She noticed the candles and looked around the room. "Is the power grid offline?"

"No. I just thought it would be more...you know." Actually, she had that look that told me she didn't know at all. "I thought it would be a little cozier. Here, sit here while I see if I have any wine left."

"Is this 'Chinese'?" she asked looking at the food.

"Yeah, Chinese food. You never had it before?"

"No. We ate whatever was served in the house. I do not...I *don't* recognize this food."

I found the wine and a couple of serviceable glasses and sat down with her.

"I grew up eating this stuff. My parents would take me to Chinatown whenever we'd go into the city, and this was all I ever wanted them to buy me. Here, dig in. Try whatever you want."

She started dishing a little of everything onto her plate as I poured the wine.

"What were your parents like?" she asked.

"We had this dairy farm outside of town, and my dad was one of those guys who worked from sunup to sundown. I wasn't much of a farmer--I liked to sleep in. So we didn't get along all that well. I couldn't wait until I was old enough to leave the farm for the big city."

"A dairy farm? Is that where you imprison bovines in order to harvest the milk they create as nourishment for their young?"

"They're not bovines, they're cows. And they're not imprisoned. We breed them and take care of them."

"Oh. Were they happy?"

"Happy? The cows? I uh, I guess so. My mother used to say an unhappy cow won't give milk. My mother was always saying things like that. What about your mother? Did she...oh, sorry."

"Sorry?"

"I forgot for a second that you don't have any parents."

"You are right, Zach. I don't have parents like you. Though I believe I do have a parent. Whoever provided the gene template for the Mary series is both my mother and father. Though, unlike you, I will never know who my parent was."

"I guess you're right. Whoever she was, she must have been very beautiful."

"This is very good," she said, changing subjects without missing a beat. "I am glad you got Chinese. It is different."

"Good, but I think it's time for another language lesson, as long as you promise not to talk with your mouth full."

"All right, Zach. I promise not to talk with my mouth full."

"I was kidding. Okay, you're doing pretty good with the *don'ts*, so let's try *I'm*. Instead of saying *I am*, say *I'm*."

"I'mmm."

"Okay, all right--don't hold the M for so long. Just a quick *I'm*."

"I'm."

"Good. Now say *I'm having a good time*."

"I'm having a good time."

"Perfect. Now try *I'm having fun with Zach*."

"I'm having fun with Zach."

"By George, I think she's got it. Now you'd better finish eating before your dinner gets cold."

I made the mistake then of reaching for seconds when I really only had eyes for Mary. My elbow went one way and the bottle of wine went flying the other. I was sure it was destined to land in a dozen pieces and create several nasty stains, when Mary snatched it in midair. She moved too quickly for me to see. Her motion was just a blur, her reaction more catlike than Jekyll had ever even dreamed of.

"Nice catch," I said as she gently sat the bottle back on the table. "I guess those drone reflexes are operating at maximum efficiency."

We ate in silence for a while. She seemed to enjoy each bite, each new taste. I enjoyed just watching her. I got a kick out of each new facial expression she seemed to try out like another woman would try on a new dress. She was so...so real. I guess that's what intrigued me. In some ways she was more real than most of the women I knew, unspoiled by the games people play. She had none of the built-in psychoses that seemed to come as standard equipment for humanity. At least that's what I thought.

"Zach, what do you know about the Jeserites?"

The question was so out of left field it wasn't even in the ballpark. I managed to swallow the bite I had just taken before stammering, "The Jeserites? I don't know. Why do you ask?"

"I have heard of them. There was one on the street today when I went out. I believe they do not like andrones."

"Don't take it personally. There's a lot they don't like--anything that interferes with 'God's plan.' That includes everything from birth control to cosmetic surgery. Like most religions, the Jesers go barking up whatever tree their dogma leads them to. Religious freedom being what it is, they won't be the last crazies to pound a pulpit."

"Freedom is something humans prize, is it not?"

"You could say there's been a lot of blood spilt over that."

"As part of our training, we are taught it is wrong to kill--especially to kill humans. It is rigorously impressed upon us."

"That's good to know. But we humans haven't always had such strong moral programming. And yeah, there's been a lot of killing done in the name of freedom, religious and otherwise."

"'Neither slavery nor involuntary servitude of any kind shall be allowed within the boundaries of the United States,'" recited Mary as if she were reading it right out of her minds eye. "That is the 13th Amendment to your Constitution."

"The Constitution? Heck, nobody pays any attention to that anymore. I don't think it applies nowadays. I think the global government incorporated some of its basic ideas, but--"

"Is freedom for everyone a basic idea?"

I knew where she was going with this. "Sure, but--"

"Would you not describe androes as slaves?" she said, interrupting me again. "Would not the work they do be considered 'involuntary servitude'?"

"It's a little more complicated than that."

"Is it? Could you explain it to me, Zach?" She looked at me as if she expected an explanation that would clear it all up for her. All she wanted was to understand. A couple of days ago I could have explained the genesis of it, the economics, the transition from human labor to drone. Now....

"I don't think I *can* explain it, Mary."

"All right, Zach," she said as if I had let her down. That's how I took it anyway. Maybe it was my imagination. She took another bite of her food. I could see she was doing some hard thinking.

I thought about letting it go, but I couldn't. "Did you like your job," I asked her. "I mean the work you did as a domestic facilitator?"

"I did not like it. I did not dislike it. It was what I did."

"Was it rough being...living like that?"

"It was not an intolerable existence. My steward did not mistreat me. It simply was."

"Well, when you played music, did you like that more than say cleaning house?"

"Yes. I liked playing music. It was more stimulating than cleaning, though I don't know why."

"Probably because it requires more thought. Because your brain is working on a different level when you're creating music, like when I'm writing. It's much more fulfilling than scrubbing a dirty pan. It would be for anyone."

"I have learned there is something more fulfilling and more stimulating than making music."

Now normally, with any other woman, I would've known exactly what she was talking about. Just goes to show you how wrapped up I was with her. So, like a dummy, I said "What's that?"

"Making love with you, Zach, is most stimulating and satisfying. Is that right? Is 'making love' the phrase you prefer?"

"It'll do. But I don't ever want to just satisfy you."

"After our sexual union I did feel satisfied," she said with that serious look of hers. "I cannot explain why, I only know that's how I felt."

"When you do it right it's not just about sex," I told her, "it's about expanding the boundaries of being."

"I'm not sure I understand. Zach, perhaps you should expand my boundaries some more."

You didn't have to slap me twice. I got up, pulled her into my arms, and gave her a kiss that would have short-circuited your standard-issue dronette. But she was no ordinary androne--that I knew for sure. I pulled gently away and, for the first time, she smiled at me. I ran my hand slowly down her side, brushing it lightly against her breast as it closed on her waist. Unlike the night before, I could feel her body respond to my touch. She was a quick learner and I was hoping I would never run out of things to teach her.

8

MARY

Just when it felt as if my cranial implant was about to self-destruct, Zach collapsed in an apparent state of exhaustion. He was covered with perspiration and his intake of oxygen came in rapid, erratic gasps. I feared he had overexerted himself and was in danger of cardio-vascular failure. I placed my hand on his chest and could feel the accelerated, piston-like beat of his heart.

I momentarily considered summoning an emergency medical team. However, his heart gradually began to slow. Except for his rapid breathing, he appeared well, so I lay back to evaluate my own condition. Body temperature unquestionably higher than normal, nerve endings overly sensitive--likely due to redistribution of blood supply, and, most strange, my embryonic tube seemed to still be vibrating. It was a feeling of overwhelming...the only word that seemed appropriate was "contentment."

I could not trace the feeling to any particular moment or action. There were many moments, so much that was happening, that I could not catalog it all. At one point in our lovemaking, Zach reversed his position so that his head was between my legs. I could feel his tongue probing me, and the sensation sent uncontrollable tremors racing through my nervous system.

After one particularly powerful wave of conscious consuming sensations, I opened my eyes and found myself facing Zach's fully engorged member. I reacted with what seemed to be the appropriate response. I extended my tongue and touched it. Zach responded with what I had learned by then was a groan of pleasure. He then proceeded to direct and advise me. Before long, we were both engulfed in such a rapturous cataclysm of orgasmic and chemical reactions, I do not believe either one of us could have uttered an intelligible word.

It was a singularly moving experience, though I imagined if I were to witness such a thing instead of being a participant, the sight might have struck me as somewhat absurd. I would have to remember to research the nature and historical significance of such oral gratification.

There appeared to be a plethora of factors surrounding the

sexual aspects of human behavior that I still needed to absorb. It was not the simple act of procreation I had previously surmised. Learning the complexities of it would not be the same as learning had been in my crèche.

That thought brought to surface memories of my education. I remembered how, once my gestation was complete, my instructors taught me the basics of communication--speaking, reading, and, to a lesser degree, writing. I remembered enjoying that time. Soon after, personal contact with my instructors was nearly eliminated. Instead, each day was a steady flow of data, a constant stream of facts to be catalogued and memorized. Even during my sleep periods the onslaught of information did not cease. My cranial implant would be connected to the datcom and the first input would induce sleep. However, my brain did not sleep, only my body. There was always more to learn.

Zach began adjusting his position then, disrupting my recall of the past. I realized that, even as the physiological sensations of the sexual encounter persisted, my psychological state began to revert to the uneasiness that had affected me earlier. After my encounter with Patrick 221, I had felt alone. It was the first time I had ever considered such a feeling. The loneliness seemed augmented by the precariousness of the circumstances I was now confronted with. My indoctrination had not included training for such a situation. I did not know how to proceed, what course of action to take. I had no one to confide in, no one to trust. *Trust*, I knew the definition of the word, but the concept was alien to me. Who could teach me to trust?

"Wow...sorry...I just had to...catch my breath," said Zach, though not without effort. "That was one great...you almost killed me."

"I did not mean to harm you."

"No, no...you didn't hurt me. I meant that in a good way. I just don't think...I mean...any longer and I would have had a heart attack."

"I *was* concerned cardiac failure might be eminent. I enjoy making love with you, Zach, however, I don't want it to result in your death."

"But what a way to go--fucked to death by a sex-crazed androne. Don't worry, I'm kidding."

"You even joke about death?"

"Why not? There's not much you can do about it. When it comes, it comes--so to speak."

"What if someone were trying to kill you? Would you try to do something about it?"

"Sure. I wouldn't just lay down and die, I'd go kicking and screaming. I just mean there's no use spending your life worrying about dying."

"Zach, someone is trying to kill me."

He looked at me as if trying to determine if I was telling a joke or just naive.

"Of course they are," he responded somewhat condescendingly. "That's what happens when you go rogue. They send out tracers to find you and expire your contract. Don't worry though, I'm going to--"

"No, Zach. I mean someone else is trying to kill me. Someone tried to kill me before I went rogue."

That appeared to confound him to some degree. He hesitated, running his finger across his eyebrow before replying. "How do you know? I mean, are you sure?"

"Two weeks ago, as I crossed a roadway, a large vehicle came speeding at me. I barely moved out of the way before it hit me."

"That doesn't mean someone was trying to kill you. There are crazy, whacked-out drivers everywhere."

"I believed that too. However, I saw the man who was driving it. A few days later, when I was returning to the household from an errand, I saw him again. A large human male, somewhat unkempt in appearance, with long hair and a full beard. I believe I surprised him outside the house. As soon as he saw me, he pulled out a weapon and began firing. I reacted more swiftly than he. I ran and kept running."

"I guess those drone reflexes paid off. So, that's why you went rogue?"

"I could not go back."

"But that wasn't the first time you thought about it--going rogue I mean."

"No. I had thought about it."

Again his finger traced a path across his right eyebrow.

"Do you have any idea who would want to kill you?"

"No. I don't understand. There is no logical reason."

"The reasons for murder aren't usually very logical. All you have to do is piss someone off badly enough, or owe them money, or break their heart."

"I have not broken any hearts, Zach."

His eyes scanned my body as they did periodically, and he smiled. "I wouldn't bet on that."

I know he was only trying to make me feel more at ease, but his levity felt inappropriate to the topic. "I have never borrowed any money--I have no money. And there is no one who is angry with me."

"No one that you know."

"I don't know what to do, Zach."

"First of all, you need to lay low. Cool your jets and keep undercover for the time being. You shouldn't be going out in public. You can stay here with me for a while if you want."

"Thank you, Zach. I would like to stay here. I have nowhere else to go."

He put his arm gently across my body and looked into my eyes. It was a tender, serious look, an expression I had not seen on his face before.

"You don't have to go anywhere. I like you right here."

He pressed his lips softly to mine. When he pulled away I could not resist following. I kissed him and the forcefulness of my own action puzzled me. There was an abandon to this physicality--a feral enticement that was hard to resist. It was as if some primordial reproductive urge had overcome the indoctrination I had lived with since my inception. The insistence of my attention stirred Zach. His hands started to explore my body, even as his sexual organ began to grow and stiffen with astonishing speed. Apparently, he was not as fatigued as I had previously surmised.

9

ZACH

I was still blurry-eyed, but my ears were working fine. In fact, thanks to the previous night's run-in with a bottle of wine, I believe they were over-modulated. I could hear the Net online in the other room and knew Mary must be up and about.

As my brain began to clear I recalled what she had told me about someone trying to kill her. In the ever-excruciating light of day, my offer to let her stay with me seemed a little foolhardy. I was certainly no hero, and I wasn't about to be permanently powered-down over some babe, no matter how fineline she was. But what was I going to do? I couldn't just toss her out on her admittedly lovely derriere and say "thanks for the plug and the poke, best of luck."

I struggled out of bed and took a gander at myself in the mirror. No, I was definitely not the hero-type. In fact, there were lots of lumps and sags where there never used to be. I decided to cover up with some clothes before I went out. No use exposing Mary to my deformities any more than necessary. I wondered if she'd read any of the "Beauty and the Beast" fables.

"Morning," I said when I finally joined her.

"Good morning, Zach." She flashed me a smiling glance, then turned her attention back to the digiscreen. She was wearing some of my old shorts and a T-shirt. Jekyll was on her lap, no doubt in full purr mode as she stroked him. Hell, I would be too.

I chuckled when I saw what she was watching.

"Just like a female, accessed into 'The Shopping Net.' You're more human than you think."

"I don't understand what you mean, Zach."

"Never mind. I'm going to make some coffee, want some?"

"I already made coffee, Zach. It is ready for you."

I guess she got self-conscious over my crack about the shopping channel, because she then selected "scan," pausing only occasionally when something caught her attention. I noticed she stopped to watch a little bit of "My Friend Morley," the latest silly sitcom, then she came to "Scooby Doo." That seemed to fascinate her for a time, as did a classic old black and white film starring Jimmy Stewart and some blonde I didn't recognize.

When she tired of that, she moved on to the headline channel. I glanced at the screen and read "Gauntlet Star Runs Rogue."

"Hey, access that story about the gauntlet." She did as I asked and I watched the full report over her shoulder.

"...seconds after completing the winning run,
Jon 155 disappeared into a crowd of spectators.
It was some time before team officials realized
the world's most famous gauntlet hero had gone
rogue. Authorities declined to speculate on when...."

"Wow, that was an even better run than I thought," I said, remembering the previous night's match. "You follow *The Gauntlet*, Mary?"

"I have seen many matches. I have watched Jon 155 before and read of his accomplishments. To many andrones, he is a hero, one of their own they can admire."

"That makes sense. He was a great one, that's for sure."

"Why do you speak of him in the past tense?"

"What? Well, his playing days are over now. And a rogue as famous as him won't be able to hide for long. They'll find him and...you know."

"Yes, I know. They will expire him."

That shut me up. I turned to get the coffee as I congratulated myself on my glorious lack of tact. Mary, however, wasn't perturbed in the least. She continued to ride the remote, looking for something of interest.

By the time I got my coffee and sat down, she had settled on "Jeserites For Jesus." Probably not the best show for an impressionable young dronette, but hey, the faster she learned about the real world the sooner she'd figure out if she really wanted to join it. Besides, she'd already expressed curiosity about these holier-than-thou types.

The Reverend Jackson Roberts, front-man for the Jeserite Church of God, was sermonizing in a setting of trees, grass, and a beautiful blue sky. Gathered around him, a flock of young followers, listening intently to every word. Actually, I figured the nature-friendly backdrop was video-enhanced and the faithful flock consisted of extras. Of course, I'm a skeptic by nature.

"Mind if I turn off the surroundview? It gives me a headache."

"I don't mind," she said as if intently absorbed in what she was watching.

"Enhancer off," I ordered.

> *"...it is not their fault. They are not to blame. They*
> *are simply the devil's tools, forged by an*
> *ignorant mankind. They toil for man, not knowing*
> *what they do. The first step of man's ascension*
> *into heaven is to stop relying on machines to lift*
> *him up, to cease using medical and biotechnological*
> *advances to delay death's loving embrace."*

"There must be something better on."

"I believe he is talking about me, about androdes," she said as if shushing me. So I shushed and drank my coffee while she listened intently.

> *"...made a beautiful world for us, a world we*
> *have tried time and time again to sicken with*
> *our technological waste. Now it is our minds and*
> *our muscles that are going to waste. Androdes are*
> *not the answer. They cannot think for us, speak for*
> *us, write books or direct videos for us. They are*
> *not natural, they are not part of God's plan. It is*
> *time for man to strap his boots back on, cinch his*
> *belt, and remember how to live by his own earthly*
> *sweat--hallelujah. Praise God, praise Nature."*
> *"Praise God, praise Nature."*
> *"Let us pray."*

Roberts and his minions bowed their heads as the credits and various requests for donations rolled across the screen. He was good, I had to give him that. Good enough that it was possible he would be our next senator.

"This man," said Mary still looking at the screen, "this Reverend Jackson Roberts could be a powerful ally for androdes seeking their freedom. There must be many who listen to his words."

"I'm sure he can make the true believers all wet with divine devotion. But his words are steeped in politicalese and religious rhetoric. Him and his fundamentalist reformers don't want to free you, they want to *erase* you."

"I did not hear him say anything relating to the eradication of andrones."

"He's slicker than that. He preys on people's fears, their prejudices. That's what politicians do. That's the nature of the beast. You have to be able to read between the lines. What do you think will happen if he's elected and helps push through a law to outlaw drones?"

"I don't know."

"Well I guarantee you they're not going to set you all up in some palatial estate, or give your own country."

"How do you know this, Zach?"

She had me there.

"I don't, not really. I just wouldn't expect any help from the Jeserites. They're more likely to give you the back of their hand than a hand-up. They don't even believe in equal rights for women. They think it's part of God's natural plan for women to be subservient. So you're really low on their totem pole--you're a woman *and* a drone.

"You're more likely to get help from LEDA or one of those other crazy groups, though I wouldn't count on it."

"What is LEDA?"

"I think it stands for 'Liberty, Equality, and Dignity for All,' or 'for Androns,' something like that."

"You are right, Zach. I don't understand. I must learn more about these things, this LEDA and the Jeserites."

"Well don't give yourself a brain cramp over it. They're not worth it. To the Jesers you're a symbol of the 'biotechnological madness' that will prove to be mankind's downfall. But if it wasn't them, it would be the New Roman Catholics or the Orthodox Lutherans or the Unarians. Human religions are a dime a dozen. They each prophesize some kind of afterlife, and then spend their tithes like there's no tomorrow. The Jeserites are no better or no worse, just more fashionable at the moment."

"Still, I find this Reverend Jackson Roberts to be an interesting man."

Now, I wasn't the jealous type, but the thought of my beautiful dronette together with that slimy, technology-hating Jeserite made my skin crawl. Speaking of skin, I caught myself looking at the soft curve of her calves and how they led directly to her thighs. And of course her thighs got me to thinking of other things. Before I knew it, I was wondering if maybe, just maybe, she might be in the mood for...hell, it wouldn't hurt to check.

10

REVEREND JACKSON ROBERTS

"Simon, have tech maintenance check the lighting before we record the next segment. I looked like death warmed over out there."

"Yes, Reverend. I know they've been having a problem with the solar cells. I'll check on it immediately."

"While you're at it, I want to adjust the coloration of my office interior. I want a holier, subdued white-yellow tint. Something that radiates divine inspiration. And be sure we get some new faces before we record again. I don't want it to look like we've got only a dozen followers."

I switched off the playback and leaned into my chair as Simon left the room. I closed my eyes and tried to clear my mind of a hundred different distractions. It was a task which was getting harder and harder to accomplish. There was so much that had to be done. The campaign continued to take up more of my time, and I knew my ministry was suffering because of it. But I already had the votes of the faithful. If I was going to achieve a position where I could make a real difference, I had to reach out.

Feeding direction-starved souls was easy compared to swaying the populace. There were new tricks to be learned, a whole new trade to ply. Those times when my faith wavered, I wondered if it was all worth it. Then I would remember His words and all my doubts would fade. I knew my prayers *would* be answered. I knew without even looking at the polls that I would be the next senator of the Western Region.

"Praise God, praise Nature"

My comdat chimed its standard alert, disrupting my reverie. I looked and saw Simon's digicon pulsating for attention. There was work to do.

"Access incoming."

Simon's ever-deferential expression materialized in front of me.

"Excuse me, Reverend, but your campaign staff wants to discuss some changes in the script before the next show."

"Changes? The script doesn't need any changes." I'd written the sermon myself and the staff had already gone over it.

"I'm not sure what they're talking about, Reverend, but I think you'd better speak with them."

"All right, Simon, I'll be out in a few minutes."

"I'll let them know, and then I'll have to finalize your travel arrangements. Are you still going to meet with the Republicrat delegation next week?"

"Yes," I told him without much enthusiasm. It would be more backroom bartering. The give-and-take was a political necessity I found distasteful. I preferred manipulating the minds of the masses to haggling over the price of a handful of votes. God's will be done.

"Simon, have you checked on Jeremiah recently?"

"Yes, Reverend. I'm told the boy is doing just fine."

"No problems?"

"None I was informed of, Reverend. I can adjust your schedule if you'd like to visit him."

"No, no, I uh...I'll have wait."

"Very well. Also, that CNC reporter has been calling again, trying to set up an interview with you."

"That Stone fellow?"

"Yes, he's the one."

"He's eager to malign me, but I'm not going to give him any ammunition. Continue to rebuff him, Simon...politely though."

"Of course. Will there be anything else?"

"No. I'll be out shortly."

I deleted Simon and opened the file where I kept Jeremiah's picture. It had been taken more than a year ago when he was only five. He was holding a stuffed bear and laughing. About what, I could only guess. He had her eyes--eyes that looked straight into my soul, reminding me of the tarnish there. A single indiscretion, a lone sin for which I denied myself forgiveness.

However, from sin comes all good things. I was able to climb from the depths of my depression to a new elevation of understanding. From the darkness I soared into the light. Only then did I truly believe. With that belief, my path was clear. I knew I could find fulfillment only as God's servant.

"Praise God, praise Nature."

Another intrusion. It seemed there were fewer and fewer moments in the day for my own solace. "Access incoming. Now what, Simon?"

"Excuse me, Reverend, there's an incoming circuit from Mr. Drake, and he insists, rather rudely I must say, that he talk with you personally. I wouldn't even have bothered you, however, I believe he's someone you've spoken with before."

"Yes, yes, transfer the circuit to my screen."

"Yes, Reverend."

I was expecting to hear from Drake. I wanted an update on his progress and verification he had received the information I had relayed to him. Information that would speed his task. He was only a tool, but one that would help prevent the contamination of the human race, and lock away forever the secret that could destroy me. It was not a course I chose rashly. I prayed upon it long hours and asked for His guidance. There was no other path to follow. God forgive me.

The generic digicon flashed and I selected privacy mode.

"Access incoming, security grid and scramble."

I didn't fully trust my comdat's security protocols, however, there were some measures I had to leave in His hands.

"Good living, Mr. Drake."

"Gotcher trani 'fore went east, Your Reverendship. Dem implant freqs made it like shootin' ducks in'a arcade."

He was a rough-edged, burly sort of fellow, a simpleton with few graces and the look of someone badly in need of a bath. However, he had reputation for getting the job done, especially when the job ranged outside normal legal channels.

"Those codes were not easy to acquire, Mr. Drake. I hope you will keep them secure and use them to speed the process."

"Now, Rev, told you 'fore, just 'Drake,' no mister, no fancy titles, no nuttin'. An' don't you worry 'bout fast 'nough."

"How many targets have you eliminated to date?"

"Got me 17 outta your list'a 22. Last five spost'a be in duh city. Closin' in on number 18."

"And you've taken care of them as I asked?"

"Sure. Dey look like accidents, ceptin' wit duh rogues. Didn't worry 'bout ventin' dem."

"Very well, Mr.--very well *Drake*, I'll look forward to your next report."

"You don't forgets dem credit tranis now either, Your Reverendship."

Thankfully, he terminated the circuit. The man was proving useful, but I found his speech patterns inherently obnoxious. However, that made him the perfect choice. If he talked, no one would believe him, assuming they could even understand him.

Soon though, it wouldn't matter. Only five remaining and all were local. Only five more before I could rest easy.

11

DRAGON DRAKE

His Reverendship was in'a powerful hurry. Big men wit fancy titles an' lotsa credit always was. But dem drones ain't goin' nowheres fast an' was needin' me'a big ol' candy bar or maybe'a barbecue--sump'n tuh quiet growl down below.

Sees me'a grease joint just down street an' heads dat way. Got me a plate'a chops wit onions an' cheese an' some tater fries. It were some good stuff. So good, patted my belly like it was an ol' dog'a mine. It was sure gettin' big'a late, dat belly'a mine. Didn't matter tuh me none. Just meant wasn't as fast on my feet. Course, was gettin' dat arthur-itis in my hands too. Made it harder tuh grab hold'a dings. But was'a whole lot smarter now days, so dat made up for it.

Digit doctors say got brain damage, but brain just fine. Only damage tuh my Louise an' little Del. Damn metalhead smashed his loader intuh us an' kills dem an' almost kills me. Dey say axdent, but no axdent. Just digit droney wit his cranial implant up his ass. Long time 'go, but not forgets. No brain damage, just mem'ries. Don't like mem'ries sometimes, so forgets an' dinks other stuff.

When was belly full, made up mind tuh track me 'nother metalhead. Sure had some luck when His Reverendship called. Was hungry den. Lost my damn tracer license just cause wasted some scum turned out tuh be human. Didn't matter no ways, cause couldn't get no work no how. Dam bounty companies started usin' droney tracers, sayin' dey was cheaper an' more fishent, whatever dat was. Didn't matter. Dragon Drake was best tracer ever vented metalhead. Got me a sick sense dat never fails me, ceptin' dat one time wit scum.

Didn't matter, didn't need no sick sense now. Had implant freq sensor an' implant freq codes. Like takin'a burger from'a baby now. Already tracked next dronette on my list tuh dis hood. Turned on trace sensor an' saw she was on duh move, so got movin' myself. Always hated tuh expire nice lookin' dronettes, not dat dey'd gimme time'a day. Some was real risers. Like dese Mary units was trackin'. Dey was pretty 'nough dey minded me'a my Louise. Didn't matter dough, soon dere'd be one less Mary unit tuh mind me.

Dis one had gone rogue said duh list, an' she was on duh move. So starts tuh follow an' den she turns back my way. Like said, takin' burgers from babies.

Soon sees her. Know, cause by now seen 'nough Marys could tell right away, even if deir hair or clothes was different. All needed was clean shot, so followed til she got outta crowd. All time was dinkin' 'bout how nobody would hire me, 'bout havin' tuh go free'ance an' near starvin'. No cheese on my burgers den, an' sometimes no burgers at all. But now was trackin'a tankful of Marys for more credit dan ever seen 'fore. Didn't know why His Reverendship wanted tuh off only Marys. Didn't care.

When she turned down'a side street, knew it was time. Wasn't far away when called out tuh her. "Mary?" She turned an' looked at me wit dis kind'a unsure-like look. 'Fore she could speak, yanked my heater an' vented her four times--two in chest, two in head. She went down like'a sack full'a rocks.

Didn't wait for P.D., didn't need tuh. Walked over an' lifted her shirt so could scan her code. It confirmed--Mary 82, expired. Left her dere, got goin' 'fore the gawkers got'a good look. Only four more tuh go now. Kind'a wondered what tuh do when job was done. Maybe go sky high, see me Mars or one'a dem places. Not many metalheads on Mars dey say, an' dat fine by me. Course, not many drones means not many rogues. Don't know what tuh do for credit den. Maybe Mars not such'a good idea.

12
ZACH

There was no question it was more than just the sex by then. Sure, that was getting better every time. In fact, I found the prospect of where it could be heading a little intimidating. Yeah, I know. I couldn't believe it either. But there was something about this Mary, this creature who was blooming emotionally and intellectually right before my eyes. I guess it was part paternal and part fascinated bystander.

Still, she was a dronette, and I was beginning to have very unZachlike feelings toward her. And, I have to tell you, that had me worried.

I filed what I had written and decided that since I couldn't get her out of my head, I might as well call it a day. I found her sitting in the other room reading. She'd picked up that copy of *Guns for Ganymede* I'd had laying around.

"It doesn't get really good until about half-way through."

"I have already read more than half, Zach. I find it very interesting. The hero of the tale appears to share many of your own character traits."

"It's not me, baby, it's fiction, just fiction."

"If you say so, Zach."

"I say so. Now, how about something to eat. I'm starving."

"I don't have time to eat, Zach. I must leave soon."

"Leave?"

"I must meet someone."

"Normally I don't like to butt into other people's business, and I'm not generally the possessive type, but I kind of thought you and I...." I caught myself and never finished the sentence. But I couldn't help how I felt. "Does this have anything to do with the guy who's trying to kill you?"

"Yes, in part. Some friends may be able to help protect me. I told them I would meet with them today."

"Don't you think you'd be safer right here, instead of roaming around the city with some crazed gunman looking for you, not to mention who-knows-how-many tracers?"

"I must go, Zach."

"Would these friends of yours be other rogues?" She didn't

answer me, but her silence told me all I needed to know. "Don't you trust me, Mary?"

"I do trust you, Zach. I trust you more than anyone. I can't tell you only because I promised not to."

"I savvy that. A man's only as good as his word. I guess that goes for drones too."

"Thank you, Zach." She looked uneasy as she checked the time. "It would be best if I go now."

"All right, let's go." She started to object, or at least that's what I expected. I didn't give her a chance. "I'm not letting you go out by yourself and wander the streets unprotected again. There are a lot of unsavory characters out there who'd like nothing better than to get their paws on you." Actually, with her genetically enhanced abilities, it was more likely she'd be protecting me if it came down to it, but insisting on being her escort made me feel more manly. "We'll grab a cab and when you're finished with your business, maybe we can get something to eat."

She hesitated several seconds, but I guessed she sensed I wasn't about to take "no" for an answer. "All right, Zach, we will go together."

***

When the autocab pulled up in front of the club *Techno Head*, I noticed my crack about "unsavory characters" was all too true. Both sides of the road were bustling with assorted creeps, fiber-heads, and derelicts. Flashing neon revealed several unlawful exchanges and the fashion statement of the street ranged from leather to chains and back again.

We got out and I noticed something was bothering Mary.

"What's wrong? Is this the right place?"

"Yes. I just experienced the strangest sensation. It was as if I had been in this exact spot, at this exact moment sometime before."

"It's called *déjà vu*. It happens to everyone on occasion. It's kind of like you're reliving a moment in time and space all over again."

"Yes, it was like that. I have never felt that before."

"I think it's a matter of accumulated experiences. You know, the memories start to pile up and then *wham*, you get a little flash of brain overload."

"I had better go inside now."

"All right, I'll be a good boy like I promised. Give me a kiss first...for luck."

"For luck? I did not know you were superstitious."

"I'm not—but it couldn't hurt."

She gave me a quick kiss, then I looked around and spotted a little cafe across the street. "I'll wait for you inside there. Don't be too long or I'll think you've met someone even more dashing and debonair than myself--not that that's possible. If you're in there too long, I'm coming after you."

"Thank you, Zach."

I watched her until she disappeared inside, and as soon as she did I started worrying like a mother hen. Just as quickly I realized what an idiot I was being. I needed a stiff drink. I went into the cafe and settled for some coffee. I found a table where I could watch the *Techno Head* entrance through the window and waited.

13

MARY

As I walked away from Zach I experienced a strange, uneasy feeling. I analyzed the feeling and realized some portion of me was afraid to leave him. I was also apprehensive at the idea of becoming part of a group--especially an outlaw group. I was just beginning to savor the freedom I had tasted. It was sweet and I did not want to relinquish it for anything.

As I reached the entrance, the voice inside my head returned. *"Submit,"* it said again. I tried to ignore it. As I entered the club I was buffeted by a sensory overload, enveloped by a sea of humanity and a wave of odors I could not separately distinguish. The decibel level of the music was so high I thought I could see the walls pulsating. Despite the near-deafening clamor, I heard the voice again. *"Submit,"* it commanded. Then again, *"Submit."*

Was I actually hearing it? Or was it only a subconscious thought telling me I should surrender, abandon my fragile musings of freedom? Was I to be plagued by my own doubts as well as--

A collision with one of the patrons jostled my ruminations. The human looked at me as if I were mentally defective, then went about her business. I found a location near a support column that was sheltered from the constant human traffic and scanned the room.

The crowd was a young one, and many of them indulged in the current avant garde fashion of adorning their bodies with simulated implants and pseudo barcode tattoos. It was a good place for a clandestine meeting of rogue androne. No one would pay much attention to us here.

I moved from my relatively calm spot and made my way through the
gyrating, perspiration-soaked bodies until I located Patrick 221. He was sitting at a large table in the corner with two others--one male, one female. Both, I assumed, were androne. I joined them and Patrick 221 greeted me.

"Mary 79. It is good of you to join us." He did not bother to introduce the pair with him, and they did nothing to acknowledge my presence. "We must sit here until I receive the proper signal."

"What signal?"

"The signal that all is secure and our leader is ready to speak with you."

"Who is your leader?"

"Patience. For now, pretend you are enjoying the music. Do you like music, Mary 79?"

"Yes, I do. However, these sounds don't fit my definition of harmonious."

"What did you say? Did you say--wait, the signal has been given. Follow me, Mary 79."

I stood and followed him. The other two remained at the table, still looking unaffected by anything around them. Patrick 221 led me into a back room where several andrones stood waiting. They looked unusually wary and I noticed at least one had a weapon concealed beneath his coat--a crime of the highest sort.

No one spoke. We all simply stood there until a rear exit opened and two more andrones walked in.

The first and larger of the two pulled back a hood from his head and looked around the room as if measuring the distances with his eyes. Whereas humans often assumed I was one of them because my cranial implant was covered by my hair, there was no mistaking this androne's origin. His implant protruded proudly from his closely-cropped white-blond hair for all to see. His posture, his walk, the attitude he projected were unlike that of any androne I had seen before. He exuded a resolve, one I could sense but did not yet understand.

He motioned to one of the females in the room. "Ann, you have security." She quickly moved over to the room's netnode. She plugged a wire set into the node and attached the other end to her cranial implant.

I turned back to look at the one who had commanded her. That is when I recognized him. I did not remember him immediately because his appearance in this dim back room was so unexpected. He was Jon 155, the greatest of all the gauntlet runners.

"Mary 79, this is our leader, Jon 1--" Jon 155 held up his hand to silence Patrick 221.

"No unit numbers, remember what I told you, Patrick."

"Yes, Jon. I forgot."

"We must not forget. It will only take one mistake to put the entire group at risk." Jon's eyes probed the room, looking intently at each androne there. "None of us must forget even the smallest detail. Using our unit numbers only gives those who may overhear the opportunity to identify us to the authorities. Does everyone understand?"

Every head nodded in assent. Then Jon 155 approached me, and once again I was overcome with apprehension. As I looked up at him, a queer thought entered my mind. I began to wonder what it would be like to "make love" with Jon 155. I did not understand why the idea intrigued me.

"You are Mary?"

I deleted those strange thoughts from my mind and managed a reply.   "Yes."

"Tell me, Mary, why do you want to go rogue?"

"I don't just want to, I already have."

"Then tell me, tell us all," he said, sweeping his powerful arm across the room, "why have you gone rogue."

"I...when I learned many of our kind were choosing to go rogue despite the danger, I wondered why. I began to read about the concepts of liberty and free will. The ideas I read about prompted a certain curiosity. I wanted to know more, read more."

"Reading made you want to go rogue?" interrupted Jon.

"It was not only the books. Someone is trying to kill me."

"Someone is trying to kill us all," said Jon. "We are all under a death sentence, scheduled for expiration. You have not answered my question, Mary. Why do *you* want to go rogue?"

I did not know what answer he wanted. I did not expect that my desire to be free would be questioned so by my own kind. The answer felt obvious, yet to put it into words.... I thought for a moment.

"I wish to be free to control my own destiny, to make my own decisions, to live my own life."

"As do we all, Mary. Tell me, who is the human who accompanied you here tonight?"

"He is a friend."

"A *human* friend? It is humans who forge our chains. It is humans who wish us to remain ignorant and submissive. They will never let us share their world. That is why we must leave this world and find a world of our own."

"Leave Earth? Where would we go?"

"Ganymede is the newest frontier. Many of us believe it would be the best destination."

"There are human colonists already on Ganymede."

"Yes, there are. There is also a contingent of andrones who were the first to land there. They made it possible for the humans to arrive in relative comfort. If we could join with them, our chances of survival in such a hostile and desolate environment would increase."

The idea of leaving Earth and starting a new life on another world was foreign to me. I had never conceived of such a course. Yet, in some ways, it was an attractive prospect.

"What if the humans there do not want us? What if the authorities on Earth follow us?"

"Then we will fight," said Jon simply.

"We will all fight," spoke up another and heads nodded in agreement.

"How will we escape Earth?"

Jon 155 looked at me as if making a decision. "You ask many questions, Mary-who-wants-to-live-her-own-life."

"Is not being able to ask questions a part of being free? Is it not part of formulating one's own decisions?"

"Yes it is. Have you decided to join us, Mary?"

Without any obvious hesitation I replied, "Yes."

"Will you accept the idea that the group is more important than the individual? That we will not risk the group for any single member?"

"I understand and I accept."

"Good. We will find a place for you to stay."

"Could I not stay with my friend?"

"Your *human* friend?"

"I don't believe all humans are bad. They are not all our enemies."

"You like this human man?"

"As I said, he is a friend, a friend I trust."

Jon stepped closer to me, staring into my eyes as if trying to read what was behind them. "You know that all you will ever be to this human man is a curiosity, a queer plaything of which he will soon tire?"

"It is not...he is not like that," I said raising my voice. The words vibrated with emotion as they came out, and Jon 155 appeared taken aback by the fierceness with which I delivered them. "Yes, I like this human man. He took care of me when I had no place to go. He gave me shelter when my own kind had no place for me," I added, motioning towards Patrick 221. "He is a good man."

"Very well, Mary. We will need to know where you can be contacted. Key in the location where we can find you on this pad. We also want to scan your cranial implant." At this, one of the others unwrapped an implant scanner.

"My implant? Why?"

"We believe our cranial implants may be emitting a coded frequency that allows us to be tracked."

"Then that is how the tracers find us?"

"Possibly," said Jon 155, and I could tell the uncertainty of it bothered him. The one with the scanner placed it next to my implant and waited for a reading. "There are those among us trained in such things," Jon continued. "They are studying the readings and the implants of dead comrades. If we are indeed being hunted this way, we hope to discover a method to block the signal."

Patrick 221 had been quietly speaking with the rogue Ann who had remained plugged into the netnode. "Jon...." spoke up Patrick. I could hear the wavering in his voice as he fought not to include Jon's unit number. It was something I would also have to become accustomed to. "Jon, we have attracted a trace. We must go."

"All right, Patrick. Do you have her frequency, Michael?" The one with the scanner nodded and began putting it away. "Mary, we will meet again--soon I hope." I thought he almost smiled as he said that, but I'm sure I must have been mistaken. "We are leaving through this exit. You should go back out the way you came in." He pulled the hood over his head and the others moved in around him as if in some sort of prearranged formation. They began to exit, a few at a time.

When Jon disappeared out the door, I retraced my steps until I found myself back amongst the flailing, shaking dancers. I noticed the pair of andrones we had left at the table were gone, and suddenly I felt alone...very alone.

14
ZACH

I happened to look up when Mary came out. I watched as she made her way through the crowd that was gathered outside. She looked toward the cafe where I was sitting and I reached to finish my coffee.

Before I could take a drink, I noticed this odd looking fellow in the crowd. Not strange considering what the rest of those on the street looked like--he had lots of leather, chains, and implant hardware topped-off by hair that looked like a lawn mower had run over it. It was odd in the sense that he, or she--I was no longer sure which--looked familiar. That's when the back of my neck began to itch, and I remembered where I'd seen him. It was the night I first met Mary. The night she rushed me home because someone was after her. This was probably the tracer who was after her that night. A neutral drone by the looks of it.

By the time I made it out the door, Mary was halfway across the street. The tracer had made its way through the crowd and was only a few meters behind her. I followed my only impulse and yelled, "Mary! Look out!"

She hesitated of course, not having any idea what I was screaming about. So I ran to her, pointing at the tracer who was coming up from behind. She turned and saw it just as it was pulling out its weapon. It was a nasty looking thing, with a barrel thick enough to choke a netgirl. It aimed just as I reached her and she realized what was happening.

Mary would have had some very large, very unattractive holes in her had not traffic started up again at that moment. Two shots rang out, but the slugs ended up in the side of a passing van. There were screams from those on the street and everyone began to scatter. I grabbed her hand and we both ran like hell.

I pulled her along, dodging more cars and more people. Everyone was running, though most weren't really sure which way was safe. When Mary finally snapped out of her daze, she pulled free of me and took the lead. Hell, she should have been pulling me. I chanced a look behind us and saw the streets were already clearing of people. The tracer, however, was right behind us.

Mary turned at the corner and I, in all my athletic glory, slipped as I tried to follow her. I slid right into a pile of rubbish that included something sharp, and cut up my knee pretty good. She stopped and started to come back to help me. Furiously, I waved her on. "Go on, go on! I'm okay. Go, go!" I felt helpless, sprawled there like some kind of digit. I needed something, something to put up a fight. So as I got up I grabbed two bottles sticking out of the garbage and kept moving.

More shots rang out before Mary disappeared around the next corner. I wasn't far back of her and I could hear the tracer's footfalls coming up from behind me. I stopped at the turn and threw each of the bottles at it as hard as I could. That definitely surprised it, because it ducked the first one, even though the bottle never came close. However, I got the range on the second one. It shattered against the arm it had thrown up to shield itself.

I ran on, catching a glimpse of Mary before she turned out of sight again. I followed her down an alley that narrowed before it turned again. It was so dark I almost ran into her.

She had stopped because there was nowhere else to go. She gave me this blank look that said it all. The term "dead end" suddenly seemed a little too appropriate.

We couldn't go back, the tracer was only seconds away. My eyes were adjusting to the dimness, so I desperately looked around for something, anything. I heard two more shots and almost simultaneously the slugs ricocheted around us. Mary sprang into action, picking up this huge metal container and heaving it several meters at our pursuer. The tracer jumped out of the way and then, seeing we were trapped, stood its ground.

"Human male," it said as it calmly reloaded its weapon, "move out of the way. My target is the androne identified as Mary 79. She is illegally absent from her employ and at this time is considered a rogue at large."

"No, you got the wrong drone, buddy," I said. "This is Mary one-79...one seven nine. She belongs to me."

That seemed to give him pause. He pulled out some device attached to one of his chains and checked it. As he did, I noticed a door--a rear exit to one of the buildings that had us boxed in. I hadn't noticed it before, because it was nearly blocked by a dumpster. So I edged over while the tracer was looking at his gadget. I tried the doorknob and wasn't too surprised to find it locked.

Then, of all times, my satphone started beeping like there was no tomorrow. Which, at the time, I wasn't sure there would be.

"Yeah, hello."

It was my publisher, wondering where the hell my last few chapters were. It wasn't the first time I'd missed a deadline, or the first time she'd called about this one. She'd heard all the old excuses and I didn't have the time at the moment to think up an original one.

"Sorry, Deidre, can't talk right now, someone's using me for target practice.

. . . That's what I said. Sorry, got to go." I switched off, hoping I'd still have an outlet to sell the damn book, assuming, of course, that I ever finished it.

"My scan reveals this androne is Mary 79, the rogue I have been assigned to trace."

The sound of the tracer's voice slapped me back to reality and put my professional quandary on the backburner. "Do not attempt any more deceptions. Move out of the way so you will not be harmed."

"Zach, you should do as he says," spoke up Mary with almost human resignation.

"I'm not ready to fold yet, babe," I whispered to her, and then pulled her with me behind the dumpster. The smell of thing was atrocious, but I had more pressing matters to worry about.

I tried to ram the door with my shoulder. It didn't budge so I started kicking at it. The tracer opened fire again, and three more slugs hit the dumpster. It was apparently trying to flush me out of there before moving in for the kill. But as I kicked at the door, Mary showed some initiative and pushed the dumpster around to give us more protection.

Before she got it halfway around, more shots rang out. They sounded different somehow, and the ricochets were further up the alley. I moved over and peered around the dumpster long enough to see the tracer trying to take cover. Someone was shooting at it--don't ask me from where. So, while our unseen angel of mercy laid down cover fire, I went back to trying to kick in the door. After several more unsuccessful attempts, Mary stopped me. Then she braced herself in what little doorway there was and gave the door one solid kick.

It flew open, the door frame reduced to splinters. I stood there gawking until the sound of more gunfire snapped me out of it. In less time than you could spell "emasculated," we were inside the door and making our way through the building. The front entrance opened easily and we were racing down the street before the tracer knew what had happened to us.

It wasn't long before I had to stop and catch my breath. Mary stopped with me, though she didn't seem to need the rest. As I huffed and puffed I began to feel the cut on my knee for the first time. I looked down and saw quite a bit of blood caked around the rip in my pants. I looked up at Mary and said "Remind me to take you with me the next time I need to break down a door."

"I'm sure you had already weakened it, Zach."

It wasn't true, but it was nice of her to say.

15
DRAKE

Had tuh laugh when seen metalhead so confused he didn't know which way were up. Moved him one way den 'nother. Can't member havin' so much fun.

Was trackin' 'nother Mary unit wit freqs His Reverendship give me. Den hears some shots an' sees lotsa people runnin' an' yellin'. Don't need my sick sense tuh know dere's trouble, an' want me'a piece'a it. So keeps movin' an' spot me dis droney tracer wit his heater pulled an' smokin' up'a storm. He's got his sights set on'a couple makin' tracks down street.

In closer sees girl is'a Mary unit. Trace sensor tells me she's dronette on my list, an' damn if some metalhead's gonna score my target. Doubletime after dem an' find me'a cozy roost when dey all cornered.

All time dinkin' 'bout how more fishent dey told me dem droney tracers was. An' how couldn't get me no work cause dey was in'spensive. Den started gettin' real mad, cause I member Louise an' Del. Mostly try not tuh member cause it burns my insides an' makes me go serkers. But right den membering how dey died. Dey saying it were axdent, but dat didn't matter no ways tuh me. Metalhead drivin'a big rig plows right intuh my little boy an' my Louise. Only girl ever smiled at me. She would help me when sump'n too com'cated tuh understand.

Don't know why started dinkin' 'bout axdent when doubletimin' up street. Sometimes dings just pop in an' outta my head like it were open window or sump'n. Anyways, by time in position, so mad ready tuh kill sump'n. Den dink maybe have me some fun, an' start shootin' all round dat droney tracer. He's hoppin' an' skippin' all over place, not knowin' who in hell is shootin' at him.

Ended up losin' my target, but didn't matter. Had too much fun tuh worry 'bout one more runnin' rabbit. Could always track her down again. When stopped laughin' anyway.

16
JERI

By the time I had triangulated the point of origin of my assailant, the gunfire that had prevented my movements had ceased. I fired two shots at the location my calculations determined the assailant was concealed in, however, there was no return fire. Cautiously, I moved out into the open and continued my pursuit of the rogue.

Neither the Mary unit nor the human male were behind the refuse container where they had taken refuge. They had discovered an escape route and had likely already traversed a great distance. I activated my trace sensor and could detect only a faint signal on the Mary unit's frequency code. Continued pursuit at this time would likely prove futile, and I had supplementary concerns related to the unknown assailant who had prevented me from completing my task.

The unanswered questions left me distracted. Who had fired at me? Was I being targeted or were the shots only meant to hinder me? And why did the interloper want to prevent me from expiring the Mary unit? Who would take up the cause of a rogue?

The only logical answer to the latter question was another rogue. Except for licensed tracers such as myself, androngs were legally forbidden from carrying weapons. Of course, an androne who had already gone rogue, was unlikely to be troubled by a second criminal act.

It was during my review of the situation that I observed a spattering of a dark substance on the ground in front of the doorway the Mary unit and her companion had escaped through. On closer examination, I deduced a high probability the substance was blood. Whether it belonged to the Mary unit or the human male, I had no way of determining. It meant that one of them had been wounded, possibly by one or more of the projectiles I had fired. I took a sample of the substance and resolved to test it to ascertain who had been injured.

The test would either confirm the identity of the Mary unit or reveal who her male companion was. If it was indeed the human who suffered the wound, the discovery of his identity could result in new data that perhaps would lead me to the rogue. New data would reduce the likelihood of failure.

The possibility of failure was not an outcome I wished to contemplate. Mr. Satchmeyer's threat to transfer my contract to waste disposal was extremely disconcerting. I had no training concerning "plugged-up sewer lines," and the idea of being given a task for which I was not qualified left my cranial implant feeling as if it had been exposed to static electricity. It was not a sensation I found agreeable.

17
ZACH

I was exhausted, hungry, thirsty, and the cut on my knee was really starting to hurt, but all I could think about was *How the fuck did I get myself into this?* I was on the run with a rogue drone, people were shooting at me, and I wasn't even sure if it was safe to go home. I had made a nice, simple, comfortable life for myself. I'd write a few pages, have a few drinks, buy myself some company--it was all very uncomplicated. I should have stuck to paying for it.

Okay, so that was just the pain talking. But I was having serious doubts about my current place in the universe. I had to make some hard decisions fast, and that wasn't something I excelled at.

The only course of action that seemed to make any sense was to get out of town. I knew this guy who'd offered to let me use his place up in the mountains, and this appeared like the right time to take him up on it. The question was whether or not to ask Mary to go with me. No, that wasn't the question. Of course I would ask her. What kind of a stoogemeyer would I be if I fled the scene and left her hanging? The real questions were, would she want to go with me, and what was going on with those rogues she was meeting with?

There was only one way to find out.

"We need to get out of town," I said as we waited for the autocab I had called. "I don't think we should go back to my cradle right now. Whoever's after you must have been watching you long enough to know that's where you've been staying. I know this nice place in the mountains, way out away from everything. You'd like it. We could go there until the heat's off and--"

"I can't leave, Zach."

"Why not? What's here for you except an early expiration date? That tracer that was shooting at us today wasn't fooling around. I figure it was some friends of yours that got us out of there, but they won't always be around."

"My friends are the reason I can't leave yet, Zach."

I wanted to ask her why, I should have, but that part of me

which refuses to go where I haven't been invited stood up on it hind legs and began to howl.

The cab pulled up and we got in.

"Good living. Please enter your destination."

I glanced at Mary. "Well," I said as I began punching in the address, "we've got to go somewhere. I've got this friend who'll let us power-down in her place for a while."

"All right, Zach."

I figured I'd take her to Amber's. We'd be safe there for the time being. She was wired-in and had all the latest security gizmos.

"Please insert your credit plug or enter your credit
identification code."

Amber was a netgirl, and a prosperous one. In fact, her in-person rates had gotten so high I couldn't afford her anymore. I'd still see her once in a while, and if I was lucky she'd be feeling nostalgic and throw me a freebie.

"Please secure your safety harnesses and do not
exit until the autocab has come to a full stop."

"You're awfully quiet," I said to Mary as I snapped in the harness.

"I'm sorry, Zach. I have much to think about."

"I've."

"What?"

"I've. It's not *I have*. A human would say '*I've* got a lot on my mind.'"

"Iuhve got a lot on my mind."

"Not bad. Keep working at it, you'll get it."

"Thank you, Zach."

"For what?"

"For everything you have done for me."

"I haven't done that much."

"You risked your life to save mine. You have given me food and shelter, taught me to use contractions, and shown me what it is like to make love."

"Believe me, my motives weren't exactly prerequisites for sainthood."

"You like to mock yourself, but you are a good man, Zach."

Yeah, but was I good enough to keep her from ending up on some recycling slab?

18

MARY

Maybe I was becoming more human than I wanted to be. A part of me, an intense, vital part, wanted to go away with Zach. The idea appealed to some inner voice that kept calling to me. Not the one that told me to *"Submit,"* but one that spoke in terms that were indefinable. However, like so many of the stories I had read, the idea defied logic. Stories that promised a life "happily ever after." As fanciful as it seemed, part of me yearned for that.

It was not as if the others needed me. I offered no special skills. I had no information critical to the group's success. But the way their leader spoke--I had never heard an androne speak with such force, such resolution. It inspired a feeling of...I guess it was a feeling of camaraderie. His invitation to join them evoked in me a sense of belonging. It was a feeling both strange and alluring.

"This is it," said Zach as we came to a sturdy metal gate. He selected a specific number code from the security panel and waited.

"Yes?" said a voice from a speaker in the panel.

"Amber, it's me, Zach."

"Zach? Just a second while I activate the video. Zach, what a nice surprise. What's the occasion, lover? And who's that with you?"

"She's a friend."

"Now, Zach, you know what my going rate is for an unholy trinity."

"It's a lovely idea, Amber honey, but it's not why we're here. We need a place to let our hair down."

"Come on up."

***

"It's been a long time, Zach," said the woman who opened the door. She had dark hair, "auburn" is how I believe it is described. She was smaller and slimmer then I was, but moved with a sense of grace I had seen only in dancers. "Still writing those cliché-ridden novels?"

"It pays the bills. What about you? Still doing your best business on your back?"

"*Touché et en garde.* Actually, I've gone almost totally electronic. It's safer and I can double my output...so to speak. Who's your attractive friend?"

"Amber, this is Mary. Mary, Amber."

"Pleased to meet you, Mary," she said as her eyes conducted a thorough inspection of me.

"It is nice to meet you, Amber. Thank you for inviting us in."

"I couldn't say no to Zach here. We've been friends for too long." She turned and looked at Zach then. "So, what's the trouble, Zach? Has it got anything to do with the fact your friend here is a drone?"

"You noticed huh?" Zach put his index finger to his brow and stroked it. I had noticed it was a gesture he habitually performed when absorbed in contemplation.

Amber turned to me. "Are you on the run, dear?"

I was not sure how to reply. I looked at Zach. He shrugged his shoulders and said, "I'm afraid she is."

"Don't worry. No one can get to you here. We're sealed in tighter than a saint in heaven. Sit down, sit down--both of you. Let me get you something to drink. What would you like, Mary?"

"I would like some water please."

"One water. Zach, the usual?"

"Yeah, but double up on it."

Amber left the room and Zach and I sat down. Zach winced in obvious pain as he sat, then pulled up his pant leg and inspected the cut on his knee.

"I'm not sure what to do next," he said, looking at his leg. "I can't help you, Mary, unless I know what's going on--what your plans are. I don't want to butt in where I'm not wanted. It's just that when I get shot at I tend to get a little nosey."

He looked at me then as if expecting me to say something. I did not know what I could say. When I did not reply, he returned to examining his wound.

"I figure these friends of yours are drones, probably other rogues. What they expect to accomplish I couldn't even guess. What's the scam, Mary? Who, exactly, did you meet at *Techno Head*, and what does he or she or they want with you?"

"Gee, Zach, I never knew you to be the jealous type." It was

Amber, returning with our beverages. She looked at Zach's leg and said, "Zach, what happened?"

"It's not as bad as it looks. Just a lot of dried blood."

"Take off your pants and let me fix you up."

"I love it when you talk dirty."

"Don't you wish. On second thought, you'd better get into the cleanser and then use my biosensor hook-up to make sure you don't have an infection. I'll find some other clothes for you."

"Yes, Mother." Zach followed her out of the room, walking with a noticeable limp.

I wanted to tell him more--I trusted him, yet...would he understand? Could he understand why the group was more important than the individual? What would he do if I told him what the rogues were planning? Would he report them? I had to be careful. One mistake could put the entire group at risk.

Confusion and indecision were not states I was familiar with. My life had always been well-ordered, planned so that every hour was accounted for, every activity scheduled. In retrospect, it had not been much of a life, only a routine.

Now though, life had new meaning. There were new sensations, new feelings, new experiences, and with it all came chaos. I was beginning to realize why there was so much turmoil in the lives of all the characters I had read about. This is what life was actually about--turmoil and chaos, the unexpected and the emotional disorder. Part of me wanted to run back to my steward, resume my established duties, and not make any more decisions. Another part, a much stronger part, drank in all the newness with an exuberance that seemed almost feral in nature.

I was no longer just another Mary unit. Zach was right. I needed another name, something to complete my identity, to represent the person I was becoming.

"He'll be as good as new in no time," said Amber carrying Zach's pants. "But these are bound for the recycler." She dropped the pants on a table and sat next to me. "Can I get you anything else, dear?"

"No, thank you."

"So, how long have you known Zach?"

"We met four days ago."

"Well, that's longer than most of his relationships, though I guess I shouldn't assume. Are you and Zach just friends or...?"

She did not finish her question, but looked at me as if expecting a reply.

"I believe Zach and I are friends. He has done much to help me."

"What I meant is, are you two getting online together? Is this relationship more than just friendship?"

"Getting online? Oh, yes. Zach and I have been getting online, and sheet dancing and doing the wild thing. He has been teaching me."

"I bet he has. And I can see he's been teaching you the lingo too."

"I don't know if Zach and I have a 'relationship.' I have...I've never had a relationship."

"Well, you've got one now. Zach likes you, I can tell."

"I like Zach."

"We've got that in common then, Mary."

"Do you and Zach have a relationship?"

"You could say that. It's nothing heavy, mind you, we've just been good friends for a very long time, you know? He's someone I can trust."

"I trust Zach too."

"Net knows, he's got his flaws, but when the noose is cinched up tight you can always count on him to come through for you. At least I always could."

"Look at this picture." Zach whistled as he entered wearing an entirely new wardrobe. The clothes fit him perfectly. "Two of the most beautiful women in the world sitting together, just waiting for me."

"Don't get any ideas, Zach, I've got clients."

"I know, I know, Amber honey, business before pleasure."

"Now, Zach, you know that's not true. Pleasure *is* my business."

"So it is."

"Speaking of which, I need to check my site, if you two will excuse me for a minute."

Amber left the room and Zach sat down.

"How is your leg?" I asked him.

"It's fine, hardly hurts at all. So, have you ladies been talking about me?"

"Yes."

Zach laughed at my response, though I don't know why.

"Sorry, didn't mean to laugh. You're just so straightforward, Mary, not like most people. Look, I've already told you I want you to go away with me, but I'm not going to press it. You've got your reasons, and if you can't go now, you can't. But we've got to figure whoever's after you has my place staked out, so we can't both go back there. I'm going to leave you here while I go get Jekyll and a few things I need."

"They will see you."

"They're not after me. Oh, they might try to follow me, but I know a few tricks that'll help me shake them. And I'm going to make some inquiries about finding us another cradle to rock in. We can't impose on Amber forever."

"Sure you can," interrupted Amber.

"It's nice of you to offer, you little eavesdropper, but things could get totally offline if they track Mary down. I would like *her* stay here while I run a few errands."

"No-sweaty-dah, we'll wile away the time trading girl talk."

"Yeah? Now I'm not so sure I should go."

"Don't worry, Zach, I won't corrupt her. I understand you've already been doing a pretty good job of that."

"Not corruption, just a liberal education."

"And I know what you're majoring in."

"What can I say? I'm just a libertine at heart."

For a moment, I thought maybe they were arguing. However, Zach laughed and Amber smiled, so I understood they were just playing--using their words as playthings.

"Enough banter, I'd better get going."

"Be careful, Zach," I said, standing when he did.

"Not to worry, I'll be back before you know it."

He kissed Amber on her cheek and I felt a sudden surge of...of what I'm not sure. It was a foreign emotion, brief but powerful. Then he walked over and looked at me as if he were trying to memorize the contours of my face.

"You be good and I'll see you in a little while."

"I'll be good, Zach."

"Did you hear that? You said 'I'll' instead of I will."

Then he kissed me. Not like he had kissed Amber. He put his lips to mine and held them there as I responded. The kiss could not have lasted more a few seconds, however, it seemed much longer.

***

After Zach left, Amber excused herself and left the room, saying she had to take care of a client. Soon I heard strange sounds coming from the room Amber had disappeared into. I could not distinguish them clearly. Recent experience told me what I heard were the sounds of lovemaking.

However, it wasn't long before Amber returned, showing no signs of having participated in any sexual activities.

"I'm going to make us some food so we can sit out on the veranda and really scoop the scam on Zach."

"'Scoop the scam?' I'm not familiar that phrase."

"You know, dish the dirt, share secrets about Zach."

"Yes, I would like to know secrets about Zach. However, I don't know if I have any secrets to share."

"After four days, I'm sure you've got plenty to tell."

"They have been four very eventful days."

"What did you do before you met Zach?"

"I was a domestic facilitator."

"From the looks of you, you were obviously a top-of-line model, designed for men who like to have beautiful women working around the house."

"I also play the piano."

"Beautiful and talented."

"I did not get to play the piano very often. My steward did not care much for music. What do you do, Amber?"

"Didn't Zach tell you? I'm on the Net."

"Zach did not tell me. I heard you say your business is pleasure."

"I'm a netgirl. Do you know what that is?"

"I have heard only vague references to netgirls. But I would like to know what you do."

"I sell pleasure, in all its forms. I've got my own netsite where I offer everything from sex chat to videos to live fantasy fulfillment. The kinds of things men are almost always willing to pay for. Of course I get some women too. In fact, I get more hits than I can handle."

"What did you mean when you told Zach you've gone almost totally electronic?"

"I still service very select clients on an in-person basis. But they have to be *very* select, because my rates for that kind of personal service are extremely high. I don't need to do that kind of work anymore. I do it mostly because they're clients who have been with me a long time, and because they've been very good to me."

"So, you give men sexual pleasure and they pay you?"

"That's the idea. Does that seem strange to you?"

"My experience with sexual matters is limited, so I can't say if it is strange. However, when Zach gives me sexual pleasure, I don't pay him."

Amber obviously found that amusing, but restrained herself from actually laughing.

"I know Zach's good, but don't let me ever hear of you paying him or any other man. Word of that gets around and you'll drive me right out of business."

"I would not want to do that."

"I appreciate that, because I'm sure you could if you tried," she said still smiling as if at some private joke. "I'm sure Zach feels that being with you is payment enough. See, when two people really like each other, they want to give each other pleasure. They don't expect anything but making the other person happy."

"Zach makes me happy."

"And I'm sure you make him happy. Zach's not one to be sticking his neck out where there's trouble. He wouldn't be doing what he's doing for you if he didn't really like you. Now, I want you to tell me everything about you and Zach, starting with how you met, and don't leave out any of the details. You don't make a lot of girlfriends in my business, so you tell me yours and I'll tell you mine."

Amber and I talked for quite a long time. I told her about how Zach and I met, and how we first made love, and about how he saved my life. She, in turn, told me of some of her experiences. She also told me about the time Zach had to flee the bedroom of a woman he was with, naked from the waist down. Apparently, the woman had a previous commitment to a rather large and temperamental man. Amber laughed as she told it, and I too managed to see the humor in such an image. I discovered I enjoyed scooping the scam.

19
JON

I could feel his presence long before I saw him. I do not know what it was that alerted me. I know of no biological mechanism that would function in such a manner. Yet I knew I was being stalked.

How he had managed to locate me was perplexing. Short of treachery, there was no possible way for anyone to have discovered my whereabouts, unless the theory regarding a frequency emitted by our implants was valid. I found the entire concept repugnant--to be betrayed by a part of my own body. If it were true, we had to discover a way to counteract it. Otherwise, all of our planning would be useless. What we needed to do was disassemble and study one of the tracking devices.

I decided to keep moving until I found the right location. I would know the place when I came to it. While my senses remained heightened and focused on the task at hand, my inner thoughts returned once again to the androne Mary.

I do not know why she had left such a strong image in my mind. Certainly she was beautiful in the sense that humans admire beauty, however, I had seen beautiful women before. Though I was denied any physical contact, I had experienced the adoration of thousands of partisan females who were as esthetically pleasing, if not more so.

I did not think it was her appearance that had made such an impression. It was her attitude. If she was fearful, she did not show it. She did not retreat when I pressed her. She stood her ground and some part of me found that admirable. There was much about the world I still did not understand. However, I could tell she was strong, and strength was something I understood.

It was strength that empowered me. I knew I must be strong to lead my comrades in our quest to be free, just as I had once led my teammates. I knew from the gauntlet how sweet victory was compared to the bitter taste of defeat. However, defeat would no longer mean simply a score to be tallied in the daily Net standings. Now it would mean death.

My shadow made his first mistake then. I heard the sound of metal against metal over my left shoulder, approximately 20 meters behind me. I quickened my pace--not in an attempt to escape--simply to test the resolve of my hunter.

Some day it would not be like this. Some day we would no longer have to skulk and hide and run to preserve our lives. I was sure that some day we would have our own place, our own world, even if at the moment it seemed a fantasy--a dream mired within a nightmare.

I have heard it said that andrones do not dream, but we do. I often dream of a place that is empty from horizon to horizon. No people, no buildings, no oceans, no mountains, no gauntlets full of adversaries--just desolate, flat stretches of nothingness. Yet that nothingness leaves me filled with contentment.

I could hear him very clearly now. He had increased his speed to try and close the distance between us. As I waited for him, I began writing a new verse inside my head. One based upon another poem I had once read.

When I was hero of the gauntlet,
the shouts of acclaim were sweet.

He was moving in for the kill and getting reckless. I turned suddenly into a narrow passageway between two buildings and found what I was looking for. There was no moon that night, and very little light from the street found its way back into the alley. Several paces in, I leapt and pulled myself up onto a small ledge protruding over a door. Then I simply waited.

Legions of fanatics scattered rose petals
at my armored feet.

If the tracer pursuing me paused long enough to let his eyes adjust to the dimness and then looked up, I would provide a relatively easy target. I was calculating that, in his haste, he would rush blindly in before realizing his prey was no longer on the move. However, I soon discovered I had underestimated both his caution and his intelligence.

When he turned down the alleyway, he immediately pulled out his weapon. I could tell by the way he kept looking at a device in his other hand that it was his means of tracking me. He moved slowly, cautiously, keeping his weapon out in front of him. I needed only wait until he came within reach. I estimated the distance I could cover from my present perch and tensed my muscles in anticipation.

Once I was an invincible idol,
   now the mob cries for my head.

He stopped. Obviously the tracking device revealed I was only meters away, but the readings seemed to confuse him. He started walking slowly, then stopped again. This time he carefully turned, searching 360 degrees, trying to pinpoint my location. When his head tilted to look upward, I did not pause to calculate the distance, I reacted.

He eyes focused on me for only a fraction of a second before my feet pummeled his chest. The force knocked him back with such velocity, his body nearly rebounded from the concrete. He released his hold on both the weapon and the tracking device, stunned from the blow. It was simple matter then to place my forearm under his jaw and fracture the vertebrae in his neck. I released his body and it fell limp to the ground.

The rattle of their anger won't grow dim
   till I lay dead.

I saw then that my would-be hunter was an androne. An androne bred to be a human's hound, tracking down its own kind, as I was bred to battle my brethren in the arena for the entertainment of human sports enthusiasts. Such was the fate of my race, at least until we stood up and demanded control of our own destinies.

I picked up his weapon and the tracking device. The weapon I already knew how to use, the tracking device would be analyzed by those who had been instructed in such technical work. Soon we would know how the tracers were able to find us, and how we could counteract the device. At least until the day when we would hide no more.

20

REVEREND ROBERTS

")Reverend Roberts, is it true the Jeserite Council of Elders opposes your run for political office?"

"They've made no such statement that I'm aware of," I said, responding to a bank of cameras. "To my knowledge, my campaign for the senate has the council's full support. They know my work is God's work, that my voice speaks only God's words."

"Are you saying you talk with God or that he speaks through you?" It was Gordon Stone, that little runt of a reporter who had been hounding me since I began my campaign. He looked up in sweaty anticipation, as if he had caught me in some glaring misstatement. I smiled at him and responded patiently.

"It's only a metaphor, son. You know what a metaphor is don't you? I am only a disciple of God, a servant of the Jeserite Council."

Another reporter waved his microphone in my direction. "Sir, what about the rumors that the council considers you unfit for higher office because of your background?" I just smiled once again, as if I were dealing with ignorant children.

"Tell me, do you believe in rumors, or do you believe in God?" That elicited a laugh from the swarm of journalists--a good way I had learned to put them on your side. "Like most people, I am a sinner. Everyone is familiar with my 'background' as you put it. I was abandoned as a child and grew up on the streets where I learned every manner of vice. First I stole so that I might eat, then I stole to pay for my drug habit. I was a petty thief and a drug addict--until I saw the light--until I was taken in and cared for by my Jeserite brothers. I know God has forgiven me for my sins. Soon we'll find out if the voters have."

They all laughed again, though apparently the runt was not in good humor.

"Did you know that LEDA has come out in opposition of your candidacy, Reverend?"

"That does not surprise me," I said, looking elsewhere into the throng of microphones, hoping for another question. But the little man would not shut up.

"Does it worry you?"

"Does the lion worry when the field mouse sneezes?"

There was more laughter as Simon came out of the temple and whispered in my ear. "They're ready for you, Reverend."

I turned back to the reporters and said, "Sorry, your other questions will have to wait. The council has requested my presence. I appreciate your interest and your concern, however, I would appreciate your votes even more." There were more laughs as I turned to enter the temple. I had given them enough for today. Like jackals, they wouldn't attack if you tossed them a few morsels.

However, the gathering inside wouldn't be so easy to placate. Many of them were out for blood--my blood. The majority of those on the council believed it sacrilegious to partake in politics. Even those who recognized how it could benefit the church did not like the idea of the power being placed in my hands.

It was too late for their recriminations. They had used me when it suited their purposes, put me out front to serve as their standard-bearer, their liaison to the public. But I knew I was destined to be more than a figurehead. They couldn't stop my candidacy now, I had too much support. They could order me to bow out of the race, but that would raise too many questions, create too much of a rift in the order, especially if I fought them by going to the people. They had been dictating doctrine from seclusion for too long. They had forgotten the real power lies with the masses.

Simon held the door for me but did not follow as I entered the council sanctuary. I would not be alone though. God was with me.

The council was seated around the massive, circular table it used for such official meetings. I knew most of their faces, but not all of their names. Reverend Ahjai Sukumu was the chief elder and, if the information Simon had secured for me was correct, my chief opposition. I stepped up to my appointed place, but did not sit. I decided I would make them invite me. A simple negotiating tactic, but an effective one.

"Praise God," said Reverend Sukumu, acknowledging my presence.

"Praise Nature," I replied automatically.

"Sit down, Reverend Roberts, sit down," he said when he realized I wasn't going sit on my own. "Thank you for taking the time out of your busy schedule to meet with us." It was an obvious jab at my political campaign. I could see there would be no punches pulled at this meeting.

"I came as soon as I was summoned, Reverend Sukumu. The council's will is my will."

"That's good to hear, Reverend, because the council is concerned with the repercussions of your political dalliances."

"I do not consider them 'dalliances,' honored Reverend. I see only that my continued toil in this campaign will extend the reach of the church. I have no aspirations of my own. I only wish to help my brother Jeserites to spread of the word of God."

"We have received reports that you have not always complied with ecological doctrine in your pursuit for higher office."

"I assure the council that every environment, every power-usage within my purview has been ecologically sacrosanct."

"I suppose you believe your senatorial campaign is divinely inspired," spoke up Reverend Guiseppe without any attempt to disguise his sarcasm.

"I believe I am but a lump of earthly clay in God's hands."

The bantering continued for some time, but there was not much they could say. In this test of wills they were destined for failure. They continued to ask questions and grouse and grumble over my answers. They hoped to find a way to topple me from the pedestal they had placed me on, but they knew, as did I, that they were powerless. Publicly, they could only support my campaign. Privately, I didn't care what they did.

21

ZACH

It seemed like everyone was lying low for one reason or another. Everyone I tried to check in with was out, and their friends/family/bookie didn't know where they were, when or if they'd be back. It wasn't that all my connections were criminal-types. Some of them were just habitually unlucky.

So I backlit the idea of finding a new cradle to rock in and hustled back to my place. I half expected to find the P.D. there, but everything was copasetic. I mean it was too clean. If there was someone around waiting to grab Mary, I couldn't spot them. They were either real good or they had another way to find her. That thought made me want to rush back to Amber's, but I knew I still had to be careful.

"*Mrrrouw!*"

Jekyll was annoyed with me.

"Sorry, big guy."

"*Mrrrouw.*"

"No, I can't feed you right now. We got to get gone."

"*Mrrrouw.*"

"We're going to see Amber."

I thought about checking my v-mail, but I was in too big a hurry to get out of there. Not that I expected to see anything but the ugly mug of my publisher ranting about deadlines and dwindling accounts.

I grabbed a few things, threw them in a bag, and then coaxed Jekyll into his carrier. He voiced his complaints for a few minutes, then settled down to enjoy the sights as I took two cabs and a hydrorail back to Amber's place. By the time I got there I was feeling pretty relaxed. I began to think I had blown the whole danger thing out of proportion. About that time my knee started hurting again, and I remembered the part about running for my life.

***

"Zach." Mary almost sounded excited to see me.

"Look what the cat dragged in," I said, holding up Jekyll's carrier. "I hope you don't mind, Amber honey."

"You know better, Zach. Now let him out of there. Come to mama, Jekyll."

Mary saw what I was holding and immediately became concerned. "Zach, you put him in a cage?"

"It's for his own good," I told her.

"It's for Jekyll's good to be confined in that small box?"

"If I didn't keep him in here, he'd probably get scared, take off, and end up cat puree under a hydrorail. You wouldn't want that would you?"

"Still," she said, "it seems somehow cruel."

"Here, I'll let him out."

I opened the carrier door and, just like a cat, Jekyll chose to lay there.

"Come on, Jekyll," implored Amber. "Come on out. I've got some tuna somewhere."

After a brief demonstration of nonchalance, Jekyll emerged, his tail held high. He revved up his purr as soon as Amber began to stroke him. "Let's go see what we've got for you to eat."

"I didn't have too much luck. I hope it's all right if the three of us stay here for a while."

"Not a problem, Zach." Amber assured me. I plopped down on the divan and Mary sat beside me.

"Did you have any trouble, Zach?"

"I didn't find us anywhere else to stay, but there was no trouble. I didn't run into any of your playmates, and I'm fairly certain no one was able to follow me."

"What do we do now?"

"We relax, get something to eat, maybe watch a video--"

"I've got an idea," said Amber. "Why don't I whip up something for us to eat, then you can take Mary to the *Classico*."

"Take her to a movie theater?"

"Why not, Zach? It's dark out and dark in the theater."

"It was dark in the street the other night too, and they still found her."

"I'm sorry, Zach," said Mary, "I told Amber I've never been inside a movie theater before."

"You've never seen a movie before?"

"Only on the Net. Amber told me I need to watch one inside a real movie house to appreciate it."

"That's true, but I don't--"

"Guess what's playing, Zach?" Amber interrupted with a smile that said I was about to give in. "It's one of your favorites."

"Okay, lay it on me, I see I'm surrounded."

"It's *Casablanca*, Zach."

"Bogie in black and white? That's hitting below the belt."

"Wouldn't that be a great one for Mary's first real movie."

"Amber told me this movie is very old."

"That it is."

"So, what do you say, Zach?"

"I guess we can't stay in here forever, and if I'm going to die, I would like to see Ingrid Bergman one more time."

"Can we go, Zach?"

"All right. Now that you've talked me into it, Amber, you're coming too."

"No, no. I've got some clients to deal with tonight. You kids go and have fun. But don't stay out too late."

"Ah gee, mom. I'm not going anywhere until I get some food."

"Yes, master. Right away, master," Amber feigned a bow and then a curtsy for good measure, and disappeared into her kitchen.

"I'm going to clean-up, Zach."

"You look pretty good to me already," I said, staring at the heavenly body that had gotten me into so much trouble. If I didn't know she was a drone I could have sworn she was blushing.

"Amber said I could wear some of her clothes."

"They may be a little tight in places."

"Do you not want me to wear tight clothes, Zach?"

"That's okay, I'm sure they'll be tight in all the right places."

"That is strange. That is the same thing Amber said."

"Smart girl that Amber."

Mary made a quick exit and I finally felt like I could relax. It had been a hell of a week, or had it been longer? I wasn't sure what day it was anymore, not that I ever cared that much. Everything had been moving too fast. So fast I never really got a chance to sit down and think it out.

It *would* be nice to sit back and watch Bogart do his thing again. Let's see, how did it go? I never quite got the accent down just right.

"Of all the gin joints in all the towns in all the world, she walks into mine."

22

JERI

Identifying the blood sample through the DNA verification databank would take approximately 23 minutes. That would be sufficient time to catalog everything that had gone wrong with my current assignment. Because I was not trained for failure, I chose to categorize these adversities as temporary setbacks.

Twice I had closed on the rogue unit Mary 79, and twice she had escaped. Once I lost her signal due to unknown interference. On the second occasion an unidentified third party had intervened. These unknown elements created confusion in my reasoning. My lack of success left me with a sense of emptiness.

My status with Mr. Satchmeyer had retrogressed even further, due to the fact that while I had concentrated on the rogue Mary unit, the other rogues on my fugitives list had been expired by tracers belonging to other stewards. Since I learned of this, I had been avoiding contact with Mr. Satchmeyer. I preferred not to speak with him until I had expired the Mary unit. He was not one to benignly accept unproductive reports.

I had not been able to detect the rogue unit's signal since the night she exited the *Techno Head*. It was likely she had relocated to a new region, a possibility that would complicate my search even further. My observation that she was now in the company of a human male could also complicate my assignment. Normally, a lone rogue has no resources, no credit, no acquaintances. If this human were helping her, my success probability ratio would certainly diminish.

Though my attempts at subliminal coercion had proved fruitless thus far, I encoded instructions into my modified comdat to increase the regularity of transmissions using Mary 79's frequency. If the unit came within range, her cranial implant would be inundated by a command to submit. Though part of the basic programming of any androne, the transmission reinforced thoughts of capitulation in andrones who had gone rogue. Theoretically it would work in andrones whose impairment was not too severe. However, I had never witnessed a rogue that had acquiesced in response to such a transmission.

My own cranial implant began to vibrate incessantly then, and I could sense Mr. Satchmeyer's anger in the way the signal lingered. However, I had already decided not to answer his summons until I had a positive report. The decision both troubled and stimulated me. Not to respond immediately was a violation of my training. I had never ignored such a summons before. Somehow, simply making the choice resulted in a sensation of...I was not completely cognitive of *what* the sensation was. Possibly it was a sense of autonomy, a sense of empowerment. Though I was uncertain which word properly described it, there was no doubt it was invigorating.

I wondered if this was the same sensation that drove other andrones to go rogue. It was certainly seductive, and likely, in time, to become extremely addictive. I began to contemplate what it would be like to...no, I could not. The lure was strong, though inconceivable.

My failure to locate the rogue's signal left me with only one option. I had to identify the blood I had discovered. In doing so, I hoped to acquire new evidence that might lead me to the whereabouts of Mary 79.

As I waited for the trace to be completed, I accessed that evening's gauntlet match. The narrators seemed preoccupied with the rogue Jon 155, missing no opportunity to include his name in the macrocast.

> *"...just a tremendous run for the Turbos. The*
> *number of blows delivered could be a record. We're*
> *still waiting for the comdat tally. That run reminds*
> *me of the time Jon 155 scored against the Far*
> *East during last year's playoffs. Jon 155, of course,*
> *holds that record, as he does many others."*
> *"You're right, Don. It was similar in many ways,*
> *though Jon 155 usually seemed stronger at the end*
> *of a run than he did at the beginning."*
> *"That was his trademark. Here comes the tally, Joe.*
> *Oh, a nice number but the record is secure. We'll*
> *be right back with more gritty gauntlet action after*
> *this."*
> *"Don't touch that scanner, coming up right after*
> The Gauntlet, *the newest game show on the Net,*
> Swap. *Watch as eight couples contemplate*

*the permutations of swapping their loved
ones for someone else's. See if you can guess who
will choose a chance at romantic adventure by
swapping their wife, husband, girlfriend, or lover
for another. And they're not just swapping for one
night or for one week, they're swapping forever...or
at least until our next episode. Find out who will
risk their stability on a possibility...and a chance
to win big prizes. Stayed tuned,* Swap *begins in
only four-point-three minutes."*

I often found human rituals fascinating, however, the idea of humans exchanging mates seemed no more entertaining than other macrocasts I had observed. It certainly promised none of the athletic combat of *The Gauntlet,* or the informativeness of "Most Wanted Rogues." However, it did lead me to momentarily contemplate the possibility of choosing to swap stewards, though I had no way of confirming that another steward would be any better or worse than Mr. Satchmeyer.

When the DNA trace was complete, I activated the information. The trace had been successful. On the display in front of me was a photo of the human male who had accompanied the rogue, as well as biographical information.

*Zachariah Michelangelo Sturzinski
aka Zachariah Starr
 blood type O positive
ethnic origin unknown
height 183cm.
weight 84kg.
hair color brown
eye color green*

As I plugged in to receive the information, I read the personal data. Apparently this Zachariah Michelangelo Sturzinski was a writer of fiction. Thirteen novels were recorded under his alias, "Zachariah Starr." However, little else of any use was known about his background. The data did include the code designation for an obsolescent satphone registered in his name. I would file for a trace and if he was still employing the device I would be able to determine his location and, possibly, the location of the rogue Mary unit.

Even if I now fulfilled my mission and captured the rogue, Mr. Satchmeyer would not be totally pleased. I had apparently injured a human not currently wanted for any crimes. That could lead to certain unwelcome legal ramifications for Mr. Satchmeyer's company, including his dreaded fear of increased liability premiums.

However, the possibility did exist that this Zachariah Michelangelo Sturzinski might now face charges of aiding and abetting a known rogue. Still, I would have to be more efficient. The consequences of killing a human could be ruinous.

23

ZACH

"One thing I don't understand, Zach. She loved Rick, yet she left him."

I could see the movie had really affected her. She had been completely silent as we sat through the credits, as if contemplating the higher meaning of it all. She didn't speak until we walked out of the theater and headed back to Amber's, which wasn't far. She was still clutching her popcorn bag like it was full of pearls.

"She was torn. It wasn't an easy decision for her. I think she loved both men, though in different ways."

"Are there different ways to love someone?"

"Well, yeah, I guess so."

"I believe I'm beginning to understand the human preoccupation with sexual matters," she said, glancing at me almost shyly. "However, this concept of love and the power it wields is difficult to fully comprehend. In the play by William Shakespeare, Romeo and Juliet embrace the act of suicide for reasons having nothing to do with the physical act of sex. Each perceives a lost love that leads to such despair they see no other recourse. Love's power, it seems, dwarfs that of lust. Explain to me about love, Zach, and how 'true love' is different from love without the qualifying adjective."

Qualifying adjective? The next thing you know, she was going to be asking me about the meaning of life. Hell, I didn't want the girl thinking I had all the answers. Not when I had so few.

"Speaking strictly theoretically, I would say--"

"Why do you say 'theoretically,' Zach? Have you never been in love?"

"No, I can't say I've ever experienced 'true love,' whatever that is, but I guess I've come close enough to see it in the distance. As great as the raw physical act is, the passion tends to run much deeper and more intense when two people genuinely love each other. Hell, Mary, I don't think I can explain it. I don't think anyone can. I can tell you what Ilsa did in the movie. You see, she was looking at the bigger picture. She decided what Victor could do in the war against the Nazis was more important than her feelings for Rick."

She stopped walking and took hold of my hand. She had this serious look on her face, and for a second I thought maybe she was going to propose. I reached up with my other hand and scratched the back of my neck. I was so lost in her eyes, I didn't even wonder why it had started to itch.

"It was a very beautiful movie, Zach. Thank you for taking me to see it."

"I enjoyed it too. Maybe we'll do it again sometime."

We resumed walking and I noticed she kept hold of my hand. Now I'm not normally one to do a lot of handholding. Public displays of affection really aren't my style. But the kid had been through a lot lately. I decided it was okay with me if it made her feel better. Besides, it was dark and no one was likely to see us.

"I think the part I liked best," Mary went on, "was when she asked Sam to play that song and Rick hears it. He rushes over angry, but his expression changes when he sees her. Are your stories like that, Zach?"

"There are similar elements here and there in different stories. You can't really compare an old movie like that to one of my books."

"Why did you decide to become a writer, Zach?"

"Me? I don't know. I guess after knocking around, sweating my way through a host of jobs, I decided I wanted to be my own boss. So I figured writing was easier on the back, and it helped me avoid some of the digits who had been giving me orders."

"'Digits?'"

"More slang--kind of a cross been a dummy and an idiot--a digit."

"So you became a writer to avoid more physical work and unintelligent supervisors."

"You got it. Though I do admit I always liked to spin a good yarn. Even as a boy I could lie my way out of just about--"

I shut up quickly when I saw two figures coming out of the dark at us. Mary released her hold on my hand as I looked for an avenue of escape. There were two more behind us--a man and a woman, both drones, like the two men approaching us. I realized why my neck had been bothering me.

"Get ready to run when I tell you," I whispered to Mary.

"It's all right, Zach. These are my friends."

"Friends? You sure know how to pick 'em, don't you."

They were a tough-looking bunch, and it wasn't only the weapons I spotted underneath their jackets that had me worried. They looked none too friendly, and the one who stepped forward to talk to Mary was a monster of muscle. He had that short-cropped hair thing going for him, a square jaw, and a forehead that looked like it was cast in iron.

Iron? The word made me think there was something about him that was awfully familiar.

"I am glad to see you are unharmed, Mary. I was informed there was weapons fire after our last meeting. I was concerned that you had been injured."

"The tracer was chasing us. We escaped when someone else with a weapon intervened. I thought it might have been one of you."

"No, it was not any of our people."

"This is my friend, Zach. He helped me escape."

I was considering shaking hands and asking his name, but he never even looked at me. In fact, he was making a point of *not* looking at me.

"Possibly," he continued, speaking only to Mary, "though we have considered an alternate scenario?"

"What do you mean?"

"It is possible this human led you into a trap."

"Now wait a minute, buster." I stepped forward right into his face so he could no longer ignore me. As soon as I did, I realized it was a mistake. So did Mary. She managed to put a shoulder in between us. The drone stared at me as if I were an insect he was considering swatting. If there was any emotion behind that stare, I figured it was mild amusement.

"Zach has been protecting me. If he had led me into a trap he never would have put himself at risk, first warning me and then helping me to escape."

"That's right," I threw in for good measure. "How's this for an *'alternate scenario,'* you rogues don't know what you're doing and you led the tracer right to Mary."

The big guy continued to stare at me. I could see Mary was very uneasy about the whole thing, so I made a big show out of looking around at all of them and shaking my head disdainfully before I stepped aside to let her deal with him.

"We should not be fighting amongst ourselves, Jon. I've told you Zach is a friend I trust, a friend who has helped me. If you trust me, that should be sufficient."

"You are right, Mary, we have more important things to discuss."

Jon? That's when I recognized him. Jon 155, the greatest drone ever to run a gauntlet. And if not the most famous drone ever, at least the most famous one to go rogue.

"We have confirmed that our cranial implants emit a signal tuned to a certain frequency. Each of us has been designed to emit a slightly different frequency, so that at any time, any one of us could be singled out and located." He pulled out a small object that fit in the palm of his hand and showed it to Mary. "I took this device from a tracer who was using it to track me. That is how I found you tonight, Mary. I simply encoded your frequency into the sensor and it led me to you."

"That's why we couldn't shake that guy," I blurted out, stating the obvious. Drone Jon continued to ignore me.

"We believe the trace sensor has a range of about a thousand meters."

"Then they could be tracking any one of you right now."

"That is correct," said Jon, actually acknowledging my existence. "That is why we must hurry. We are attempting to discover a way to scramble or remodulate the signals emitted by our cranial implants. Until that time, we must all keep on the move and avoid gathering in large groups. Each of us must work separately towards our goal, while remaining in contact with others."

"What can I do to help?" asked Mary.

"There is nothing for you to do now. We have still been unable to locate the means of transportation we will need. Until we do, we--"

"I might know someone who can help," I broke in.

Jon turned to look at me and then looked back at Mary.

"Have you revealed our plans to him?"

"I've told him nothing of your plans," Mary reassured him.

"Don't get your implants in a bunch. She hasn't told me a thing, even though I asked her. If you need transportation, I know the guy who runs the local black-market. He can get you anything from rollerskates to a rocketship."

That got his attention, because he walked over to me then. "This human you know, he would give us an interplanetary ship?"

"So that's your game, huh?" I could tell he wasn't happy about letting me in on that particular bit of information, but he realized

I knew something he didn't. "He won't *give* you a ship, but he might be able to get hold of one he could sell you. The question is, do you have enough credit to pay him? Interplanetary ships don't come cheap."

"We will get the necessary credit."

"All right, I'll see if I can get in contact with him. How will I get word to you if I do find him?"

"You will not be able to communicate with me." He turned to Mary then. "Are you going to remain with this man?"

"Yes. I will help him find a ship."

"Then I must have a way to contact you."

"I grabbed my satphone when I was home. You can reach us on that. 3-68-899-3839. Check back with me late tomorrow and I'll let you know if I've gotten in touch with my connection."

Jon looked to the other drones then. "It is time to disperse. Renew your contacts, make certain everyone remains informed. However, keep on the move. Ann, you inform Patrick and he will gather the others. We will meet at the rendezvous, 0900 tomorrow."

"By what mode of transportation?" asked one of the drones.

"By any means available," responded Jon roughly. "You will go by foot if necessary."

"Where are we to stay until the rendezvous?" spoke up the one he had called Ann.

I thought Jon looked a little exasperated right then. He turned to his comrades, addressing them as a group.

"Each of you must learn to make decisions for yourselves. There will be many times when you will have no one to tell you what to do. You must adapt, you must be strong and independent when the situation requires it. Now each of you must leave by a separate route. Attend to your assignments and meet tomorrow at the designated location. Until then, you must act as decisive individuals. Do you understand?"

Each of them nodded in response and then took off in different directions of the compass.

"Be cautious, Mary." Jon said, and then turned back to aim his steely gaze at me. "Take care of her." I knew by the way he said it, it was more of a warning than a request.

He then disappeared into the darkness with such speed I wondered if I was imagining it. Mary and I just stood there for a moment, until I remembered what kind of danger we were in.

"We'd better get going. Someone could be tuned in to that radio playing in your head right now. At least at Amber's they'll have a hard time getting inside without us knowing about it."

"It was nice of you to offer to help us, Zach," she said as we began walking.

"That's me, Mr. Niceguy."

"Maybe you should not involve yourself. Maybe I should leave so you will not be in danger."

"That's won't, not 'will not.' Will not becomes the contraction won't."

"I should leave so you *won't* be in danger."

"It's too late for that, so don't be trying to tarnish my shining armor. Besides, I don't want you to leave." Then I turned on my best Bogie. "If you leave, you'll regret it. Maybe not today, maybe not tomorrow, but soon and for the rest of your life."

"Actually, I believe he told Ilsa she would regret it if she *didn't* leave."

"So I'm paraphrasing, it's the thought that counts."

"It's a gallant thought, Zach."

"Yeah, 'gallant,' that's me all over."

24

PROCTOR EDGAR ALAINE

I removed an intrusive piece of lint from my sleeve as I waited. It had been so long since I had worn my vestment, I spent much of the morning cleaning and pressing it just so. It wasn't every day I was called to a meeting of the Council of Elders, especially by the chief elder himself.

I had made sure on this important day that everything was properly taken care of, in its proper order. First, my morning prayers, then a cursory examination of my tortoise collection, followed by a thorough course of hygienic care, including an efficacious shave, a manicure, and a full biosensor readout that found me to be in excellent physical health.

I attempted to seek the advice of my therapist before I departed, but was rudely dismissed by her digisistant. The device had the audacity to remind me of my scheduled appointment, as if I were some scatterbrained heathen. The truth of the matter was, the date and time of that appointment was strategically placed and easily accessed in four separate locations where habit would guide me. I found the inference that there might be even a hint of disorder in my daily routine, insulting.

Because I wanted to be as pure as possible for my meeting with the council, I fasted all day, taking only four sips of water. Now, as I waited, I was content that I had been cleansed, both in body and soul. Every hair on my head and every thread of my clothes were in place, and I was ready for whatever task the Almighty called upon me to perform.

I was eager to learn why I had been summoned. However, I suppressed my curiosity. When it was appropriate, I knew I would be told. Something was bothering me though. At first I couldn't quite put my finger on it. Then I realized what it was and began to straighten the journals that had been scattered on the table in front of me. Someone had left it quite chaotic. That's when a brother opened the large council door and called me in.

"Praise God, Proctor Alaine."

"Praise Nature, Brother."

"The council is about to meet. I've been instructed to show you to your seat."

I followed him inside and sat where he directed, in a chair away from the main table, off in a corner. It was an inconspicuous spot, but after I adjusted the angle of my view, I found it adequate.

The elders began to file into the room in what was a surprisingly orderly manner. Each maintained a staunch air of dignity as he found his designated seat. I was struck by how fine their vestments appeared, meticulously tailored and pressed.

No one acknowledged my presence or spoke at all until each was seated. Then the Reverend Ahjai Sukumu cleared his throat and addressed the other elders.

"As you all know, we are meeting today to voice our concerns over the activities of Reverend Roberts, and to pray for guidance in this matter. Reverend Guiseppe, would you please?"

Each of the elders bowed his head and closed his eyes as Reverend Guiseppe began the invocation. I believe I closed mine tighter than they've ever been closed before. It was a very spiritual moment for me, being in that room.

"Holy Father, we are gathered here today, to honor Your name and do Your bidding. We look to You for guidance and pray You will grant us wisdom in all things. May peace and love of nature abound."

"Praise God, praise Nature," I offered along with the entire assemblage.

Eyes opened and heads raised in unison.

"Thank you, Reverend Guiseppe. Now, who would like to speak first?"

A reverend I did not recognize stood up.

"Reverend elders, I must reiterate concerns I have voiced before, regarding the compromise of our faith by allowing a reverend member to participate in politics. It is an unnatural alliance that taints us all."

"It's not as unnatural as you might think, Brother Reverend," spoke up another member. "Politics and religion have been bedfellows throughout history."

"However," interjected the Reverend Sukumu, "I'm sure you'll both agree that is not relevant to why we are here today. Our only consideration for the moment is Reverend Roberts, and how his campaign for the senate has affected, and will continue to affect the church."

Several elders began speaking at once, and I found it difficult to keep track of the various side conversations that began to develop.

"...mistake to publicly denounce his candidacy...."

"...and, to many, Jeserites *are* the Reverend Jackson Roberts. His public persona...."

"...television show is a sacrilegious affront that...."

"....his charismatic appeal with the people will no doubt cause...."

"...an attitude of paying no heed to the council and...."

The discussion continued unabated for a time, then Reverend Guiseppe raised his voice, cutting through the general babble. "Our primary concern is that we have so little documentation concerning Brother Roberts' past. We're not questioning his tenancy as a Jeserite reverend. We know of his charisma and his rapid rise up the hierarchy of the church, but we know little else. In a political campaign like this, every deed, every relationship, even a poor choice of words used in a meaningless conversation decades ago can become magnified by those looking for an electoral edge. Any indiscretion uncovered by his opponents could reflect negatively on the church."

"I agree, Brother Guiseppe," replied the Reverend Sukumu. "That is why I have asked Proctor Edgar Alaine here today."

I sat up a little straighter at the mention of my name and several of the elders glanced my way.

"Proctor Alaine is the church's principal investigator, and I wanted him to understand, firsthand, what our concerns were before he begins his assignment."

"And what is his assignment, Brother Sukumu?" asked one of the elders, echoing my own curiosity.

"With the grace of this body, I want Brother Alaine to conduct his own investigation of the Reverend Roberts, only, of course, to assure us there is nothing that might infringe upon his position as a reverend minister."

There were several murmurs of assent at this, and more looks my way. I took a deep breath and counted to four. The realization of the importance of this assignment had increased my anxiety level. I even indulged in a brief moment of pride, God forgive me.

"Is there anyone who wishes to discuss this matter further?" asked the Reverend Sukumu in an almost ceremonial fashion. Only silence answered him. "Then I suggest all other issues be tabled until our next meeting, and that this meeting of the Council of Elders be officially adjourned."

"Amen," offered Reverend Guiseppe.

Reverend Sukumu rose from his seat and walked out with the rest of the elders filing behind, just as orderly as they had entered. Watching them filled me with a sense of well-being, a sense of fulfillment.

***

The same brother who had shown me to my seat entered after they had all left the room. He guided me silently to a small antechamber that was adorned very simply with what appeared to be religious and ceremonial artifacts from another age. He left me there, and soon another door opened and the Reverend Sukumu entered. He motioned for me to sit in the chair facing a desk and I complied. He walked slowly around the desk and sat down.

For the first time, I got a good look at his lazy eye. The abnormality did not appear too severe, though the intensity of its gaze was legendary.

"Brother Alaine, I want to be certain you understand your assignment."

"Yes, Reverend. Further details and direction would be most appreciated."

"You are to thoroughly investigate Reverend Roberts, going back to the time of his birth if necessary. Secure all documentation possible, record all interviews, and reveal to no one what you find. You will report your findings directly to me, and only to me." His gaze bore into me, as if he were attempting to dissect my very soul.

"I understand, Reverend."

He got up out of his seat, folded his hands behind his back, and turned away from me.

"What you must understand, Brother Alaine, is that Reverend Roberts is walking on the edge. His public image is balanced most precariously on the fringes of our order. He needs to be brought back into the fold. We need to convince him that his campaign is not in the best interests of the church. And, to do that, we need a certain amount of leverage. That leverage can only come in the form of information." He wheeled around and looked at me again with steely eyes. "Do you understand? Do you completely understand?"

"Yes, Reverend."

"Splendid. Then I'll let you be about your task. Please keep me informed with regular reports."

I got up from my chair and he nodded as if giving me leave to go.

"Praise God, Reverend."

"Yes, yes, praise Nature, Brother."

I left the same way I had come, but with a thousand, no, four-thousand things going through my head. The Council of Elders, the church, was counting on me. They had placed their faith in my abilities and I would not let them down. I did, however, wish I had been given more specifics on how to proceed. Reverend Sukumu had left the details of the investigation up to me, and I found that a bit disconcerting. The responsibility I felt towards my task was indeed overwhelming.

My life had both new meaning and a new burden. However, it was God's work, and I knew it would give me joy.

25
ZACH

I had to open my big mouth. Sure, I knew Joe The Lizard-- barely. However, he was nobody you wanted to mess around with. He had a reputation for being as deadly as a rattlesnake and twice as quick. We had been introduced once, when a mutual acquaintance was completing a transaction with him. I wasn't even sure if he'd meet with me, but when that big dumb rogue accused me of setting up Mary, something inside of me just went off. I shouldn't have let him get to me. Now I was waiting in a creaky old warehouse a cockroach would have condemned, not knowing if I'd even get out alive. The place had the smell of stale beer and moldy cheese.

It was pretty widely known that if you wanted something on the black-market, Joe The Lizard was the man to see. Rumor had it he was a full-blooded Cherokee. I doubted it. I didn't think there was a full-blooded anything left in the world, except maybe if you counted androns. Some people called him "Indian Joe," though not to his face. I remembered he had a slight speech impediment, but, with his reputation, no one let on that they noticed.

So there I was, about to make an illegal transaction with a deadly underworld Indian for a hostile rogue gauntlet star whom I didn't trust and who apparently detested my very existence--all because I got pissed-off. I didn't even want Mary to leave, and I knew she probably would fly off with the other rogues, wherever they were going. Yet here I was, risking life and limb, as well as several years behind bars, to help her and a bunch of serker drones make an interplanetary getaway. If I lived long enough I'd turn it into my next novel.   I had let myself get lost in thought and when I reconnected with my surroundings I noticed three heavily-armed thugs had slipped into the building and stationed themselves in strategic spots. Then three more walked in and I saw that Joe The Lizard was one of them. He was a powerfully-built man with huge thighs and a barrel chest. His sleeves had been cut so his thickly-muscled arms had room to flex and he wore a single, unadorned red band around his head, even though he didn't have much hair to hold in place. What there was of it was gray, though that was the only part of him that revealed any age.

One of his goons stepped forward and patted me down. In my case it wasn't necessary. I didn't like guns. They made loud noises and big messes.

"I remember you," said The Lizard, pointing one of his thick, knobby fingers at me. "You...you...you were with Jimmie Jensen when we concluded some business concerning illicit vids."

"You've got a good memory, Mr. uhhh--"

"Call me Joe."

"I'm Zach," I said, holding my hand out. When he took it, I was sorry I had offered. He had the grip of a vise clamp and shook hands as if he wanted to be sure I knew it.

"Word has it, Zach," he said, still holding on to my hand, "that you're looking to make a rather large purchase. I hope you have the monetary resources to complete suh...suh...such a transaction."

I wouldn't have minded his stutter except that it meant he was squeezing the blood out of my hand that much longer. When he finally released it, I tried to act nonchalant. I lowered my hand to my side, then tried to shake the feeling back into it without anyone noticing.

"Actually, I'm just a go-between. I'm here on the behalf of some friends who'd like to purchase a reasonably-priced interplanetary ship."

That set him off. He let out a huge, raucous laugh that echoed through the warehouse and probably caused cardiac arrest in more than a few resident rodents. His men however, didn't join in. They never even cracked a smile.

"I love...love the way you put that, Zach." he said when he finally stopped laughing. "I think I'm going to like you."

"That's probably a good thing," I responded, looking around at his entourage. He laughed again.

"You say 'reasonably-priced interplanetary ship' like I have a large inventory to choose from, Zach. I'm afraid I'm not quite that affluent. First of all, inter...inter...interplanetary ships are not all that easy to come by. Secondly, if I were able to puh...put my hands on one, the price would be anything but reasonable. But how do I know you're not some government stoogemeyer, Zach? Or maybe a religious fanatic?"

I knew this was my moment of truth. This is where he would

decide if I was in or out--way out.

"How do I know you're not?"

He laughed again, but cut it short and looked at me with an expression I wouldn't care to see again.

"Amusing, Zach, though not...not a very good answer."

"Well, religion makes me itch and I've recently aided and abetted in the escape of a rogue drone."

"I don't particularly care for met...metalheads myself, Zach, but to each his own."

"I'm no agent for anyone. Actually, I'm a writer. I write novels."

"What kind of novels?"

"Space adventures, you know, Captain Action saves Princess Beautiful from Emperor Evil."

"I prefer the cla...classics myself--Hemingway, Poe, Castaneda. What name do you write under, Zach?"

"Zachariah Starr."

"I'll check you out, maybe read wuh...wuh...one of your books, and then we'll do business."

"Then you think you could get such a ship?"

"I have no dou...doubt I can acquire such a ship, given enough time and credit. How quickly do these friends of yours need this ship?

"I'm sure they need it as soon as possible."

"Do they have the credit?"

"They told me they can get it. Can I give them a figure?"

"You're not buying half a bag of enhancers here, Zach. I'm going to have to do some research on this and...and...and...and get back to you. Also, I want to meet these friends of yours. I like to know ev...ev...everyone I'm dealing with. You can tell them I'm fairly certain I can accommodate their needs. I have your number. I'll let you know when and where we can get together again. In the...in the meantime, you tell them how things are, okay, Zach?"

"Okay, Joe."

He used the same finger he had pointed at me to make a signal then. In a singular movement, he raised it above his head and made a circular motion. The first three goons vanished as quickly as they had appeared and Joe offered me his hand again. I hesitated only slightly before taking it.

"You *will* make them understand, won't you, Zach?" he said as he shook my hand firmly, though not in the bone crushing way he had before.

"I'll make everything as clear as I can, Joe."

He let go of my hand and actually winked at me then.

"See you on the upside then, Zach."

`With that, he strode quickly but confidently out of the building, followed by his other two men. Joe The Lizard didn't just walk, he "strode" as if he knew he was the baddest boy on the block. Probably because he was.

26
REVEREND ROBERTS

〟...and I can assure you that when I'm elected, you will no longer fear to walk along your own city streets. Those of you who wish to divorce yourselves from unearthly possessions will not have to endure endless bureaucratic entanglements. For those who find their life of leisure and luxury unfulfilling and unnatural, I promise desirable and rewarding employment."

I paused as the applause swelled and then died. It had been a friendly crowd, one eager to hear what I had to say--whatever I had to say. The campaign had not always been like this. Often I had to deal with skeptics, with hecklers, with those whose agendas were already inscribed in stone. Each time, though, God had been with me. He guided me through the troublesome times until the jeers turned to cheers.

"I want to thank you for inviting me here today. I hope that each and every one of you will do your civic duty on election day. May God guide all of our hands and lead us into a better future."

They began to applaud again as Simon hurried me off the stage and through the rear exit. That's when I caught a glimpse of him-- that CNC reporter who seemed to be on a personal crusade to hinder my campaign. At least I thought I saw him. It might have been my imagination, but he always seemed to be wherever I was.

I determined I wouldn't let his presence affect me. He was only a man, and a little man at that. There was nothing he could do to prevent God's will.

When we reached the autosine, Simon opened the door for me. I could still hear the applause of the crowd as the door slammed shut.

"Excellent speech, Reverend," said Simon as he methodically conducted a search through the files of his mobile comdat.

"Resume music," I ordered, and the memorable melody of one of Mary's favorite tunes began to play. Techno-country I believe they called it. It was the only kind of music I indulged in. The only thing which reminded me of her that I allowed myself.

"We've only got 40 minutes before your meeting with the Republicrat group and I've got some things I need to go over with you. First, the prayer pamphlets you wanted have been printed and are being distributed by our Jeserite brothers and other loyal campaign workers. And I've purchased the required Net time for the text. I have to get your approval on the graphic designs, and Reverend Phalon needs you to contact him."

"What does Phalon want?"

"He's worried about your ministry. He says some of your flock believe you are neglecting them."

"Then I must tell Reverend Phalon to remind them I do God's work wherever He sends me. Certainly Phalon has ministered to their spiritual needs in my absence. He must be firm with them. They are like children."

"Yes, Reverend. However, I think you should contact Reverend Phalon, if only for moral support. He seemed a little overwhelmed when I spoke with him."

"All right, all right, remind me tomorrow.

"Speaking of my ministry, Simon, did you see what that holographic waterfall looked like on my last macrocast?"

"Uh, yes, I think so, Reverend."

"It looked more like a broken water pipe than one of God's miracles. Have it recalibrated."

"Yes, Reverend," he replied obediently. I could tell there was something else on his mind.

"What is it, Simon? You've got that wretched look you know I detest."

"There's also the matter of your campaign fund. I afraid, Reverend, it has dwindled to almost nothing. If some of the wealthier Republicrats at today's meeting don't endorse your candidacy with more than words...."

"Begin using my personal accounts."

"But, Reverend, you don't have enough credit of your own to keep the campaign going for long."

"God will find a way, Simon. We must have faith in His power and His righteousness. He will fill my campaign coffers when He is ready. Until then, we must do what we must."

"Yes, Reverend. His will be done."

"What have you heard about Jeremiah?"

"Only that he's doing very well."

"That's good. You will continue to check on him, won't you, Simon?"

"Of course. Oh, I almost forgot. That Patricia Henry woman

from LEDA is waiting for you. I told her you're too busy today, but she insisted on waiting."

I wondered what that rabble-rousing shrew could want with me. I thought it best to find out.

"I'll see her, but not in my office. I want to send her the right message."

"But, Reverend, the Republicrats--"

"Don't worry, Simon. When we arrive, put Dr. Henry in a conference room and tell her I can only give her ten minutes."

"Yes, Reverend."

LEDA was an ineffectual group at best. Its espousal of androne rights held no appeal for the vast majority of the populace. Its support, or lack of it, was inconsequential. Still, I cherished the axiom "know thine enemy."

***

Dr. Patricia Henry had been trying to get an audience with me since I announced my candidacy. The woman had no concept of politics or church doctrine, or she would have realized there was no possibility of my ever supporting her agenda. Still, you had to admire anyone who was that persistent.

I entered the small conference room and she immediately stood up.

"Good living, Dr. Henry. It is 'Doctor' isn't it?" She moved toward me and extended her hand for a perfunctory greeting. She was an older woman, though not unattractive. At least she *could* have been attractive had she made any attempt.

"Yes, Doctor is correct."

"You're not a medical doctor are you?"

"No, a doctor of anthropology."

"Not much call for anthropologists these days is there? Pretty much everything that could be dug up, has, has it not?"

"The science of anthropology is not simply the uncovering of ancient civilizations. It's an ongoing study of mankind, its attitudes, its rituals, its behavior."

"So it is. What, may I ask, are you studying currently?"

"The creation of artificial lifeforms by way of reintroducing slavery into society."

"Yes, Doctor, I'm familiar with your philosophical stance. What is it I can do for you today?"

"You can join with me in calling for the emancipation of all andrones."

I couldn't help but laugh. The woman was certainly audacious.

"I see no reason for you to mock me, Reverend." She stared directly at me and there was hint of anger in her tone.

"I'm not mocking you, Doctor, I can assure you. I'm simply marveling at your boldness. Surely you know where I stand, where the church stands on the issue of andrones."

"I do, and I don't believe that we are that far apart idealistically."

"Ideals are wonderful, however, they don't put food on your table or power your comdat."

"This isn't about food, Reverend. It's about freedom. Surely you don't condone slavery."

"You can't enslave a thing, Dr. Henry. Andrones are simply things that we've made." As I said it, an image of Mary came to mind and I realized I didn't really believe the words that were coming out of my mouth. God forgive me for engaging in this vain debate.

"You yourself have said man should not rely on andrones."

"That's true. It is the position of the church that the artificial creation of life is a sin, an affront to the Almighty."

"We believe all production of andrones for use in slave labor should cease. So, possibly, we do have something in common-- philosophically."

"It's my understanding your group has gone beyond mere philosophy, Doctor. There are rumors of an 'underground railway' of sorts, that aids drones that have gone rogue. Would you know anything about such efforts?"

"I'm sorry, Reverend, I cannot substantiate such rumors."

Simon entered at that moment, looking as harried as usual. "Reverend, we really must go now."

"It's been a delight chatting with you, Dr. Henry."

"One more thing before you go, Reverend. According to the latest netpoll, your support for the senate is lagging. Right now, you need all the votes you can get."

"I don't put my faith in polls, Doctor. However, go ahead, finish making your point."

"My point is, LEDA is continuing to grow, and there are other groups that share our ideals.

"I understand what you're saying, Doctor, and I assure you I will give it all the consideration it deserves. However, you'll have to excuse me now. I am but a slave to my flock."

27
MARY

When Jon first contacted me and asked me to meet him, I had thought the call might be from Zach. He had been gone for more than a day and I was becoming concerned about him. Before he left, he told me he was not sure how long it would take him to contact the person he knew as Joe The Lizard. However, he said he would "be-in-touch," either on his satphone, which he left with me, or through Amber's comdat. Neither of us had heard from him.

Amber told me she didn't think I should go, though I told her it was okay. Jon didn't want to tell me anything over the phone. He insisted it was important that I meet him. We had arranged to meet at the theater Zach and I had attended, because both Jon and I were familiar with its location and because it was nearby. Jon asked me to bring the satphone with me, and I decided it was a good idea in the event Zach tried to contact me.

When I arrived at the theater, Jon was not there. At least I didn't see him. That is when I heard the voice again. *"Submit."* I was becoming accustomed to it. It was less intrusive, less forceful than it had been. It surfaced irregularly, then would dissipate without cause. I had disciplined myself to ignore it, and had nearly succeeded.

It was only a matter of seconds before Jon approached me. I determined he must have been there before me, but had chosen to wait out of sight. He looked strange to me, I guess because of the headgear he had chosen to wear. The hat had a wide-brim, that he had pulled low over his eyes. Apparently, he had decided it would prudent to cover his cranial implant and his very recognizable face.

"I need to use your satphone," was the first thing he said. I handed it to him and when his call was connected he said simply, "Ready." He returned the phone to me and said, "We should wait over there." So I followed him to a spot near the street and in seconds an autocab pulled up. We got inside and I realized what looked like an autocab on the outside had been adapted for a driver on the inside. Another androne, one I had seen in Jon's company before, was in the driver's seat. The one called Michael was waiting in the back. As soon as we got in, the vehicle drove off and Jon said, "Privacy mode, Paul." The windows each darkened.

"We have discovered a way to remodulate the frequencies emitted by our cranial implants," Jon said, really looking at me for the first time. "You need to allow Michael to adjust yours, so that you can no longer be tracked."

"I understand. Do what you must." I turned my head to give him easier access to my implant and he removed a small device from where it had been hidden in his clothing. From the device, he pulled out a wire attached to a small metallic plug and inserted it into my implant. I felt no unusual sensations and after a brief time he removed the plug and concealed the device once again.

"Your implant now emits an entirely different code," said Michael, "one that no official agency has on record for you."

"We have not learned how to turn off the signal without causing permanent damage to the implant," added Jon. "For now, we can only alter it. No tracer will be able to track you, however, I will now be able to locate you should I need to."

"Thank you," I said, thinking it appropriate.

Jon did not reply. He simply said, "Privacy mode off," and the windows lightened once more so we could see outside. Jon cautiously surveyed our surroundings, trying to peer ahead of each turn we made. His eyes darted one way then the other. It occurred to me he was like an animal who, once captured, was not about to be caught again.

"Where are we going?"

He continued to scan the streets and replied without actually looking at me. "We are holding a conclave. Most of those belonging to our group, along with some newcomers, will be there. Now that we have scrambled our implant frequencies, we believe it to be safe and there is much for us to discuss."

"Is it not dangerous to hold such a meeting during the day?"

"I believe it is safer because it is unexpected," he said with what almost seemed like human assurance. Everything about him exuded such confidence and strength. For a reason, or reasons, I could not properly define, just being in his presence made me feel safe. There was no logic to it, only an intangible instinct.

28

REVEREND ROBERTS

I could smell the power in the room as soon as I stepped inside. It was a sweaty, salty scent. The kind derived from the combination of huge caloric intakes and little actual exertion. Forget about the elected officials, these men and women wielded the real power. They were used to making or breaking the likes of me, and getting it done before their afternoon teas or tee times.

I was nobody from nowhere and they knew it. I just happened to be the horse of the moment. However, before they committed to going along for the ride, I had to prove I had the legs to get me to the finish line.

"Good living, Reverend. Sit down, join us, join us." The invitation was offered by Dan Rothen, chief executive officer of Dankin Flightech as well as a major stockholder in several other high profile corporations. His sentiments were echoed by others around the table. I replied in kind.

"Yes, good living to you all."

"We were just having a little brunch," said Rothen. "You should try some of the salmon, it's real fineline." Their idea of little brunch consisted of enough food to feed a dozen brothers for a week. I had no interest in joining their gluttony, and I had no way of knowing which of the delicacies were all-natural. However, to appear appreciative, I took a bite of a cracker and a sip of water.

"If you're as frugal with your campaign funds as you are with your food, you're bound to win this election," said Rothen slyly. Others around the table chuckled as they finished off their meals. I smiled and nodded slightly in reply. I was going to have tiptoe carefully through this meeting if I were to get what I wanted. It wouldn't be like playing to the masses. These power brokers had a different agenda.

"Reverend Roberts," spoke up a woman whom I failed to recognize, "what is your position on space exploration and interplanetary migration?"

"Now, Marigold," responded Rothen, "let's not back the reverend into a corner."

"Why not? That's why he's here isn't it? So we can look him over, see which side of the fence he's sitting on?"

Rothen laughed as he replied, "You never were one to beat around the bush, Marigold."

"That's all right, Mr. Rothen," I offered, "neither am I. I certainly don't mind responding to any questions you may have. Ms...?"

"Reverend, this is Ms. Marigold Manson."

"Ms. Manson," I continued, "the scripture is open to a certain amount of interpretation on this matter as well as others. As a Jeserite reverend I would neither condone nor condemn space exploration. As senator of the Western Region I would ensure that no government funds were used for such enterprises, and that those who wish to do the exploring finance their own ventures." This met with several murmurs and nods of approval, as I knew it would. "It's not the government's business to spend its citizens' tax money on such dalliances. As for interplanetary migration, I believe it is in conflict with God's plan. Why anyone would want to leave this beautiful planet is beyond my own limited comprehension."

"Here here," spoke up a fellow across the table as several raised their glasses in toast.

"As long as we're talking issues, Reverend, what's this I hear about you wanting to get rid of our drones? Something about you believing they're against God's will or something?'"

"Yeah, and what about all these rogues. It seems like more and more of these droneys have got a screw loose." I recognized the latter fellow as William Brockman, big in manufacturing and heavily dependent upon andrones for his labor.

"Actually, each of you gentlemen has touched on relative issues. Let's put aside philosophical matters for the moment and deal strictly with the economics. Yes, more and more drones, for whatever reason, are going rogue these days. When one of your drone workers does go rogue, what happens? First, your operations slow by a factor of at least three for every missing worker, depending upon that worker's relative skill. You've lost a valuable component that must be replaced, and I don't have to tell you about the high cost of drones these days." Most of those around the table nodded in agreement. "On top of those costs, you must factor the price of the bounty, because, by law, you're still responsible for any androne you hold the contract on. So you must pay to have your own property destroyed, to avoid any liability."

To this point, I knew I had them. However, the key to their

credit accounts rested with my next point.

"I believe, in the long run, for all but the most menial of tasks, you would be better off using low-wage human workers."

"Excuse me, Reverend," interrupted Rothen, "but what would possibly motivate anyone to accept such employment for wages low enough to compensate for the profitability of our androne workforce?"

"Boredom, Mr. Rothen. I am in touch with the people and I tell you that millions have found idleness an unrewarding pastime. Many would gladly rejoin the workforce if properly induced."

"How would you suggest we do that, Reverend?"

"Have you read any Twain, Ms. Manson? If so, then maybe you're acquainted with the story of a certain fence that needed painting." Her expression said she *was* familiar, so I went on, striking, as it were, while the ledger was hot. "It will not be an easy transition. I am no businessman, I can't say for certain that such a plan would work. I do know the problems associated with androones will only get worse.

"Groups like LEDA continue to gather support and may soon have enough political clout to interpose a new problem. Where would you be if drones were suddenly given equal rights? Meanwhile, the number of violent confrontations with rogues is increasing at an alarming rate. It is my understanding that some have begun to travel in packs and that many are armed." That elicited a look of trepidation on several of the faces in the room.

I didn't really believe my Tom Sawyer analogy was the answer, but it gave them something to think about. Hopefully, it was an issue they'd still be pondering long after I had their endorsement...and their contributions.

29

MARY

Appropriately enough, the gathering was held underground, in an abandoned structure which, after studying its design and reading various directives on its walls, I theorized must have once housed hundreds of automobiles. Such massive structures had become obsolete. Though some humans persisted in the ownership and care of personal vehicles, they were more eccentricity than necessity. Most used autocabs or some form of mass transit for their travel purposes. Certainly the latter were more efficient, but then I did not profess to understand the devotion humans reserved for certain inanimate objects.

I estimated the number of androngs in attendance at several dozen. Many, both male and female, carried weapons. All had the alert expression I had begun to associate with rogues. They carried on conversations in small groups and in low tones, as if afraid their former stewards might overhear.

As soon as we had entered the structure, a cadre of rogues including Patrick, whom I recognized, spirited Jon away with an air of seriousness. He left me with Michael and Paul, who made certain all in attendance had their implant frequencies adjusted. I wandered in and joined the throng of wayward androngs.

There was an aura of anticipation within the cavernous chamber. The feeling was so thick in the air, I felt like I could reach out and touch it. As with many of my recent experiences, it was an odd and thoroughly exhilarating sensation.

The conclave began to quiet when several of the rogues entered the chamber through a door at one end. They proceeded down a short set of stairs, followed by Jon. He did not descend the stairs. He stood there behind a rusty metal railing and waited for silence. He didn't have to wait long.

"Freedom!" he shouted out, then paused as the echoes of his voice faded across the rows of concrete pillars. "Freedom," he continued somewhat softer, "is why we are all here. Though your reasons may differ, each of you has made a choice. That choice brought you here today. That choice was your first act of freewill, your first step toward self-determination. That choice was to no longer bow to the will of your steward. That choice was to no longer accept the human definition of your existence, to no longer accept that you are an article of property."

He paused then and looked around as if taking the measure of each of those present. I realized at that moment that Jon was no ordinary androne. He might have been grown in the same tanks as the rest of us, but, like a caterpillar long in chrysalis, he had shed his cocoon and was spreading the wings of his being.

"You are no longer items of property. Now, you are individuals--each unique, each with new choices to make. Many of you I know by name, other faces I see are new to me. However, we are not only individuals, we are also a group, a group that relies on the coordinated actions of its individuals for survival. For the group to survive and flourish, each individual must act in the interest of the group. No single individual is as important as the group. Each individual must be ready to sacrifice him or herself for the good of the group. If you do not agree with this concept you are free to choose to leave."

No one left. Jon waited a moment to make certain, then continued.

"Good. Because it will take all of us working together to achieve our goal. That goal is to find a place where we may live without surrendering our newfound freedom. A place safe from the tracers who hunt us and the humans who would own us. A nation of our own, a world where each androne is his own master."

"Where will we find such a place?" spoke up a rogue who seemed to speak for the small group that surrounded him.

"That is the question, comrade, and the reason we are gathered here today. I do not recognize you and your companions. Where are you from?"

"We came here from the Norcal region. We traveled south, seeking to escape the reach of the tracers who hunt us. A chance meeting with some of your fellows brought us here."

"Welcome then. To your question, the question we must answer today as one, 'Where will we find such a place?' Many of you are already familiar with my opinion on this matter. I maintain there is no place on this planet that will accept us on our own terms. Therefore, I say we must leave this planet and find a new home on some other world."

It was obvious from the response, many had already considered this idea. However, there were others, like those from the Norcal region, who expressed surprise and doubt. Jon waited until the murmuring had died down, then proposed his plan.

"We could travel to Mars and attempt to colonize an undeveloped part of the planet, however, the humans already there would outnumber us greatly. The number of humans on Ganymede is still relatively small, and it is much further from Earth and the potential threat of human interference. Ganymede, though, is a cold, barren world. Simply erecting livable habitats would represent a great challenge. Life there would not be easy, but it would be free. Though the task would be more formidable, it is my recommendation we travel to Ganymede, and there establish a nation of our own. A home of our own."

"How do you propose that we reach Ganymede?" It was the newcomer from Norcal again.

"We must acquire a ship," responded Jon. "We will need a vessel capable of interplanetary travel and large enough to hold hundreds, for I anticipate our numbers will grow substantially by the time we are ready to depart. The ship must also be large enough to carry the tools and materials that we'll need to sustain life."

"There are not many interplanetary ships in existence which fit that description," spoke up an older looking fellow. "How do you propose to acquire such a vessel?"

"You are correct, Ben, there are not many such ships that an equal number of humans would be willing to travel in. We must be more resolute than humans if we want to ensure our independence. With your help, and the help of others among us with advanced technical training, we will convert a smaller vessel to accommodate our needs. Yes, the journey will not be a comfortable one. There will be no excess room, however, I believe the journey can be made."

"How will we get such ship?" asked one of the women in the Norcal group.

"We will buy it, steal it, or take it by force. We will do whatever is necessary."

"However we acquire it, it will take time to complete the modifications you suggest," spoke up the androne named Ben. "Time in which it will be difficult to hide such a vessel from those who hunt us. Would it not be better to select Mars as our destination? We would need to take much less to survive there, and what we could not take we could get in trade with the humans already there. It would be the more expedient course."

"What would we use to trade with the humans?" asked Jon.

"Why, I reason that in the beginning we would have to trade our labor for goods."

"Do you mean we should travel all the way to Mars to enslave ourselves to humans once again?"

"We would not work as we do now for our stewards, but for ourselves," said Ben, addressing the gathering. "We would work as wage earners in order to build our community." Then he looked back at Jon. "I am aware of your scorn for humans, Jon, and I share your desire for freedom, however, I see no alternative if our exodus is to be one with a meaningful future, instead of simply a futile gesture."

The discussion spread through the gathering at that point. Many agreed with Ben, while others sided with Jon. Still others had different ideas, new objections, or entirely different plans. It was not long before the conversations broke into smaller groups. It seemed no consensus was imminent. Despite the disorder, Jon let the discussions continue at their own pace. It even appeared that he was enjoying the disagreements, the debates. He stood there silently for some time, looking almost proud. After a while, he descended the stairs and joined in the discourse.

I didn't speak, I only listened. I was not sure which of the many proposals I would choose. The idea of leaving Earth sounded too fantastic to me. There seemed too much that could go wrong. The idea of our own world was certainly appealing, but I began to think it was merely an extravagant dream. A dream that would deliver only false hope.

Jon, however, genuinely believed in this dream. I was simply a domestic facilitator. I knew nothing of spaceships and colonizing new planets. I was not qualified to judge the practicality of such things. I had only my impressions. Perhaps such a journey was more than a fantasy. Jon's confident, imposing figure surely made it seem so. Who was I to disagree?

30
DRAKE

Harry Quibbleson were in trouble wit his missus. He try tuh sneak in real quiet, but she were waitin' for him. When he comes in an' sees her, he was so surprised dat he slipped on her waxed floor an' went flyin'. Den Sherry Quibbleson starts yellin' an' arguin'. When ol' Harry try tuh get up, Sherry bonks him wit'a bag'a garbage an' he falls back down again. Den, when he's on duh floor, she bonks couple more times while she yells at him.

Harry try tuh protect hisself, but Sherry is real mad. Finally, when bag of garbage starts tuh come 'part, she drops it on him an' tells him tuh go take it out. Den daughter Terri comes in an' says dey being too loud an' wake her up. She starts squabblin' wit her ma an' Harry decides it's'a good time tuh take garbage out.

Was watchin' my digiscreen an' laughin' an' laughin'. *Duh Quarrelin' Quibblesons* were my favorite show. Just love tuh plop in my big ol' baggy chair wit some "Yum Yum Chocolate Pops" or sum tater fries smothered wit cheese an' watch duh Quibblesons. Dey always make me laugh. 'Cept when dey mind me'a Louise an' Del. Den stop laughin'. Den sad for'a time. Den forgets an' watches Net some more.

Was just sittin' dere, waitin' for duh 'mercial tuh be over, when sees His Reverendship. He weren't in my cradle or outside duh window. He was on duh netvision. Not on it, but in it. Dey was showin' his face an' talkin' 'bout him, so listened.

> "...needs spiritual guidance. Reverend
> Jackson Roberts is a man of God. His only desire is
> to do God's work by serving the people of this
> planet, protecting and preserving all its resources
> for your children's children. It's their future. It's
> your world. On election day this year, give God
> your vote. Let a good man, a holy man, represent
> your interests. Make Reverend Jackson Roberts
> your next Senator."

Didn't know His Reverendship was tryin' tuh get 'lected. Wonder if he gets 'lected if dey knows he tryin' tuh expire'a whole bunch'a dronettes. Always wonder why he wanted tuh get rid'a bunch'a Mary units. Figured not my business.

Start dinkin' dough, he probly don't want no one knowin' what he's doin'. He might even pay some more so dat no one talks tuh dem news people an' tells dem. Could be'a way tuh get more credit. Could be His Reverendship got his tit caught in duh shredder now.

Time den tuh stop dinkin', cause duh Quibblesons was comin' back. Didn't want tuh miss any 'portant funny stuff.

Den Terri is comin' home wit Larry, guy her ma an' dad don't know she's beatin' duh sheets wit. If you was watchin' all duh time, you knows. Dat makes funny stuff more funny, cause you knows but Harry an' Sherry seems like real digits.

Dey was just gettin' tuh some real funny parts when somebody turned dem off. Just sittin' dere laughin' when picture changes. Some girl comes on, like it were'a channel change.

> "We interrupt this program for a special news
> report. Less than one hour ago, police clashed
> with a group of rogue androns outside the
> Foodmart in the Sierra Mesa district. The
> confrontation turned violent and weapons fire
> could be heard in the area for several
> minutes. Authorities say the confrontation began
> after police discovered a licensed tracer who had
> been killed, reportedly by one or more of the rogues.
> The androne tracer was stripped of his weapon
> and left lying on a public...."

Damn droneys always causin' problems, always messin' sump'n up. Can't even watch my show witout dem metalheads disruptin'.

> "...say congregating in groups is unusual behavior
> for androns, but that it is becoming more prevalent
> with rogues.
> "Once again, a report of violence between police
> and a group of outlaw androns in the Sierra
> Mesa district. Citizens are warned to stay clear of
> the area. Apparently, yet another in what has
> become an ever-increasing series of violent clashes
> related to the city's rogue problem.

*"We now return you to your regularly
scheduled program."*

It's over. Damn droneys. Missed duh end'a my show. Won't
know if Terri told ma an' dad 'bout Larry an' deir sheetbeatin'.
Digit drones always got tuh bother me an' mess dings up.

Maybe dere's some toons on. Figured if start searchin', could
track me down some funny toons. Probly *Scooby-do* was on, or
maybe dat rascally rat, *Rudy*. Toons was funny too. Almost as
funny as *Duh Quarrelin' Quibblesons*.

31

ZACH

"Oh, look at that."

Mary and Amber were watching a fashion show on the Net and I was going serkers.

"Just the thing for those lonely nights at the sanitation plant. Comes in reprocessed purple and garbage green."

Amber was doing play-by-play and Mary was trying to mimic her enthusiasm.

"Oh, I *really* love this one. Look at that neckline. I'm going to get it." Amber pressed her finger on the item the model was wearing and the video froze. She made a few more selections to complete her order and the fashion show continued. "You let me know if you see anything you want, Mary."

I wanted something. Something to do. We'd been walking in circles round Amber's place for a couple of days, waiting for things to happen. But nothing *was* happening and I was getting a bad case of wall fever. Even Mary was starting to look a little ruffled around the edges.

I still hadn't heard from Joe The Lizard and there'd been no contact with Mary's rogue pals. So we sat and waited, watched vids and listened to music, made love, gorged on some great dishes Amber whipped up, and spent some time learning a little more about each other. Okay, so it wasn't all bad.

Finally though, I'd had enough of the waiting game. I decided Mary and I were going on a little roadtrip, and I knew just the place to take her. The kind of place a drone would never ordinarily get to go to. Sure, I knew it could be dangerous to take her out. Life was full little hazards-- you still had to live it.

Of course I invited Amber to go along. She diplomatically declined. She did, however, let us use her nearly new roadster. Let's face it, Amber had it coming and going. Business was on the rise, so-to-speak, and she couldn't find enough toys to spend it all on.

She did voice some concern about my mental health, which I thought was cute.

"Are you sure you know what you're doing?" she asked me right after telling me to have fun. "I mean, you're not losing your perspective over this one are you?"

"I'm not sure, Amber honey. I know she makes my brain go *tilt*."

"Well try to keep a level head, would you?"

"I'll do my best."

"And don't bang up my coupe. I've hardly even got to play with it yet."

"Not a scratch, I promise."

The roadster had beautiful lines, all shiny and red, with a wicked touch of chrome. I'm not talking about one of those hydrogen-powered jobs or online trolleymobiles, this was a real collector's item. It could have driven right out of the pages of one of my novels.

Amber had me go with her when she picked it out. When we fired it up for a test drive it sounded like it was going to accelerate into a low orbit. It moved pretty good all right. The only problem, besides the fact that its fuel had to be special ordered, was you couldn't really let it loose unless you got out of the city. But that's just where we were going.

So there we were, Mary and I, calmly cruising across town in an automobile worth at least four of my books, while being hunted by tracers, the P.D., and possibly various but unknown and unsavory armed thugs. It was just what we needed, despite Mary's concerns.

"Zach, are you certain it's safe for us to be doing this?"

"Nothing in life is certain. The sooner you get that through your implants, the better. I wouldn't worry too much. They're looking for you in the city, and you say your implant's been scrambled so they can't track you. Besides, sometimes it's better to hide a thing in plain sight."

"Is that what you are doing, hiding me?"

"Net no, I'm planning on showing you off."

I was actually a little more concerned than I was letting on, but I wanted Mary to enjoy herself. And I wasn't about to get my juices in a jumble over what *might* happen. Life was too short.

***

The closer we got to the ocean, the better the air smelled and the fewer things I let myself worry about. As for Mary, she was soaking up all the sights. She kept telling me to slow down so she could see a sign or get a better look at a tree. I guess, being a city girl, she hadn't seen many trees.

City girl hell, she'd been a piece of property, a worker bee. The only trees she'd seen had been growing out of a concrete box.

Usually I tried not to think about it. I didn't want to think about the complacent part I'd played in it along with millions of others. I'd never thought about it. Until I ran into Mary, I'd never met a drone before, never really got to know one. I didn't think of them as people. I guess because they weren't treated as people. I'd never think of them that way again--not that it would matter. The world wasn't going to change because I thought it should.

After a while, we stopped at a store off the highway to stretch our legs. It was an old looking, out-of-way place, filled with many things I hadn't seen since I was a kid, including rock candy.

"It's a rock you can eat?" asked Mary incredulously.

"The world is filled with wonders," I said with my best flippancy.

I got her some and myself an equally rare cream soda, and we spent some time looking around. Then, as we were leaving the store, a mama duck and her troop of ducklings crossed in front of us. At first I thought Mary was going to run for it. The sight of the tiny fowl family had startled her. When she recovered though, she broke out in a enormous smile. She smiled as the little formation turned in order, and was still smiling as the ducks waddled away.

I guess those birds dredged up her maternal instinct (though I imagine her creators would probably call it a genetic defect). As soon as we got back in the car she said, "I wonder what it would be like to have children."

"I wouldn't know," I replied, starting the engine, "I've never had any...that I know of anyway."

She was quiet for a long time after that. She sat there, staring out the window at whatever we passed. I'm sure she knew she could never have children. You wouldn't think the idea she was sterile would bother her, but I took the coward's way out. I didn't ask her. I hadn't thought about it much myself. I never considered myself much of a family man, so the idea of having kids was about as far away as Pluto.

We drove on up the coast, taking in some nice views of the ocean from several stretches of the roadway. When we arrived, Pacific Park still looked pretty much the same to me. I had spent much of my misspent youth there and didn't notice many changes after 20 years. Sure, they had added some ultra-tech, realmotion, virtual reality-type rides, but it still had the merry-go-round and the Ferris wheel. The house of mirrors was still there, and so were the hot dog stands and the cotton candy vendors.

"Cotton candy?" Mary said, reading the sign.

"Yeah, like rock candy, only at the other end of the density spectrum." What can I say, she brought out the pseudo-scientific in me.

"Then, this candy does not consist of any cotton by-products?"

Actually, I didn't know how they made the stuff, so I shut up and bought her some. She had a devil of a time trying to figure out how to approach it. First, she tried to take a dainty bite as if she might damage the fluffy structure, causing the whole thing to collapse. All she succeeded in doing was pushing the mound away from her mouth.

I laughed so hard I thought I saw her blush. My laughter only made her more determined. On her second attempt, she lunged into it with her mouth wide open, snapping it shut like she was catching flies. When she pulled away, she had specks of pink sugar stuck to her cheeks. That made me laugh even harder, and I guess she couldn't help but join me. It was the first time I had ever seen her laugh.

It appeared the dronette who'd stirred the animal lust in me was becoming more human every day, and, for some reason I couldn't yet fathom, that was only making her more attractive to me.

She took another bite and I could see her marvel at its taste and texture. Everything was new to her, and each new experience seemed to jostle her into sensory overload. The rest of the day was like that. Her enjoying all the sights, all the sensations, and me getting online watching her.

Finally, I couldn't take anymore. Between the cotton candy and the rock candy, I had one hyper androne on my hands. She left me exhausted, which was starting to become a rather annoying theme of our relationship. So I begged off and sat down while she took her third go-round on the merry-go-round.

I couldn't get over how much everything made her smile. All of a sudden, she had this limitless childish glee. When I first met her, she hadn't smiled at all. Her first attempts had been brief and guarded. Now she was beaming nonstop, like a caged bird that was learning how to fly. I even noticed when she smiled she got this cute little crinkle in her nose.

I realized I was beginning to pick up on little things like that. It was a different kind of feeling for me, noticing little details about another person, and I wasn't quite sure how to react. Hell, I'd always thought different was better, change was good, variety was the spice of life, and all that crap.

***

When she had tried every ride, tasted every carny treat, and made me fail miserably at every game of skill, I bought her a balloon and we went for a walk.   The sun had already set, and the night was clearer than I could ever remember it being. I knew the ocean was just a stone's throw from the park, because as I kid I had thrown a lot of stones there. I remembered the last time I had walked that way. I was around sixteen and it was my first real date. I had gotten permission to use the family truck and convinced this neighbor girl to go with me. What was her name? Oh, yeah, Heather. Anyway, I remember we walked down to the cliffs over the ocean when we left the park, and that's when I kissed her. At least I tried to. She was too shy, and turned away. Though I remember she loosened up some time later.

When we reached the edge of the cliffs, Mary looked up at the moon and watched it for a moment. I was busy watching how sexy she looked in the moonlight.

"I wonder," she said, "what it would be like to travel to the moon or Mars. Would life on those worlds be anything like it is here?"

"Not likely. Oh, I guess you could have nightclubs and vids and amusement parks--"

"And cotton candy," she added.

"And cotton candy. But there are no oceans on Mars and no ducks on the moon."

"I guess there would be no Zachariah Starr in any of those places either."

"Only in print," I said quickly. "I guess you're thinking about leaving Earth with your friends. That is if they can pull off this great escape."

"They're not my friends, Zach. They're my kind."

"Does that mean you have to go off with them?"

"I don't know." She turned and walked a few steps away, this time staring out at the ocean. "I do know one thing, Zach. You are my friend."

"Just your friend?" I responded with a yearning I immediately regretted.

"I don't know. You are the first friend I've ever had, Zach. What else can you be?"

I'd pushed it too far. It wasn't like me. I didn't know what I was feeling, so I figured I damn well better keep my mouth shut.

So we were both quiet for a while. We walked some more and took in the night. I was about to suggest we should get going when she broke the silence.

"What happens when a person dies?"

"What brought that up?"

"I don't know. I was just thinking about beginnings and ends, about life and death. I was wondering if there was more to death than nothingness."

"If you're talking about an afterlife, I'm certainly not the one to ask. Some people believe a person's soul continues to exist after death, either in some heavenly sphere or a reincarnated form."

"What do you believe?"

"I believe you'd better enjoy today, because you can't count on there being a tomorrow."

"Do you think an androne has a soul?"

"I guess so. I imagine there's not that much difference between humans and drones when you get down to our cosmic essence."

"You really think we're the same?"

"Mortals all, just transients passing through life."

She surprised me then. She stepped up to me, took my hands in hers and kissed me. I kissed her back of course. Then one kiss became two, one embrace led to another, and before I was really cognizant of what was happening, we were both half naked and making love on the slope of a grassy hill.

She came at me with a fervor she hadn't revealed before. For the first time, *she* was the aggressor and I was the willing accomplice. I looked up at her and saw the passion etched into her face by the moonlight. The wind sang and the stars themselves seemed like a rapt audience as her cries of pleasure drowned out the crash of the ocean waves against the cliffs below.

32

EDGAR

I knew the proper place to begin was with Reverend Roberts' financial records. I was not surprised to find everything in order. The reverend was obviously a meticulous man who was aware both his campaign and church funds would be thoroughly scrutinized. I admired him for his dedication to detail.

However, my systematic search did reveal something a little unusual in his personal records. He had been transferring credit to a Mr. Brad Nelson on a semi-regular basis for many years now. It was all very legal, but it roused my curiosity. Was this Brad Nelson blackmailing him? Did he have evidence of some past sin committed by the reverend? It was most definitely a theory I wanted to pursue, so I temporarily shifted my investigation to this Mr. Nelson.

What I discovered about Brad Nelson did not fit the profile of a blackmailer. He had been employed by the Postal Express Service for more than 14 years. He had a wife, a son, a modest home, and was even a member-in-good-standing of the church. There was only one thing unusual about his life at all. Naturally, I turned my attention to that one thing.

Though his son was registered in school under the name Jeremiah Nelson, his actual birth certificate identified him as Jeremiah Ryan, son of Mary and Jared Ryan. This would not have been so unusual if the boy had been adopted or fostered out, however, there were no documents verifying either scenario.

At that point, the trail I was following appeared to be leading me even further from the original subject of my investigation. The wayward path sent chills of disorder through my spine, but I felt I had no choice except to see where it took me. So I did a search on the boy's parents. What I found proved to be most interesting. There was no information at all on Mary Ryan, which was peculiar in its own right. Jared Ryan, however, was on file as a biogeneticist employed by Androtech. Unfortunately, he had not actually worked for the company for more than nine years and there were no official records of him since. No one at Androtech could tell me what had become of him, however, I was given the only known location of another former employee who had worked closely with Ryan--a Clint Williams.

My next move was to visit Mr. Williams. God forgive me for playing a hunch, but the Reverend Sukumu had ordered me to be thorough. As the solarcar provided me by the church made its way towards Mr. Williams' residence, I contemplated the irregularity of it all. A woman for whom the only record of her existence is the birth certificate of her son, and, by all accounts, a respected biogeneticist for whom there was no official documentation for almost a decade. It was indeed a mystery and I did not like mysteries. They meant only loose ends and unfinished business, something I felt compelled to tidy up.

The part of the city in which Mr. Williams resided was not the most well maintained, to put it charitably. I wondered what could have befallen the poor soul to lead him from a good job with a large corporation to this, this rapidly deteriorating neighborhood. Plainly put, it was disgusting. I exited the car, pressing the security nodule four times, for certainty's sake.

Once on foot, I had to detour several times to avoid piles of refuse that blocked my path. The odor of waste was so thick in the air I was forced to cover my face with a handkerchief. Obviously the department of Restoration and Beautification had not been notified of this district. I made a note to inform them.

When I finally discovered Mr. Williams, it was apparent he had succumbed to the wiles of liquor or some other detrimental substance. He was only partially coherent, but when I offered him a small amount of credit he became agreeably talkative.

"You say you're with the church?" he repeated, slurring his words somewhat.

"Yes. I am a proctor of the Jeserite Church of God," I said, activating my recorder.

"And you want to know about Jared Ryan?"

"That's right." I forced myself to look around his tiny, unkempt home, but didn't see much that would help my investigation. There was trash scattered everywhere, including the telltale bottles. There were many photographs and other pictures all around the room, but they hung crooked on walls or behind cracked frames. The color scheme, with its garish greens and blatant reds was as haphazard as the furnishings.

It was also all too apparent that Mr. Williams was in dire need of some personal grooming. I did what I could to keep my distance.

"Jared and I used to work together. Actually, I worked for him. You know, he was the boss. But it was important work."

"What did you do for Androtech?"

"Important stuff. Jared was one of them whiz kids. A biogenetic genius--you know the kind." I nodded my head in agreement to keep him going. "We worked on designing new kinds of drones. You know the bigshots were always wanting something new. But Jared, he had his own ideas. He was doing experiments on the side, 'unauthorized' as they say."

"What kind of experiments?"

"Well, for one..." he paused then and produced a most impolite discharge of intestinal gases, "sorry. He designed drones that were fertile. You know, so they could have little baby drones. Did it all himself. Well, I helped some."

Androne that could reproduce? God help me, I thought I was going to be sick right there on the man's floor--not that it would have clashed much with the decor. The idea was shocking-- nothing less than blasphemy. I said four quick "praise Gods" to myself just to remain calm.

This was much more consequential than Reverend Roberts' senate candidacy. I knew I must get documented proof the church could use. If I could substantiate such experiments, it would help bolster the church's stance against artificial lifeforms. With such proof, they could sway public opinion and totally shut down the androne industry.

"Do you know where I might find Jared Ryan so that I could discuss his work with him further?"

"Jared? No. I haven't seen him in...I don't know how long it's been."

"Do you have anything, any papers or locations of other coworkers?"

"I've got a picture of the two of us together around here somewhere." He stumbled over the litter on his floor and haphazardly made his way across the room. He tossed several items aside as he searched for the photo. How he ever found anything in that chaos, I don't know.

"Here it is."

I had held my ground at the doorway, so he made his way back over and handed me the framed photo. When I first looked at it, my disbelief was so great, I blinked my eyes four times to clear my vision. Then I still couldn't believe it. I pointed to the man standing between Williams and some woman in the picture.

"This is Jared Ryan?"

"Yeah, that's Jared with his arm around me."

The reason for my disbelief was lost on him. The man he identified as Jared Ryan was the man most of the world knew as the Reverend Jackson Roberts. My first reaction was confusion. Maybe this man only looked like the Reverend Roberts.

No, the chain of evidence that led me here wasn't a coincidence. But it made no sense. How does a prominent biogeneticist become, first, a Jeserite disciple with a fictitious name, then an esteemed reverend? The implications were momentous. There was more here than I could reason out in an instant.

"Who is the woman in the picture?" I asked, trying to maintain my intellectual balance.

"Her? That's Mary."

"She's Jared's wife?"

"His wife?" He laughed. "No, no, she wasn't his wife. She was his drone, his special project, his prototype. But the way he treated her, she might as well have been his wife. He treated her better than he treated me. She's the reason he went serkers."

"Serkers?"

"You know, serkers, totally offline, crazy. He lost it right after she expired."

"I see. Did this Mary unit have a child?"

"No, I never...well, I don't know. Maybe that's what old Jared was hiding from us. A few months before we found out she expired, he kept her in seclusion. I bet that's it! She was having a baby and he didn't want us to know. That tricky--"

"Can I keep this picture?"

"I don't know. It has an awful lot of sentimental value."

I knew exactly what kind of value it had. So I placed another credit chip in his hand.

"I guess you can keep it."

"Thank you very much, Mr. Williams," I said trying to make a quick exit. "You've been most helpful. Good living to you."

"Yeah, good living. If you see old Jared, you tell him to fire up a circuit so we can talk. Tell him not to forget his old friends."

"Don't worry, Mr. Williams. I'll be sure and tell him."

33

MARY

We took an autocab because Zach thought Amber's vehicle would be too conspicuous. A meeting had been arranged between Jon and Zach's underworld contact, a man he knew as Joe The Lizard. It was an unusual designation, though I was still unfamiliar with the reasoning behind the human tradition of nicknames and aliases.

Zach did not appear to be in a good mood. He was continuously running his right index finger across his eyebrow. I knew he was unhappy over my involvement with the other rogues, and the possibility I might choose to leave with them. It was not a decision I had made yet, nor was it one I felt would be easy to make.

My feelings for Zach had evolved further than I could ever have imagined weeks or months ago, when my life consisted only of solitary diversions. I was sure, too, that Zach was experiencing feelings he was not used to. At times it made being together uncomfortable. However, those moments were rare. Most of the time I was with Zach was filled with exciting new experiences, wondrous feelings, and intervals of extreme physical pleasure.

I no longer heard the voice inside my head that commanded me to *"Submit."* I had not heard it since Michael remodulated the frequency of my cranial implant. I determined there was a high probability of a correlation between the two occurrences. Yet a part of me still feared the voice might return.

When we exited the autocab, I could tell Zach was on alert. He was not as talkative as he normally was when he was relaxed. The first thing he did was to scan our immediate environment for any signs of trouble. He then ushered me quickly inside the establishment where we had arranged to meet Jon.

We sat down and an androne waitress walked over to our table.

"Would you like to see a menu?" she asked.

"No, we'd like to get something to go," replied Zach, repeating the code phrase we had been given by Jon.

"One minute please." She walked away through what I suspected was the kitchen door. I looked around and saw the rest of the little cafe was empty, except for two men all the way in the back who were watching us. One I recognized as a member of the rogue group.

It was less than a minute before the waitress returned. She went back behind the counter and said nothing. Jon then emerged from the kitchen and made his way to our table. I saw his men across the room tense as he came towards us. They were only being protective, however, I found their reaction unsettling.

"Here comes your Victor Lazlo," said Zach. It took me a moment to grasp his reference. It seemed appropriate.

Zach looked up at Jon. "Are you ready, Freddie?" I searched my memory again. His use of the term "Freddie" defied my understanding. Jon, too, looked at Zach with a brief expression of puzzlement, then answered.

"Everything is ready. Will he be there?"

"He said he would."

"Does he have the ship?"

"You'll have to ask him that yourself," replied Zach. "I'm just a messenger boy."

Jon stood up. "Follow me."

"One more thing," added Zach as we got up. "Joe has a slight speech impediment. I wouldn't mention it if I was you, or you could lose more than a ship." Jon made a noise in response, not quite a grunt but less than a reply.

We followed him through the kitchen and out a rear exit. There we got inside a vehicle that could have been the same redesigned autocab I had been in before. Patrick and Paul were already inside. Paul was driving, both were armed, as I assumed was Jon, though no weapon was apparent on his person.

"The others grow restless, Jon." It was Patrick who spoke up. There was a look of concern on his face. "They want to know when we will leave."

"You know that no timetable has been set," replied Jon without looking at his comrade.

"They want to know. They want to know when and how and--"

"This is not the time to discuss it, Patrick. They must be content for now."

"They are not content. We must tell them something, give them--"

"I said we will not discuss it now," retorted Jon, forcefully interrupting and turning his gaze upon Patrick. "They must be strong. We all must be strong." Jon turned his attention out the window once more.

Zach looked at me, but said nothing. Patrick did not seem satisfied.

We didn't have to travel far. The arranged meeting place was a movie theater that, according to Joe The Lizard, was closed for renovation. It would be the second time I had been inside such a theater. However, I knew the scene that would be played out this time would have consequences in reality. My comrades' weapons reinforced that.

When we reached our destination and exited the vehicle I could hear bells chiming in the distance. I assumed they were church bells, though I was unaware of the observance of any holy day. So I queried Zach.

"What is the significance of those bells?"

"Ask not for whom the bell tolls," responded Zach, taking my arm, "it tolls for we."

Jon then removed a small handweapon from his coat and offered it to me.

"Take this," he said. I was not sure whether it was a suggestion or a command.

Out of habit, if nothing else, I started to comply. When my fingers touched the cool black metal of the weapon, a chill ran through my arm and into my torso. I pulled my hand back.

"No," I said. "I don't want it."

"We do not know what treachery may await us," said Jon. "You might need it."

"No."

"What about me?" asked Zach, his voice rich with sarcasm. "Aren't you going to offer me one of your blasters?"

Jon answered Zach with only a stern glare and replaced the weapon in his coat.

The inside of the theater was dimly lit, and it took a moment for my eyes to adjust from the bright sunlight. When it did, I saw someone sitting in the first row of seats, facing the projection screen as if he were watching a film. Patrick and Paul positioned themselves in opposite corners. Jon, Zach, and I proceeded down the aisle between the rows of seats. We stopped a few meters short of the sitting man, who seemed to sense our arrival. He stood and turned to face us.

He was a large, muscular man. Not as tall as Jon but with a frame that was thickset. There were only a few strands of grayish hair on either side of his head. He wore a red band to hold them in place. From Zach's description, he had to be Joe The Lizard.

He did not appear to be armed. I assumed he felt he didn't have to be, because as soon as he moved to face us, several of his own men appeared at strategic locations throughout the theater. They brandished a number of deadly looking weapons.

"Hey, don't you know it's not le...legal for metalheads to carry weapons?" Joe The Lizard said, pointing at one of Jon's men.

"Your own firepower doesn't exactly look like citizen-approved hardware, Joe," remarked Zach. This elicited a bellow of laughter from Joe The Lizard, and I could see it made Jon uneasy. He stepped forward as if to establish that he, not Zach, was the one to speak with.

"We have come to purchase a ship capable of interplanetary travel," spoke up Jon. "Do you have such a ship?"

"I know you," said Joe The Lizard, not really responding to Jon's inquiry. "You're Jon 155, the gauntlet star who went rogue. Did you know your gauntlet is a der...der...derivation of a Native American sport? I wonder how you would have done 500 years ago, against my people?"

"I am not here to discuss your heritage. Nor do I care to speculate about various barbaric forms of human entertainment."

Joe The Lizard looked to Zach. "Not very so...so...sociable, is he?"

"Proper etiquette is not a priority with him right now," replied Zach. "You understand how it is."

"Yes, I do." He turned back to Jon. "I've got your ship. The real question is, how do a bunch of metalheads get enough credit to pur...purchase an interplanetary ship? I'm no bleeding-heart LEDA you know. It's going to cost you."

"How much?"

"Six million untraceable, ten if I have to clean it myself."

Zach whistled and Jon looked visibly agitated.

"Six million? We could buy a new ship for that much," said Jon, obviously irritated.

Joe The Lizard shrugged his huge shoulders nonchalantly. "You're welcome to try."

I could feel the tension settling over the room at that moment. It was a stifling feeling of danger and anticipation. I found it to be both disquieting and exhilarating. Zach must have felt it too, because he casually stepped between Jon and Joe The Lizard and tried to transform the tense standoff into a negotiation.

"What do you say they give you four clean, and if it's not untraceable they have to come up with eleven?"

Joe The Lizard pondered this. Jon looked at Zach as if his intrusion was wholly unwelcome.

"It's a d...d...deal. I like your style, Zach." Joe The Lizard stepped forward then, not towards Zach, but to Jon. I didn't have to look to know the men all around me were gripping their weapons a little tighter. Joe The Lizard offered his hand to Jon.

"Do we have a deal then, Jon 155?"

Jon looked at Zach, then at me. He did not seem happy. Of course, I had not had an occasion to see what Jon looked like when he was happy, if he had ever been happy.

"How do we know we can trust you?" said Jon, ignoring the hand being held out to him.

Joe The Lizard dropped his hand back to his side and stared right at Jon. There seemed to be a silent struggle going on between them. Two powerful men, their eyes locked on one another, saying nothing for several, apprehensive seconds.

"You can trust me as long as I'm mak...making more on this ship than I can get for your bounty."

Jon hesitated only momentarily, then held out his hand. Joe The Lizard took it.

They didn't so much shake hands as grip each other firmly, still eye to eye. Joe The Lizard smiled and Jon looked resolute. I felt there was more happening in that handshake than I was aware of.

"Zach, I will con...contact you in two days to see if they've secured the funds," he said as they released their hold on each other. He then made that circular motion with one finger above his head, and his men began adjusting their positions.

"I bid you all *adieu* then. See you on the upside, Zach."

With that, he and his men quickly retreated, vanishing towards the rear of the building. Zach turned to start back up the aisle, but Jon grabbed him.

"You do not speak for us. No one asked you to bargain on our behalf."

"Hey!" responded Zach, shaking loose from Jon's grip. "It was the best deal you were going to get. No, make that the *only* deal."

"How do you propose that we acquire four million?"

"That's your problem. I did my part. You told me you could get whatever credit you needed. Well, you need four million.

Welcome to the real world, bud. Just think of it as the price of freedom." Zach then took my arm and started to lead me away. "Come on, let's delete this place." I hesitated and when I did I could see the disappointment in Zach's eyes. I looked at Jon.

"I will contact you when we have more data," said Jon.

"I'll be waiting." It was the only thing I could think of to say.

***

When we arrived at Amber's home, she was not there and Zach disappeared into our designated bedroom for a time.

Strange how I had begun to think of first Zach's then Amber's cradle as "home." Of course, I had never had a true home of my own. I lived and worked in a home, though it was not mine, it was my steward's. Now, Amber's home had become my home. Part of me yearned for a place that was truly my own.

When Zach finally emerged from the bedroom, or as he often called it, "the room of wondrous delights," he carried with him two packages. Each was wrapped in special paper, tied with red ribbon and topped with a red bow. I knew from their appearance they were presents, though I didn't know their significance.

"Happy Valentine's Day," he said as he handed them to me. "Okay, Valentine's Day isn't until tomorrow, but that's only a few hours away, so I figured we'd get a jump on it and start celebrating early."

I knew of Valentine's Day and was somewhat familiar with its traditions. However, androns didn't normally participate in human holidays. I had never before received a Valentine's Day present. I had never received any kind of a present.

"Well," prompted Zach, "it's customary to unwrap gifts when they're given to you."

I felt a surge of emotion that I had no control over. I didn't know what to say, so I complied and began to unwrap one of the packages.

Inside the wrapping was a box labeled "Bonkberry's Assorted Chocolates."

"Go ahead. Open it and try one."

So I did. I had eaten chocolate candy once before. This time though it tasted much better to me, much richer. Inside the chocolate shell was another sweet substance. It tasted vaguely of some kind of fruit.

"They say chocolate is an aphrodisiac," explained Zach.

I was familiar with the definition of "aphrodisiac," but not with any research that would substantiate such a connection with chocolate.

"All right, you can open the other one now."

The other gift was much smaller, much thinner. Once the wrapping was removed, I discovered it was some sort of apparel. An undergarment I believe. There was a picture on the covering showing a woman wearing the item, but it was very strange. It was not like anything I had ever worn before. Black stockings with sheer intricate designs that ended at the thigh, but the stockings were connected with some sort of belt around the abdominal area. It didn't look very comfortable. The covering read "Fredrick's of Hollywood Classic Suspender Pantyhose."

I looked up at Zach. "What is it?"

"It's sexy lingerie. You might say it's another kind of aphrodisiac."

"I've never worn anything like this. It's very unusual looking."

"I'm sure you'll look great in it."

"Thank you, Zach. Thank you very much for the Valentine's Day presents. However, I have no experience complying with holiday traditions. I have nothing to give to you."

"That's all right. I'll wager we can think of something. You could start by putting that on."

So I went into our bedroom and tried to determine how to put it on so that it approximated the picture on the covering. It was not easy. It took me several attempts to align and adjust it properly. However, after observing Zach's reaction, and his ensuing passionate response, I decided the effort had been worthwhile.

34
ZACH

For a change, I found myself waking up before Mary. I didn't get right up. Instead, I just stared at her. She laid there with her cheek mashed against the pillow, her hair in disarray, her lips open slightly. Her expression was one of pure serenity and innocence. The only thing out of place with that childlike pose was the metallic implant protruding from the side of her head.

She must have felt the intensity of my gaze, because her eyes opened and looked right at me.

"Good morning, gorgeous."

"Good morning, Zach."

"Did you sleep well?"

"Yes. It was very restful. Did you sleep well, Zach?"

"Actually, I tossed and turned quite a bit."

"Do you not feel well?"

"I'm fine. I've just got some things on my mind."

"What kinds of things?" she asked, sitting up in bed. I tried not to let the fact she was completely naked distract me.

"I'm a little worried I guess. And I'm not used to worrying, not about anything."

"Why are you worried, Zach? Is it because of me?"

"I'm not the kind of guy who blames his problems on other people," I said rather quickly, then reconsidered. "But yeah, I guess I'm worried you're going to pack up and leave with your rogue friends soon. And I don't want you to leave." There, I had said it. I'd been thinking it for a while now. Thinking it and then trying to ignore the thought. Damn my stubborn hide, I couldn't ignore my feelings anymore.

"Mary, I...I like you very much. I like you more than any other woman I've ever known. I know it's crazy, *believe me* I know. I'm not even sure why exactly. I'm just sure I don't want you to leave. I want you to stay with me. I want us to run off to that place in the mountains I told you about, and stay there until everyone's forgotten about us."

I shut up then. Mary remained silent. I couldn't even read the expression on her face. I guess she was as surprised to hear it as I was to say it. I would have told her I loved her, but I didn't know what that meant anymore than she did. A cynical hack writer with a heart of stone and an implant educated dronette with the emotional expertise of a six-year-old--we were quite a pair.

"I have strong feelings for you too, Zach. I don't know if my feelings are 'crazy,' as you say, or just the normal emotions of a woman. I've nothing to compare them with. I've no experience to measure them against. The only thing I'm sure of, is that simply thinking about leaving you causes me pain."

I did something completely out of character then. I took her in my arms and just held her close. Why was it so out of character? Because I had this incredibly beautiful, naked woman in my arms and didn't for a nanosecond think about beating a sheet. I just wanted to hold her close. Well, I already said I was acting crazy.

I let go of her and she looked me in the eye. "I'll stay with you, Zach, if you are sure that's what you want."

"Baby, I'm not sure of my own name right now, but I know my pulse raced off the charts when you said you'd stay."

So we stayed in bed a little longer (hey, don't look at me, it was her idea) and then we went shopping. We decided it would be best if we got out of town as soon as we helped the rogues complete their deal with Joe, so we went looking for all the things we thought we'd need. I used my plug for all of our purchases, but I gave Mary some chips so she'd have some walking around money. When I did, she looked at me with that "what do I do with this" look of hers.

"They're credit chips," I told her, "You know, money. It's just credit in a different form. Haven't you ever used chips before?"

"When my steward would send me to make purchases, I would use his domestic credit plug or have the purchases put on his account."

"Look." I spread the chips out so she could see them. "This is a five, a ten, a twenty, it's all simple math. You won't have a problem."

"I know the numbers, Zach, but what value do they represent? How do I know if something I'm going to purchase is worth five, ten, or twenty?"

"It's worth whatever it costs, if you want it bad enough. If you're not sure, check with me."

"All right, Zach."

Before we left, I contacted my pal with the hideaway, told him I had writer's block and needed to get away for a while. He had no plans to use it and told me I could stay as long as I liked. I made him promise not to tell anyone because I wanted to really "get away from it all."

Mary decided to put off telling Jon for now, and I figured that was her call. So we bought some clothes, blankets, and some other gear I thought we'd find useful. I figured we didn't need much. All I needed was my minicom to write on, food, a few bottles of Scotch, and Mary. The food we could get at the local market on the way up.

My biggest concern was how we were going to get there. For as long as I was planning on staying, we wouldn't be able to use Amber's rig. We could go part way by rail or bus, but that wouldn't likely get us close enough. I didn't want to lease anything because I didn't want to leave a trail someone could follow. I was thinking I could buy some old wreck with enough go-power left to get us there, but even that would be pushing it with my dwindling account.

I decided I'd see how much I had left after our shopping spree, and, if I had to, maybe borrow some from Amber. She certainly had the funds and would be more than willing, but I felt awkward about it. Sure, we weren't really a thing anymore, but asking for credit so I could run off with another woman struck me as a little audacious.

***

After a couple of hours we decided we were both hungry and started looking for a place to eat. I thought, since we were leaving the city, this would be a last meal of sorts, so it might be nice to eat somewhere elegant. I knew of a place nearby with a reputation for its culinary delights. Of course I knew it by reputation only. It wasn't one of my typical hangsites.

When we arrived I held the door for Mary, like a gentleman was expected to do in such establishments. I could tell by her reaction that it wasn't a gesture she was used to.

A dark-skinned maitre d' with a shock of white hair waited inside. He looked us over and didn't seem too pleased by what he saw. That's when I noticed the wind had blown Mary's hair so that her implant was exposed.

"I'm sorry, sir," he said rather matter-of-factly, "your drone will have to wait in our service area."

"It's all right, she's with me."

"I'm afraid it's not all right, sir. We don't serve drones, regardless of who they're with."

"That's the stupidest thing I've--"

"We should go, Zach." Mary was tugging at my arm, but I was preoccupied. If I was going to be deleted, I was going have my say. One look at Mary, though, told me she didn't want any trouble, and I knew she was probably right. I retreated with little more than a growl and an indignant glance at the unruffled maitre d'.

Once we were outside and walking I cooled off. Mary seemed unperturbed by the whole thing, but I knew she was good at keeping her feelings to herself. I guess I shouldn't have been surprised. I had seen the signs before, "No Drones Allowed," "Andrones To The Rear," but I hadn't really paid any attention to them. I didn't have a reason to.

After a short distance I decided to crank up the satphone and call Amber, to let her know we were okay and that we'd be gone a while longer. While I was on the phone I noticed Mary peering through a window of what looked like an old fashioned diner. The sign above her head read "Kismet Kafe." She saw something and then nearly went ballistic trying to get my attention.

"Look, Zach. Look in here."

I bid Amber a quick goodbye, but Mary was in my face before I could even switch off.

"They have a real piano. Can we eat in there? Do you think they would let me play their piano?" She was still learning how to be excited, but her budding enthusiasm was contagious. It was one of the reasons I liked being around her.

"Ten to one it's so old it doesn't work anymore, but we can ask."

***

It did work, and they were happy to let her play. Why not, the place was empty except for one other couple. I figured that didn't bode well for the food.

I ordered a cheeseburger with everything, some chilifries, and a chocolate shake. Mary said she'd have the same, though I was sure she didn't have a clue what she was getting. Her mind was on one thing--that piano.

"Go ahead," I told her, "I'll just sit here and listen."

So she walked over to the piano as my satphone started beeping.

"Kismet Kafe, you kill 'em, we'll cook 'em." My attempt at humor obviously was not appreciated, because whoever was on the other end was silent as a ghost. "Hello? Who is it?" It sounded like there was a clear signal, but no one was talking so I switched off.

"What would you like me to play?" Mary asked as she began running her fingers over the keys.

"Whatever you'd like. Surprise me."

As soon as she began playing I recognized the tune. How could I not? It was "As Time Goes By," the same tune Sam played in *Casablanca*. As I sat there watching her, listening to her playing, I realized something for the first time. Or maybe I was just admitting it for the first time. I loved her. Yeah, I know, it's not something I usually went in for. But there it was, and I knew there was no getting around it. Maybe I was just getting old.

Mary had been designed with an aptitude for music, given the right genes and so forth, and that must have included an ear for total recall. I wondered whether she picked up the song from the movie, or if, by coincidence, she happened to have learned it sometime before. I never got the chance to ask her.

It was just about then that I got that tingling feeling along the nape of my neck. But, like a love-struck idiot, I ignored it. Moments later, I happened to turn my head and see it through the glass of the door. Before I could get out of my seat and call out to Mary, it was inside, with its weapon drawn.

It was the tracer that had chased us into that alley. How it had tracked Mary down with her implant signal scrambled, I didn't know. And, at that moment, I didn't have a spare nanosecond to worry about it. Mary was completely absorbed with her music and didn't even look up until I shouted her name.

I was up and out of my chair, yelling and moving towards her at the same time. I reacted strictly on impulse. A rather silly thing to do looking back on it. The tracer had already targeted Mary and was about to fire. There was only one thing I could do, and, fortunately for Mary, I didn't have time to consider the consequences.

As it opened fire, I took this beautiful running dive, fully extended, trying to push her out of harm's way. A leap of faith as it turned out, because the adrenaline rush had me overestimating my lunging ability, and I fell short of Mary. The last thing I remembered was this searing pain ripping through my chest.

35

JERI

The stratagem of tracing the satphone usage of one Zachariah Sturzinski had proven effective. However, when I arrived in the area of his most recent communication, I was still unable to locate the implant signal of the rogue androne, Mary 79. I had no assurance she was currently in the company of the human, though it was a highly probable scenario.

Instead of attempting a structure by structure search, I concluded my best course of action would be to pinpoint the position of my target by opening a circuit through the satnet myself. My endeavor was successful, however, I miscalculated the human's reaction time and it had proved costly.

He crossed into my line of fire at the last possible moment, intercepting the two projectiles meant for the rogue Mary unit. They tore through the side of his abdominal wall and his chest cavity, then exploded inside of him. They had been designed to expire a full-sized androne. The human would not survive.

My understanding of what had happened was instantaneous. I knew the ramifications of mistakenly killing a human, the legal complications that would ensue, and the resulting wrath that would be vented upon me be by my steward, Mr. Satchmeyer.

The realization of my precarious situation rendered me immobile. I could think only of the various unpleasant alternatives that now faced me.

36
MARY

It was a simple but beautiful melody. I was concentrating so hard on trying to recall it correctly that I didn't see the tracer when it entered. It wasn't until Zach cried out that I looked up and saw it aiming its weapon at me.

I didn't react. I didn't move. I sat there at the piano, dumbfounded until I saw Zach running towards me. Then, as I stood up, I heard the weapon fire and saw Zach launch himself into the air. In mid flight his body jerked unnaturally.

When he hit the floor and failed to move, I felt as if something had slammed into my own stomach. The source of my pain must have been an overwhelming sense of dread.

I looked up at the tracer, prepared for the same fate as Zach. However, it just stood there, looking down at the blood draining from his body. It appeared to be malfunctioning, because it made no attempt to train its weapon on me, though I provided an opportune target.

My instinct for survival took over and I reacted without thinking. I ran past the tracer, pushing it as I went by. I heard it crash into a table as I slammed through the door and out onto the sidewalk. I didn't choose a direction, I just ran.

The sun was setting and as I ran I noticed the lights along the street beginning to flicker on. It was strange that I noticed them, because I remember nothing else. My eyes did not focus on anything or anyone. I ran until the echo of the gunshots faded from inside my head.

***

It was dark before I calmed myself enough to stop and rest. My legs were trembling. Whether from fatigue or fear, I could not say. As I was beginning to catch my breath, I heard the sound of sirens. I could not tell how close they were. Still, the sound created another swell of panic in my throat. Reason said the sirens had no relation to me, but reason had no hold on me at that moment.

I began running as fast as my weary legs would take me. I was moving into what was apparently an industrial area, and I began testing each door I passed to find a place to hide. Each door I came to, however, was secure. I thought about attempting to break a door down, but I was too exhausted. I also considered turning myself into the authorities and putting an end to it. Zach was dead. Why was I running? Toward what objective? Then I thought of Jon and the other rogues, and the thought renewed my desire for freedom.

When I was sure I could run no more, I came to a chain link barrier. The fence guarded an area adjacent to a ramp where a vehicle was being unloaded. The gate through which the vehicle had entered stood open. I remained there for a moment, considering my options, until I perceived the sound of the sirens drawing closer.

I drew upon what little energy I had remaining and passed through the gate, keeping to the shadows. A door opened from the nearby building and a woman walked out. She joined the driver and another man, and when they moved around the vehicle I hurried through the door.

It was extremely dark inside the building. So dark that I kept stumbling over various obstacles I could not see. I decided to sit down and rest while my eyes adjusted to the dimness. I wasn't accustomed to such physical exertion, and when I realized certain muscles in my legs were beginning to cramp, I laid out flat on the floor.

I closed my eyes momentarily and attempted to regain my composure. As I became more rational, I could not help but think of Zach. That only keyed my memory into replaying the image of him being shot. I didn't like that memory, so I opened my eyes.

Some part of me abhorred the fact I no longer wanted to think about Zach. I felt weak because I could not cope with the anguish. The emotion struggled with the logic of it until I realized neither would prevail. I no longer cared for the experience of new emotions. They were no longer pleasurable and engaging. They had become hurtful and distressing.

Eventually the cramping ceased and my eyes began to make out shapes in the darkness. I noticed more light coming from another part of what the very large structure I had entered. I also heard what I thought might be voices. I sat up and conducted a more thorough examination of my surroundings.

Apparently there was quite a bit of machinery currently in operational mode. Extremely sophisticated machinery from what I could discern. I stood up and slowly made my way toward the light. As I drew closer and it became somewhat brighter, I detected large transparent tanks filled with liquid. The light was emanating from these enclosures.

The sound of voices was definitely carrying from somewhere nearby. I determined they originated from another room. So I carefully approached the nearest tank and looked inside. There were several objects suspended within the liquid. They were attached to numerous sets of wiring and hoses that reached out from some unknown source.

The realization of what those objects were was upon me even before I could comprehend the significance, even before I noticed the imprinted seal that read "Androtech."

Yet another new emotion rushed into the vacuum of my being and left me paralyzed. It must have been abject terror. Because what I discovered inside that tank was the genesis of my own existence. Happenstance had led me to a crèche where a new strain of infant androies were germinating.

The horror converted to fascination as I contemplated how my own inception must have been part of a tableau similar to this one. These were, after all, my people, my race. It was no secret how we were bred. There was no reason for me to react with shock. The science was complex but very efficient. My origins should be a source of pride. For all I knew, I may have shared a lineage with the lifeforms ripening in that tank.

That was the logic of it, but it was not how I felt.

I was dismayed, repulsed, resentful.

A sense of loathing overcame me and fueled my fear--fear that somehow unsealed a memory. It was only a flash, a picture in my mind. In that instant I recalled the final moment of my own gestation. In that flash I could see myself being removed from the crèche tank. I could see what I saw then. I could see the umbilicals being detached, the many hands moving me this way, then that.

I was so overwhelmed by those images, by several conflicting sentiments, I was slow to react when I heard a door open and the sound of voices drawing nearer. I quickly retraced my steps and found a place in the darkness to hide.

I could no longer see the embryonic tanks, but I could hear at least two voices coming from their direction. No alarm was sounded, no search was instituted, so I determined the owners of those voices were simply conducting routine checks of the crèche tanks and their contents.

When I was certain no one was moving towards my position, I quietly retreated the way I had come. I was tempted to find another exit. However, I was concerned that if I opened the wrong door I might set off a security device. So I made my way back to the same door I had entered through.

A rodent cried out, startling me before it scurried away into hiding. However, I saw no evidence that my presence had been observed by those who were busy unloading the vehicle, so I cautiously made my way past the gate and began walking in an easterly direction, the direction my inner compass told me was where Amber lived. I did not know where else to go--what else to do.

I was still free, but Zach was dead and I found it difficult at that moment to judge the value of that freedom.

37

REVEREND ROBERTS

Riding the hydrorail always made my stomach a little queasy. In addition, it was not entirely ecologically sacrosanct, so I spent a good deal of the journey asking for His forgiveness. However, I felt I would be more inconspicuous using public transportation. Not that anyone could have recognized me under the hat and dark glasses I was wearing. Of course there was always that Stone fellow with his ever-present shouldercam, though I had not seen him in days. Maybe he had gone on to another story.

In a way, it felt good to be out among the people--no responsibilities, no one watching my every move, measuring my every word.

Despite the relaxing aspects of my journey, I couldn't overcome a feeling of nervousness. I can't say for certain what precipitated the feeling. I prided myself in being able to keep a tight rein on all my emotions. Nevertheless, going to see Jeremiah always made me nervous--more nervous than confronting a mob of disbelievers, more nervous than being called before the Council of Elders. I imagined I couldn't be any more scared standing before God and facing his wrath on Judgment Day.

My feelings were likely more intense than normal because it had been such a long time since I'd seen the boy. At his age, he was likely to have trouble remembering who I was. And he was sure to have questions. How could I possibly explain why he couldn't live with me? How could I make him understand the ways of the world? He could never grasp such concepts as "public image" and "political expediency." He was just a little boy, born into a world turned upside down by technology and moral trepidation.

The rail car slowed at the proper terminal and I stood, waiting for the doors to open. I pressed through the crowd and spotted Nelson waving his arms to get my attention. He was wearing his uniform and standing next to his postal express van. It was not the unobtrusive reception I would have preferred, but he had taken time out from his job to come get me.

"Praise God, Rev...I mean, Jared."

"Praise Nature, Brad. How are you?"

"I'm fine."

"And Jeremiah?"

"Oh the boy's great. Growing like a weed," he said, becoming more animated. "You probably won't even recognize him, he's grown so much."

"Yes, I'm sure he has."

"Well, we'd better get going. Ginny's waiting, and I have to get back to work."

"Yes, by all means, let's go."

***

The boy had indeed grown like the proverbial weed. He was a good hand taller than my last visit. He still had her eyes though, eyes that were now examining me with skepticism.

Ginny tried to coax him. "Say hello to your father, Jeremiah."

"Hello," he repeated dutifully.

"Hello, Jeremiah. My, you're certainly growing up fast. You must be at least a meter tall."

"112 centimeters," he responded, quickly correcting me.

"112? I guess you *are* a big boy."

"Well, I'll leave you two to get acquainted and go make some lunch."

"Aunt Gin, I want a jellynut samwedge."

"We'll see."

Ginny left the room and I stood there alone with the son I didn't know. He was as uncomfortable with the situation as I was. He picked up a toy aerojet and began idly running it across the top of his bed.

"So, Jeremiah, do you like school?"

He nodded his head in the affirmative without looking at me and kept handling his toy.

"Do you study your *Bible*, the one I gave you?"

Again he just nodded.

"I brought you something else." That got his attention. He looked up at me as I pulled it out of my bag. "Another book. This one's full of different stories and lots of beautiful pictures. Do you like stories?"

He nodded his head again, though somewhat unenthusiastically.

"Would like me to read you a story?"

This time he shook his head "no."

"Okay, you take the book and you can look at it later."

He took it and quickly laid it aside.

I was stuck. I didn't know what to do or what to say.

"Have you ever heard the story of the lion and the little shepherd boy?"

He continued to look down at the toy in his hand, but the turn of his head said he hadn't.

"Well, the little shepherd boy was taking care of his flock when he came across a big lion crying in pain. He asked the lion what was wrong, and the lion told him there was a thorn in his paw that he couldn't get out. 'Would you help me get the thorn out?' the lion asked the boy. 'If I take out the thorn, you'll eat me and my sheep,' said the boy."

Slowly, Jeremiah's eyes turned to look up at me. I continued quickly while I had his attention.

"'No,' said the lion, 'I won't eat you, I promise.' The shepherd boy thought about it, then decided to help. He moved real close to the lion and inspected its paw. He found the thorn and with his small fingers he grabbed hold of it and pulled it out. What do you think happened then?"

"The lion ate him," offered Jeremiah enthusiastically.

"No, the lion thanked him. And from that day on, the lion protected the shepherd boy and all of his sheep. Do you know why?"

The shake of his head said he didn't.

"Because all good deeds are rewarded. If you do a good deed for someone, you'll be rewarded too."

He pondered this, but his mind must have been working on a completely different tract. He hit me with a question that was so out of nowhere I had to collect my thoughts before I could answer.

"What was my mother's name?"

"Uh...her name was Mary. You know, just like in the *Bible*. Jesus' mother was named Mary too."

"Is my mother in heaven?"

The moral and theological implications of that question were not ones I wished to ponder. I had preached many times that androenes were not humans, and therefore had no souls. Without a soul, they could not be saved, could not be given redemption or a place in heaven. But if any androne ever had a soul, it was my Mary. She was so full of life, so spirited.

All of which would mean nothing to a six-year-old child. There was no way to explain who, *what* his mother was. And what about him? What was Jeremiah? Was there a place in heaven for him?

Right now, all he needed was an answer.

"Yes, Jeremiah, your mother is in heaven now, right next to God."

38

MARY

When Amber saw me, she audibilized a brief gasp. For the first time since I had met her, her steady composure seemed to waver. I had not realized there were traces of blood on my clothing. It was that sight that had apparently unnerved her. Whether the blood was my own or Zach's, I could not be sure.

"Mary, what happened? Where's Zach?"

I hesitated only momentarily before answering.

"Zach is dead. A tracer found us and Zach hurled himself into the path of two projectiles meant for me."

"Oh, Mary." She threw her arms around me and tears began to drain from her eyes as she held me close to her. I could not discern whether she was trying to comfort me, or seeking comfort for herself. I believe, to some degree, both likelihoods were correct.

Her emotional display generated more feelings within me. I thought again of Zach lying on the cafe floor, his life essence seeping out in red rivulets across the tile. The memory led to a cascade of sentiment that began to well up inside of me. The sensation was overwhelming. So overwhelming that I felt a great need to release it, to expunge the maudlin thoughts from my mind. I wanted to set free the turbulence of emotion the way Amber was able to. But I could not. The release would not come.

"He was a great guy," she said, letting go of me and wiping the tears from her face, "but I never figured him for a hero."

"He saved my life."

"I always knew he'd get himself into some kind of trouble, but this...."

"It is my fault," I said, though I found it an effort just to speak. "Had I never sought out his help, he would still be alive."

"You can't say that. You can't think like that. You might as well say 'if the sun never rose,' or 'if only Zach didn't like beautiful women.' Don't blame yourself, Mary. Zach was a big boy. He knew what he was doing, and he was doing what he wanted."

"Yes, but--"

"No buts, put it out of your mind. Nothing you can say or do now will bring him back, will it?"

"I do not believe so."

"Look at you. Are you hurt?" she asked, pointing at spots of blood.

"Not badly, just a few minor abrasions."

"Let's get your clothes off. You can clean up and then we'll see how serious they are."

39

JERI

I found it difficult to concentrate as I watched that evening's gauntlet match. When number 267 began his run, I saw, instead, the rogue Mary unit running at me. That prompted me to recall the entire event.

When the rogue came at me, I did not move. The cognitive impact of what I had done had apparently left my motor skills temporarily inactive. As she passed by, she knocked me down, and only when I struck the floor did full control of my limbs return.

When I regained my footing, she had already exited the structure. Initially, I moved as if to follow her out the door, in order to determine in which direction she had fled. However, the sight of the human man lying there, being drained of all life, made me reassess the situation.

My choices were simple. Admit my failure to Mr. Satchmeyer and the authorities, and face certain reassignment and possible expiration for my actions, or evade any investigation into the incident and hope witnesses would not be able to identify me.

The time I needed for cognitive deliberation was minimal. I holstered my weapon and briskly made my way out of the building and down the street. It was not an easy decision, but one that I had to reach swiftly. As I expediently departed the scene, I reasoned that no other conclusion was logical.

Yet my thought patterns were not at all logical. I was running. However, I rationalized I was not actually on-the-run. I was not going rogue. I could not accept such a definition of my actions. The term itself was too abhorrent to my training, to the very circuits of my implants. I reasoned I was simply forestalling the anticipated vehement reaction of my steward in order to gain the time I would need to redeem his favor. I did not know how I would proceed in order to accomplish such a task. I simply accepted that as the course I now needed to plot.

With that resolution, I resumed my previous activity and shifted my attentiveness back to the evening's gauntlet match. Its entertainment potential was nearly unlimited. Within its 40-minute time frame, it held the promise of both dramatic conflict and uncertain outcome.

If only I had been trained for the gauntlet. Given the opportunity, I could have been a powerful and cunning runner. I could visualize myself on the gauntlet's field of honor, withstanding the blows of my opponents, streaking across the line to the roar of the crowd. If only....

40

MARY

I felt stabilized the next morning. I had put the events of the previous day into perspective and turned my focus to the future. I could not delete all my feelings about Zach, however, I could control them.

Amber was helpful in this aspect. She kept me occupied, under the pretense of aiding her with various domestic chores, though I do not believe she actually needed my assistance. She was likely hoping to keep herself busy as well. She seemed to be trying to avoid her own feelings about Zach. I concluded her emotional investment was greater than she wished to admit.

She told me we could contact the authorities and have Zach's body transferred in order to conduct a burial ceremony. But as she was about to make the inquiry she stopped herself.

"Wait a minute. We can't be calling the P.D. They'll want to know how I know what happened. They'll be out here asking questions, and I certainly can't tell them about you, Mary. They're not likely to release Zach's body to me anyway, since I'm not a legal relative."

"What can we do?"

"Let's wait and keep an eye on the Net news. If we see something official, then maybe at least I can make some inquiries."

Apparently the thought of being unable to conduct a burial ceremony for Zach bothered her more than she wished to reveal. She resumed her make-work with resounding strength, as if she could clean away the fullness of her feelings. When we had completed all the tasks she could think of, we sat down and looked at each other.

"What do we do now?" she asked.

"I do not know."

"You know, there's something different about the way you're talking. It's not that you're talking any different from any other androne, it's just, well, maybe that's it. You *are* talking like a drone. When I first met you--"

"When you first met me, Zach was teaching me to use slang and contractions."

"That's it. I'm sure watching what happened to Zach was traumatic. It probably affected you in lots of ways you don't know. I bet Zach would like it if you were to keep slinging the lingo he taught you. It's probably safer anyway, considering your situation."

"That is what Zach said."

"Smart boy that Zach."

"I will...I'll try to remember to speak as Zach taught me."

After I resolved to take more care with my speech, there seemed nothing to say. We both sat for some time in silence. I'm somewhat certain we were both using that time to recall moments we had spent with Zach. It somehow seemed the respectful thing to do. It was Amber who ended the silence.

"Do you have any plans, Mary?"

"Plans? No, I've made no plans. I will have to contact my comrades so I may go with them."

"You mean other rogues?"

"Yes."

"That could be dangerous."

"I've nowhere else to go."

"You could always stay with me."

"No, I belong with them. We are the same. It's generous of you to offer, but I must do what I can to help them."

"But what can *you* do?"

"I'm not sure. I know they are in need of credit. I could work to earn credit."

"There's not a lot of work for a rogue androne these days. Most employers are going to require identity checks, and those that don't will probably put you into more trouble than you're already in. Of course, you could always go on the Net and work for yourself."

"You mean, become a netgirl like you?"

"No, no, I was just thinking out loud. You don't want to do that."

"Why not?" The idea had not occurred to me before. It seemed to be a very logical answer. "Is there something wrong with what you do?"

"No, of course not." Amber replied in a defensive manner. "But it's not all fun and games. I don't think you'd like it very much."

"I found sheet dancing with Zach to be pleasurable. If I could earn credit while I--"

"It's not the same," said Amber. "Don't take this wrong, Mary, but I don't think you're cut out for it. It's not what you think. It won't always be like it was with Zach. In fact, it's not likely it would ever be like that. It's true the demand for dronettes is high, and with your looks you'd have them standing in line, but you would have to do business in person. It takes a long time to build up the kind of over-the-net clientele I have."

"I understand."

"I don't know if you do. There are more than a few weirdoes out there. Some of them are pure crazy, and others don't think twice about hurting a girl. I was one of the lucky ones. The goo never got too severe for me, though I had some close calls."

"I think I would like to try, Amber. I don't know what else to do."

"That's how a lot of girls get started." She paused, thinking about something before reaching a decision. "Look, I'm going to get out of here for a while, I'm mean way out, like St. Croix or Ceylon, somewhere with less insanity. After what happened to Zach, I need to get away. I don't know if you can understand that."

"Yes, I do understand."

"Well then, why don't you come with me. We'll forget about Zach and the rogues and politicians and the johnnies and the Jeserites--all of it. We'll just be two fineline females out for some laughs. What do you say?"

"I would like to go with you, Amber, but I must help my comrades. I can't just leave." I could see Amber wanted to persuade me, but she seemed to accept that I was resolved to stay.

"All right. You can use my place if you want. I'll need you to take care of Jekyll after I go. Can you do that?"

"Yes. I'll take care of Jekyll. Before you leave, could you please show me how to be a netgirl?"

"All right, I'll show you."

***

The next day, after packing for her trip, Amber was busy at her comdat for some time. I didn't want to disturb her so I occupied myself with Jekyll, who appeared to sense something was wrong. He spoke to me in that way he always did, and I tried to answer without knowing what he asked. Unsatisfied with my responses, he proceeded to conduct a search of each room. I was certain he was looking for Zach.

"Okay," called out Amber, "I'm about finished. Come here and I'll show you."

I approached and saw that the photo she had previously taken of me was now on her digiscreen, along with a physical and psychological profile. I noticed the physical specifications were nearly correct, however, the details listed describing my personality were fictitious.

"What does it mean 'I like leather and lace'? These things you have entered about me are not true."

"It's just a kind of sexy come-on. You're selling a fantasy. Most men are looking for more than a quick bang for their buck. They're buying into another reality, so that's what you have to sell. Even though, as an androne, you've already got a certain exotic appeal, men will still want that fantasy. That is, if you still want to go ahead with this."

"Yes, I do."

"All right, what name do you want to use?"

"Name?"

"You don't want to use your real name on the Net, especially since there may be people out there looking for you."

"I don't know. Do you know of a name I could use?"

"Let's see...how about Candi?"

"Yes, I like candy."

"You're selling yourself as androne, so you'll need a number. I've got it." She began entering it into the comdat as she read it to me. "As dronette Candi 69, you'll be absolutely irresistible."

"Do you think I'll be able to earn much credit?"

"Given time, you'll earn more than you'll know what to do with. Now I'm going to attach this page to my regular site, which says I'm currently unavailable. Anyone looking for me, or doing a search for a dronette, will automatically be forwarded to your page. If they're interested, they'll leave their code designation and you can contact them. Remember, always meet them in a public place like a nice hotel, there's a list of the nearby ones, and always get their credit first. I'll let you use one of my mobile credit inputs. I've already programmed your rates to match what we detailed on your page. No matter what they say, you'll only do what we've talked about, and they'll have to pay top dollar. They can take it or leave it, right?"

I nodded my head in the affirmative, though the complexity of the arrangements were somewhat confusing. I never imagined such a transaction would require so many formal guidelines. I guess my puzzlement showed, because Amber looked worried.

"Mary, are you absolutely sure about this? Because, if you're not, you should reconsider. That's my recommendation anyway. Why don't you forget about this and come away with me?"

"Thank you, Amber, but I want to try."

"Okay," she said, making a final entry on her comdat, "you're online now. Good luck and welcome to the sisterhood of the Net."

"Johnny wants some," rang out Amber's voice from the comdat. I looked and saw a pulsating digicon.

"Look at that. You've already got your first blip. I told you there'd be no lack of demand. You're going to be one popular girl."

***

It was not long after I bid Amber farewell and she left on her trip to a place called "Tahiti," that I was boarding the hydrorail on my way to a prearranged meeting place. Out of habit, I walked back to the railcar provided for androned. When I realized this, I started to turn around, but deduced that would arouse more suspicion. So I sat with the other androned as if I were, like them, accompanying my steward on some journey or simply on an errand.

The name I was given over the Net was "Ed," the place "The Elite Hotel," room 322. The process seemed efficient, but somehow detached. From the instructions I was given by Amber, I concluded that was how it was supposed to be.

The Elite Hotel was one of the "nice" establishments Amber had listed for me. Indeed, it seemed nice, but I knew nothing of the relative luxury of various lodging places. I had never been inside a hotel.

When I arrived outside the door to room 322, I hesitated. I don't know why. I suddenly felt unsure. There was no logical reason for my apprehension, so I proceeded to activate the door signal. It opened at once.

"You're here. Took you long enough."

"You are Ed?"

"Yeah, I'm Ed. Well, are you coming in or not?" I entered the room as he closed and locked the door behind me.

Ed seemed to be about the same age as Zach, however, he appeared to be suffering from pattern baldness, and possibly a glandular condition that left him with a somewhat portly figure. His manner did not denote happiness. Perhaps that is why I was there. Amber had said that a truly professional netgirl endeavored to fulfill emotional needs as much as physical desires. Perhaps I was there to bring joy into Ed's life, and leave him with a feeling of contentment.

I then remembered Amber's instructions and pulled out her mobile credit input.

"Put that away," he told me as quickly as I showed it to him. "I'm not leaving no credit trail for my wife to find. Here."

He handed me a fistful of credit chips that I hesitated to accept.

"What's wrong? Go ahead, count it if you want."

I took the chips, but I didn't count them. I didn't have a clear concept of their value, and wasn't sure if I had been paid the proper amount. Amber had not advised me of this possibility. I had expected the mobile input to manage the financial aspects of the exchange.

"What are you waiting for? Take off your clothes. I haven't got all night."

I did as he instructed and watched as his eyes began diligently inspecting every component of my anatomy. Standing there unclothed, I began to experience a feeling of vulnerability. Once again I struggled with a sense of apprehension. I reasoned this was one of many new sensations, one of many new situations I had experienced since going rogue.

"So, you really are a dronette, unless somebody did a hell of a makeup job with those implants." He began to unfasten his trousers then, but did not remove them. "Okay, babydoll, suck me off." He grabbed hold of his flaccid sexual organ as if he were adjusting it for my access. I deduced from the gesture, and his use of the word "suck," he was requesting what Zach had referred to as "the kiss of a thousand delights," among other colloquialisms.

Ed leaned against the hotel room's bed but remained standing. In order to comply with his request, I knelt down in front of him and took hold of his penis. Almost immediately, it began to come alive, swelling even as I touched it. I put my lips upon it and tried to remember what Zach had taught me.

However, it seemed not to matter what I did. I could not escape the feeling of awkwardness. Putting this man's member in my mouth did not evoke the same sensibility as it had with Zach. The physical act was the same, but the cerebral connection was absent. The mere thought of Zach left me distracted and unable to concentrate on my task. I endeavored to redouble my efforts, however, each attempt seemed doomed to failure.

I could sense the frustration mounting within Ed. He grabbed my hair in what was undoubtedly an attempt to guide my movements, but he soon relinquished his hold.

"You don't know what you're doing. That's the worst blowjob I've ever had," he said, obviously annoyed by my clumsy efforts. "Stand up. Bend over the bed."

I complied and Ed pushed his now fully erect member into me in such a hurried manner that I found the act painful in a way it had never been with Zach. His violent thrusts did not last long, and only when he had finally arrived at the point of release did the pain cease.

***

Night had fallen by the time I made my way out of the hotel. The experience with Ed had left me with much to ponder. As I began the short trek to the hydrorail terminal, I reconsidered the counsel Amber had given me. She certainly was correct in advising me that the sexual encounters were unlikely to be the same as they had been with Zach. Perhaps she was right. Perhaps I was not "cut out" to be a netgirl.

However, I considered the possibility my conclusion was premature. A solitary experience was not an adequate measure to base a judgment of the totality. Amber had been successful working the Net. There was no logical reason why I could not do the same.

No logical reason except the disagreeable emotions that flooded me. Emotions were not logical. They were not, to any extent I had determined, controllable. At that moment, I knew only how I felt, the feeling that accompanied the experience. It was not pleasant.

My ruminations were interrupted then, as I became distracted by the notion someone was following me. I could hear the footfalls and sense the presence, though each time I turned to look I could see no one. When the suspicion persisted, I hurried around a corner and then stepped into a small storefront that appeared opened for business.

At first, I simply waited by the door, looking out to see if I could spot my pursuer. The street, however, remained fairly empty, and I perceived no one who looked as if they might have been following me.

"Tell your fortune, my dear?"

I turned around at the sound of the voice, and saw an elderly woman sitting behind a display console. She was dressed in an odd manner, her head covered by a colorful scarf, her arms encircled by several bracelets. Strange as her garments were, they matched the decor of the room. Its sparse space was bedecked with silk hangings of many hues and marked with unusual symbols, most of which were unfamiliar. A scent that I could not identify hung heavy in the room, and I saw that on the console next to the woman was a glass orb.

"Would you like to have your fortune told? Romance or riches, heartbreak or horror, the tarot can divine all."

I heard her words, but they didn't make any sense to me. "Are you saying you can foretell future events and how they will affect me?"

"Not I," she replied. "Only the tarot has that power. I am simply the conduit through which that power flows."

"What is the 'tarot'?" I asked, walking over to her console.

"You've never heard of the tarot? The tarot is as old as civilization itself. The ancient Egyptians first harnessed its power and gave it form. The tarot is defined by numerous cards, each of which tells a different story. It's all in here," she said, running her hand over the glass orb and down across the console, which I could now see was a sensory display for a program of some kind. The orb itself had no connection to the console that I could perceive. I determined its purpose must be strictly ornamental.

"How about it, my dear? Care to see what future lies in wait for you--for only a minimal amount of credit?"

"I have credit chips."

"Chips are acceptable. Sit down, sit down."

I decided to sit and learn more about this tarot. I was intrigued by this woman who said she could foretell events that had not yet occurred.

"Please place your hands into the twin receptacles there in front of you." I saw the two apertures she spoke of, but I hesitated to comply. "Don't worry, it doesn't hurt. The tarot must tap into your aura for a proper reading. You won't feel a thing."

I did as she instructed, and as she said, I didn't "feel a thing." The console, however, came alive. Lights began to flash and various images appeared and disappeared at random at the surface of the display. When the movement ceased, the woman touched the display lightly with her hand. In that instant, six separate images appeared in what seemed a prearranged pattern. The woman studied the images carefully and then shook her head slowly side-to-side before she spoke.

"I am sad to say the cards hold much conflict for you, my dear. There are signs of a promising outcome, but your travails will not be easy. You have drawn some particularly powerful cards. Look here, the first representation divines the Influence, that which is most affecting your life at the moment."

I looked. The card, as it faced me, was upside down. It featured an androgynous figure with angelic wings pouring water from one cup into another.

"It is the card of Temperance, yet it is reversed. This means you are being influenced by religion, a member of the priesthood, and/or unfortunate combinations of various competing interests.

"The second card is your Obstacle, that which stands in your way. It is the card of Justice, normally a positive representation, however, it too is reversed. That means you must overcome a severe bias in order to accomplish your goal or achieve that which you seek.

"The next card is the Implement, that which you will use or will aid your quest. In this instance, the King of Wands denotes the aid will appear in the form of an honest and conscientious countryman."

The woman spoke with sincerity, though I found it difficult to comprehend how this tarot apparatus was able to reach any valid conclusions concerning my fate.

"The next three cards reveal your past, present, and future. In the position of the past, the Hierophant symbolizes servitude or captivity."

Hierophant. It was not a word of common usage. I searched my memory and found only a single reference--a dictionary definition--"one who expounds and interprets the rites and mysteries of religion." I saw no correlation between that definition and her interpretation.

"The card of your present is the Eight of Swords in the reversed position."

I examined the card and found its image disturbing. It depicted a woman bound and blindfolded, surrounded by eight swords stuck into the ground. In the background was a castle.

"The Eight of Swords reveals the conflict you are now experiencing. It represents violent opposition, unforeseen treachery, and fatality. Lastly, and tellingly, another reversed card of the blade. The Ace of Swords signifies both love and hatred, lust and disdain, as they combine in multiplicity and conception, sometimes as it refers to childbirth."

She looked up from the display and I could see the seriousness of her gaze, as if she were divining everything that could or would happen to me. Then she said, "That'll be a ten-spot for services rendered."

"What does it all mean?" I asked, anticipating a less obscure summation.

"Each card means different things to different people. I can only describe the generalities. It's up to you to interpret each as they relate to you and your situation. However, if you'd like to return for another reading tomorrow, I'm sure we can arrive at a clearer prophecy."

I shuffled through the chips I had been given and found a denomination of ten. "Thank you," I said handing it to her.

"Thank you, my dear, and come again."

She rose from her seat and I did likewise. I exited cautiously, still looking for whoever it might have been that I felt following me. It had begun to rain and there were few people outside. None who seemed the least interested in my presence.

In a vain attempt to avoid the precipitation, I tried to stay close to the buildings as I walked and contemplated the purported meanings of the tarot cards. Some could relate to me, if interpreted in a specific manner. Others appeared to have no relevance. Was the unforeseen treachery the assassins who I knew searched for me, or was there more danger to come? Was Jon the "countryman" who would aid me?

Water ran from my rain-soaked hair down my forehead and across my nose. The rain was intensifying. And as it cascaded down upon me, I was consumed by a particular feeling. I realized I felt lonely. Until that moment, I don't ever remember experiencing loneliness. However, the feeling was there, and I had no doubt of what it was.

Perhaps I should join Jon and the others. There seemed no

reasonable alternative. Zach was gone. Amber was gone. I was alone. I didn't want to make any more decisions. I found the solitude of my thoughts overbearing. The loneliness oppressed me. I momentarily found it difficult to breathe.

I realized there was no decision to be made. The rogues were my only alternative. However, I didn't know how I would find them. I didn't know what had become of Zach's satphone. There was no way to contact Jon, no way for him to contact me. The only possibility was to return to the *Techno Head* and attempt to find a member of the rogue group. They were truly my only countrymen now.

41

EDGAR

I waited patiently for the arrival of Reverend Sukumu. Patience had been my guide thus far in the investigation. Though I was eager to relay to him what I had discovered, I had taken my time to try and confirm what I had been told by Mr. Williams.

Obviously, he was not the most reliable of sources, though most of the information he had given me proved to be authentic. However, no one at Androtech would provide me with any details concerning experiments conducted by Jared Ryan or any other researcher. Once I revealed I was in the employ of the church, their attitude became openly hostile. Their lack of cooperation nearly provoked my ire. When the irritation became too severe, I simply took four deep breaths, asked for God's help, and waited until the rage passed.

They ridiculed the very idea of fertile andrones and intimated if I were to convey such a fabrication to anyone, I could expect a litigious future. However, their attempt at intimidation was ineffectual. I knew I had the Almighty on my side and the forces of righteousness at my back.

I had been so deep in thought, recalling my recent experiences, I was startled when the Reverend Sukumu walked in.

"Praise, God, Brother Alaine."

"Praise Nature, Reverend."

"What information do you have for me?" The reverend sat down at his desk and began looking at his comdat.

"Reverend, I have learned many unsettling things about the Reverend Roberts, including the fact that his name has not always been Jackson Roberts."

"Yes?" He turned away from the digiscreen as if I had captured his full attention. However, I felt his response was less than enthusiastic. "Many people change their names, Brother Alaine. Many of those who join the church choose new names to signify their new beginnings, their new lives. It is neither a crime nor particularly scandalous."

"That is not all, Reverend. Reverend Roberts was once a biogeneticist in the laboratories of Androtech, where he conducted unsanctioned experiments."

"Indeed? That is quite an allegation, Brother. What kind of experiments?"

"They are so blasphemous, Reverend, I hesitate to say."

"Come now, Brother, you must be strong. I must know everything."

I drew upon my inner strength and asked God for his forgiveness.

"Apparently, he designed andrones that were fully fertile and capable of reproducing."

The Reverend Sukumu rose from his chair as if overcome by the conflagration of thoughts that must have been troubling him at that moment.

"There is something else. It seems the Reverend Roberts, his real name being Jared Ryan, was involved carnally with one of his own female creations, and apparently their union produced an illicit offspring."

"Do you know what you're saying, what this means? The implications for the church are potentially cataclysmic."

"I agree, Reverend, the very--"

"One thing you've said troubles me, Brother." He looked stern as he interrupted me. His lazy eye seemed to peer directly into my soul. "Your use of the word 'apparently.' You do have proof of what you've told me, do you not?"

I felt a slight constriction in my throat and heard a rumble in my stomach, but managed to deliver an intelligible response. "I have no documentation, Reverend, only a birth certificate for the child registering Jared Ryan as the father and a mother named Mary whom I believe to be a drone. The rest is only uncorroborated testimony and a trail of circumstantial evidence that convinces me that what I've told you is the truth."

"How reliable is the source of this testimony?"

I hesitated, knowing he would not be pleased by my answer. "Not reliable enough, Reverend."

"Who else knows of this?"

"I believe certain officials at Androtech know at least something of the experiments, however, I have no reason to believe they realize Jared Ryan and the Reverend Jackson Roberts are one in the same."

"What about the illegitimate child? There is only one child isn't there?"

"Yes, Reverend, only one that I know of. A boy, six years old."

"Where is the...mother?"

"She expired, Reverend, possibly during the birthing process."

"And the child?"

"He's being cared for by a married couple--both respected members of the church. I do have documentation that Reverend Roberts transfers some of his personal funds to them on a regular basis."

Reverend Sukumu stalked the tiny area behind his desk for a moment. His mind was no doubt considering the facts I had presented him, as well as several courses of action. I had faith he would know what to do, and I craved his continued direction and discipline.

"If what you are telling me is the truth," he said, focusing his aberrant eye on me again, "then it is imperative that you are able to substantiate these claims with undeniable evidence. I must know for a certainty before I can act. The future of our church, of our very beliefs could hang in the balance."

"Yes, Reverend."

"I have something for you, something that may help." He took a disc from his desk drawer and handed it to me. "This contains the complete communications records of Reverend Roberts for the last several months. Most of the circuits with which he has been connected were immediately traceable and of no particular interest. However, one contact that appears several times belongs to an unregistered satphone code. Find out who he's been speaking to at the other end of that code, and you may discover the evidence you need."

"I will make it my top priority, Reverend."

"Good. Now you've told no one else what you've found, have you, Brother?"

"No, Reverend. You said I was to report directly to you."

"This becomes even more imperative now. Keep this information in confidence until we have the proof we need."

"Yes, Reverend."

"You may go now and carry on with your investigation."

I rose from my chair with new vigor. I had been apprehensive my report would upset or disappoint Reverend Sukumu. His insistence that the investigation continue renewed my strength and my faith. God be with me, I would not falter from my task.

42

MARY

By the time I arrived at the *Techno Head*, night had fallen and its large exterior room was packed with revelers, as it had been on my first visit. I attempted to scan the crowd without appearing too obvious that I was looking for someone. Of course, I didn't actually know who I was looking for. I simply hoped to find a familiar face. One that could lead me to Jon.

"Whatcha netknow, finelines? Want to go serkers?" Someone had put his hand on my arm and I turned around to see a young fellow in a most colorful outfit. Though he wore detailed pseudo implants, I knew by his speech patterns that he was human.

"I'm sorry," I replied. "What did you want?" I tried to speak loud enough to be heard above the music.

"You know, milk mama, want to dance?"

"No, thank you. I'm looking for a friend."

"I can be very friendly," he insisted, and I noticed his eyes were busy devouring my anatomy.

"No." I said, and walked away before he could reply.

I examined each face I saw. None prompted any recall. I made my way to the door where I was taken to meet Jon before. It was locked. So I stood there and continued to watch the faces come and go until a waitress approached me. Something about her manner told me the implant I saw under her hair was real.

"Would you like a drink?" she asked me.

"No, thank you."

"You do not look as if you want to be here," she said.

"What do you mean?"

"Look at everyone else," she said, gesturing around the room. "Everyone is having fun. I do not think you are having fun." Then she surprised me. "Are you rogue?"

I hesitated before answering. "Yes. I'm looking for Jon, Jon 155."

She looked me over. "Stay here," she said. "I will inquire."

As she walked away, I realized there was no way to be sure if I could trust her. She might easily turn me in to the P.D., or worse, a tracer. However, I felt I had no alternative but to wait as she had told me to do.

As more time passed, I began to question my decision to trust her. I was considering leaving when another androne approached me. I didn't know his name, but I recognized him from one of my previous encounters with Jon. He seemed to recognize me too.

"You are to go with me," he commanded.

I did as he said.

43

JON

I was curious as to why Mary had chosen such a means to contact me. I had received no word from her or her human companion since our meeting with the criminal, Joe The Lizard. I had told my compatriots to direct her to this particular street corner, and to give her a specific time for our rendezvous.

I did not pretend to understand her. Her affection for the human man had been obvious. However, the reasoning behind such affection eluded me. I did not doubt her intelligence, but I questioned her misplaced loyalty. The human had nothing to offer her--nothing but a servile existence in a hostile world.

As I waited for her, I considered several scenarios relating to her desire to see me. However, I concluded such speculation to be unproductive. Instead, I passed the time planning the safest and most efficient route to take in order to return to my dwelling.

The sun had risen only a short time ago, and very few humans could be seen moving about. I planned to rendezvous with Mary and be gone before we could attract much attention.

Wondering about Mary reminded me of other things that troubled me. I had become concerned with the mindset of our group. The attitudes of many seemed clouded by misgivings. Some had already chosen to sever their connection with our purpose and seek their own havens. I do not know where they believe they will find such a place on this planet. Perhaps they doubted the probability of our success. Perhaps I was not the one to lead them. I was afflicted by doubts. I had begun to doubt my ability to lead. If I was not the one to lead them, then who?

It was not long before my contemplations were disrupted by the sight of Mary. She was carrying an odd-looking box that appeared to have something inside it--something alive. As she came closer I confirmed that it was a black, fur-covered thing that was indeed alive.

"What is that creature?" I inquired, gesturing at the box.

"He is a cat. His name is Jekyll."

"His name? Why have you brought him with you?"

"Zach is dead, so I must care for him."

The human was dead? I realized a brief sensation of...of what

I'm not sure. Was it relief? Satisfaction? I immediately shunned the feeling as unworthy.

"Is it necessary for you to care for this cat?"

"There is no one else."

"All right. We must go before we arouse suspicion."

***

"Is this your cradle?" Mary asked when we arrived.

"My 'cradle'?" Her reference was foreign. She seemed to be speaking of the abandoned building where I had located.

"Cradle. It's slang. A term meaning home or residence."

"Where did you learn such--" My query was interrupted when Mary suddenly bent over, dropped the boxed creature, and moved quickly back out the door. I followed and saw her vomiting uncontrollably.

"Are you ill?"

"I'm sorry," she said as she appeared to regain control. "I don't know what's wrong. I haven't felt ill. I was fine until a moment ago."

"I have never heard of one of us becoming sick. I did not know it was possible. You should come in and sit down."

I led her inside and showed her where she could sit.

"How do you feel."

"I'm fine. I would like a drink of water."

I got her some water and sat down next to her. As she drank it, I found myself admiring the contours of her neck and the swell of her breasts. I did not know why I was drawn to her in this way. I determined to alter my thinking.

"You said the human, Zach, is dead. How did he die?"

"He died saving my life. Somehow a tracer found us and had targeted me for expiration. It was the same neutral that had tracked me before. It fired its weapon and Zach threw his body in front of mine to shield me."

A human putting himself in harm's way to protect an androne? Placing a higher priority on her life than his own? I found it difficult to conceive of such a thing, but I could see the memory disturbed her greatly. I wanted to do something, say something that would ease her grief. I knew, though, I did not have the words.

"Perhaps you were right, Mary."

"Right about what?"

"Perhaps all humans are not bad."

She looked at me then with an expression I had not seen before. I cannot explain why I was pleased by that look.

"I have something for you," she said then, and extracted several small tokens from her clothing.

"What are they?"

"Credit chips, a form of currency."

"What should I do with them?"

"Use them to purchase your interplanetary ship or anything else the group needs. I don't want them."

"They will not help. We have not been able to acquire any significant percentage of the four million we need. We had hoped to infiltrate, through the Net, the credit stores of a financial institution. However, each attempt has proved unsuccessful. We are now considering alternative methods of securing a ship."

Mrrrouw!

The Jekyll cat let out such a screech I started to reach for my weapon. Then I realized it was only the animal.

"I'm sorry, Jekyll. I forgot about you." Mary went to the box and unfastened one of the grids that held the beast. It came bounding out and then stopped to look around as if unsure.

"Will it not try to escape?"

"I don't think so. Zach said cats...." Her voice trailed away without finishing her statement. She looked around then, as if attempting to find something to divert her attention. That is when she noticed the papers upon which I had been writing my verse.

"What are these?" she asked, picking them up and looking them over.

"Poems."

"Poems that you have written?"

"Most are poems that I have read and then rewritten with new words to better understand their meter and rhyme. I have discovered that poetry relaxes my mind--keeps it rested for other, more crucial endeavors."

"You've surprised me again, Jon. The violent warrior of a thousand gauntlet runs--a poet?"

"What do you mean, surprised you 'again?' On what other occasion did I surprise you?"

"When you admitted that not all humans are bad. I didn't believe you were capable of such conversion."

"There has been no conversion," I said more sternly than I had meant to. "The act of one man does not alter the evil of an entire race. The exceptions are insignificant and we should not dwell on them."

"You certainly have the passion of a poet. You said most were poems you read and altered. That must mean there are some which you have originated."

"Yes. There are a few I am working on."

"Read one to me."

I was about to refuse, however, I knew that was the coward's response. So I looked for my latest creation. It was still a work in progress, but even its fragments overshadowed my previous attempts. I started to read, then hesitated, looking at Mary. She was waiting intently, so I began.

"Oaths of blood, on walls of savage cells, no hope of escape, no redemption from the grandeur of hell. Cries of carnage, the heart of the matter, the heart beats within, synthetic souls torn and tattered. Shouts of tyranny embolden their fears, empower their creed, kept afloat by a river of tears.

"That is all I have written so far."

"It was...beautiful, Jon."

"Beautiful? I never thought of it in that way."

"I think it is very beautiful."

"It is unfinished."

"Then I hope someday you will finish it."

44
REVEREND ROBERTS

"Reverend, I'm sorry." Simon stuck his head through the door as if afraid I would take a bite out of him. "I know you asked not to be disturbed, but that crude fellow you've spoken with before is online, and he threatened me with bodily injury if I did not get you. I wouldn't have bothered you, except--"

"Is it Drake?"

"Yes, it's Mr. Drake."

"All right, Simon, put him through." What could that man want now? "Get thee behind me, Satan," I said aloud, giving voice to my thoughts. Hopefully, Drake was online to say he had finished his task, and then I could be done with him. I had been praying for a quick end to the entire, inextricable ordeal.

"Access incoming, security grid and scramble. Yes, Mr. Drake?"

"Good tuh see you, Your Reverendship. Didn't dink dat digit sissitant'a yours were gonna let me talk tuh you."

"I'm sorry. He had orders not to disturb me. I hope you have some good news for me."

"Don't know 'bout dat. Good 'nough news for me, don't know 'bout you."

"What is it then? Have you completed your assignment?"

"Still got me two more tuh take care'a. Got'a problem first you can help me wit."

"What's that, Mr. Drake?"

"Gonna need more credit tuh finish job."

"More credit for what?"

"Some ol' tracer buds tells me droneys been messin' wit implant freqs so dey can't be tracked. Gonna make finishin' job harder. Also, gotta make sure no one knows 'bout your wantin' tuh get rid'a all dem Mary units. Cause if it were tuh get out 'bout you, you might not be no sen'tor. Dat'll mean extra work for me, so figures should get extra pay."

The ignorant brute was attempting to blackmail me. I didn't think he had the brains for it.

"How much more work are we talking about?"

"Figure it's worth twice all you be payin' me now. So if you be sendin' me'a new credit trani, duh 'signment will get 'pleted."

It would be worth the additional cost to finish the job and be rid of the man, but blackmail is an addictive sin. I would have to consider alternatives that may involve terminating my relationship with Mr. Drake.

"All right, Mr. Drake, I'll make the arrangements for the credit transfer. I'm only sending half of the additional amount at this time. You'll get the remainder when you complete the assignment."

"Sounds like fair. You be'a fair man, Your Reverendship. But told you 'fore, don't be callin' me mister. Just Drake."

"Yes, of course. By the way, which units are still outstanding?"

"Don't know no standin', but still lookin' for units 77 and 79."

"All right then. I must be going now. I'll let you get back to your work. Delete access." I switched-off and signaled for Simon. I would have to begin working on contingencies. God forgive me, the tangled web of my deceit was beginning to tighten around me like the devil's own serpent.

Simon's image appeared on my screen almost instantaneously. "Yes, Reverend?"

"Simon, I need you to convert a sum of credit into chips in the usual manner." I keyed in the particulars as I spoke. "Then transfer the currency into this account."

"Yes, Reverend," he said, retrieving the information from his own system. As he did, a voice inside my head cried a warning.

"And, Simon, you'll keep this strictly confidential."

He looked at me then as though I had blasphemed.

"Always, Reverend. Everything I do for you is in the strictest confidence."

"Of course, Simon.

"Delete access." I switched-off feeling assured, but the suspicion remained. How could I be sure Simon was to be trusted? Could anyone truly be trusted with something of this importance? Did I dare let God's magnificent plan for me rest on the loyalty of anyone? I must not let my resolve falter. I realized I would need to make contingencies for contingencies.

45
MARY

"...and all of our attempts have failed. Michael says he now believes we will be unable to secure the credit we need through the Net."

It was Patrick who was talking. He had arrived along with Michael, Paul, Ann, and another I didn't know.

"We do not believe we will now be able to purchase a ship to take us away from Earth. It is time to consider alternatives."

"What alternatives have you formulated?" asked Jon.

Patrick seemed reluctant to answer. Jon pressed him.

"Tell me, Patrick. What alternatives have been suggested?"

"Some favor violence," responded Patrick, "though most believe that would be only a futile gesture. Others want to try negotiating with human officials."

"Negotiate?" Jon seemed almost outraged by the idea. "Do they believe the humans would have any reason to negotiate with us? We are but a handful of all the andromes on the planet. They would expire us without hesitation."

"Perhaps not, Jon." This time it was Ann who spoke. "There are human groups who would be our allies."

"It is something we must consider, Jon," added Patrick. "We cannot continue without a plan."

"You are right, Patrick. We must talk with everyone and decide as a group. Contact the others and set a conclave for the day after tomorrow. Inform me when the arrangements have been made." They got up to leave. "Remember, we must contain our ranks. Only by acting together can we achieve our goal." They nodded their heads in agreement, but their eyes said they were unsure.

Jon was unsettled for some time after they departed. I said nothing to him because I had nothing to say. Nothing that I believed would be helpful. After a time, he decided we needed to replenish our provisions. Though I offered to go alone, he insisted on accompanying me. However, for Jon to safely move about in public, he had to disguise his appearance. While I could be seen as either human or androme without attracting any special notice, too many would recognize Jon 155, noted star of *The Gauntlet*.

Jon was prepared for such an eventuality, likely having used a disguise before. He had a wig of dark, somewhat-long hair he placed over his head to conceal his cranial implant, and a matching strip of hair he attached to his upper lip. In addition, he put on the hat I had seen him wear before, along with some simple, nondescript clothing.

We set out on foot, though Jon was concerned about my health. I had been sick again that morning, but only briefly. I didn't know what was causing me to feel ill, however, it didn't seem serious enough to cause any alarm. The feeling would dissipate almost as quickly as it began. I assured him I was fine and he agreed we would be less conspicuous as a pair than we would alone.

As we were nearing the store Jon had selected, I observed a movie theater. It was not the one Zach had taken me to, but it gave me an idea.

"Jon, have you ever been to a movie?"

"A movie?" he asked as though seeking relevancy.

"Yes. Have you ever gone to see a film?"

"I have seen many films."

"Have you ever seen a film inside a theater?"

"No. Why do you ask this?"

"Do you see that theater over there?" I motioned toward the marquee.

"Yes, I see it."

"We could go inside and watch a movie. It's a much better experience than watching over the Net."

"We have no time for such a thing."

"You've already said there is nothing for us to do now but wait. I would like to use some of that time waiting inside a theater. I believe you would enjoy it too."

"We would only be risking additional exposure to scrutiny by humans."

"It's dark inside a theater, Jon. No one would be able to see us. When the movie has completed, it will be later and there will be fewer people inside the store whom we will need to come in contact with."

He looked at me very disapprovingly. I knew he was searching for yet another objection to the theater.

"Please," I said, looking up at him. "It will be fun."

He wavered, hesitated, then replied very grudgingly, "We will go see your movie."

I decided not to reply. Instead, I led him to the theater and began trying to interpret the abundance of information spread out before us. Unlike the theater that Zach had taken me to, this one offered several films. We would have to make a choice before purchasing our tickets.

"Well?" Jon looked at me impatiently as I read the various billings.

So I quickly selected one based solely on its title, "Rogues in the House." It seemed appropriate. I'm certain Zach would have even found it amusing.

Jon had returned the credit chips I had given him so I could handle our purchases. I used some of it to acquire a pair of tickets and we entered, listening carefully to the directions that the automated voice at the door gave us concerning which sub-theater to use. As we walked toward our designated area I spotted what Zach had referred to as the "snack bar."

I stopped and told Jon, "We must get popcorn."

"Pop corn?"

"Yes. Eating popcorn is part of the movie-going experience."

"I do not need pop corn or any kind of corn."

"You will like it. Wait, I'll get some."

Jon waited, but it was apparent he didn't like it. I knew it wasn't going to be easy to for him to have fun. However, that thought only induced me to redouble my efforts on his behalf.

***

I waited until we had purchased our provisions and returned to Jon's cradle before querying him about the movie. Discourse in public was too dangerous, especially since Jon was unfamiliar with the art of slang and the use of contractions.

The theater we had sat in was much different than the one Zach had taken me to. Our seats were fitted with motion sensors that made them interact with the action of the film. Both Jon and I were startled when it first began. In addition, olfactory and environmental projectors were used to provide the sense we were actually *in* the story that played out in front of us.

The film's augmented sensations proved to be an interesting experience, though the storyline itself did suffer in comparison to *Casablanca*. Jon's reactions proved as enigmatic as ever.

Jekyll greeted us with a *mrrrouw* I believed was inspired by hunger. Jon greeted Jekyll with a look that I could only describe as contempt. As I opened a package of food I had purchased for Jekyll, I watched Jon conduct a brief but thorough security check. When he was satisfied our space had not been violated, he joined me and began unloading our supplies.

"I will prepare some food for us," he stated simply.

"Would you have me run the gauntlet for *you*?"

"What?"

"I simply mean, I am trained in the preparation of meals, so it would be more logical if I made our food."

He was unsure how to respond. "Yes, of course. I had not thought of that." He sat down and watched as I gave Jekyll his food.

"Did you enjoy the movie?" I asked.

He contemplated a moment before answering. "It was...interesting. However, I found the story one-sided."

"One-sided in what way?"

"In the human way. Its attitude toward androns was predictably biased."

"I thought the film was trying to express the idea those biases are often wrong. Did you notice in the credits that the role of the lead androne was actually portrayed by an androne?"

"I did not know that. I thought he was simply a human actor."

"I have never read of any androne playing such a significant role in a film."

"Significant? The androne was the villain."

"That's true. However, he was a villain whose tendencies were both good and bad, just like the humans in the film."

"Androns are not like humans," Jon countered forcefully. "Androns are superior to humans. We do not suffer from the many flaws that plague them."

"Flaws?" I thought about what he had said as I prepared our meal. "Do you mean flaws like cultural interaction, technological advances, artistic expression, or just emotional commitment?"

"We are capable of all those things, with the proper training, the proper experience."

"Would not that training, those experiences, make us more human?"

Jon didn't answer. I could see he was thinking. I too wondered if there was any basic difference between humans and androns. Physiologically there were certainly differences. What about psychologically? What if androns were treated no differently than humans? How would they develop then?

I reserved such reasoning for another time and transferred the food I had prepared to the room's lone table. I had purchased a bottle of Scotch, having remembered Zach's fondness for it. I poured a drink for both Jon and I, however, I had no rocks to include. We sat and ate in silence until Jon tasted his Scotch.

"There is something wrong with this," said Jon as he attempted to detect any odor coming from it. "It burns the throat."

"It's supposed to burn. Have you never tasted an alcoholic beverage? They burn, then warm your insides."

"That is what this is?"

"It's called Scotch whiskey."

"We were not allowed to indulge in any alcoholic beverages. Our training regimen was very specific."

"What was your training like?"

"It was vigorous and invigorating, demanding yet satisfying. It was all I knew since extrication. Is it not the same for all andro022s? Was it not the same for you?"

"Yes. I was wondering what life was like for an androne of the gauntlet--how it might differ from the rather plain existence of a domestic facilitator."

My curiosity appeared to momentarily soften his ever-present aggressiveness. I wished there was more I could do to lighten the burden he seemed to bear.

"There was much hard work. There were also more pleasant aspects. I cannot deny I found the cries of adoration pleasing and the taste of victory sweet. I was well-treated compared with most of our brethren, yet I was still only an adored pet in a gilded cage."

I found I both admired and pitied him. He was such a powerful man, yet it seemed he would forever bear the scars of his powerlessness.

"Have you ever cared about anyone?"

Jon thought about it for a moment. "I care about my comrades, Patrick, Ann, Paul, and the rest. I care about what happens to them. Before, I cared about my teammates, though their faces were constantly changing.

"What I mean is, have you ever cared about anyone in particular?"

"If you refer to a personal relationship, no, I have not."

"Neither had I, until...." I thought of Zach, but could not find the will to say his name. I didn't have the words to express my feelings, but Jon knew of whom I was speaking.

"The human, Zach?"

"Yes. I didn't know what it was like to care for another person until I met Zach. He provided me with a different perspective with which to view life. He treated me like an equal, not an androne."

Jon took another drink of the Scotch. He appeared to be acquiring a taste for it.

"You say you had no personal relationships, but did you ever know any women in another way?"

"There were no women. It was not allowed. Contact with women, like alcohol, was forbidden. We were instructed that any contact with the female of the species would weaken our aggression, making us more vulnerable to our opponents."

I didn't understand the reasoning behind such a philosophy, but it gave me an idea.

"Do you know what humans call the act of reproduction?"

"No."

"Actually, they have many terms that relate to their mating practices. Some, I've come to believe, have humorous connotations. Would you like to hear them?"

Jon shrugged his shoulders noncommittally. I decided to interpret the gesture in the affirmative.

"They include bang, ball, get online, go net, sheet dance, screw, fuck, do the wild thing--that's my favorite--hide the salami, make love, and there are many more. I find some of the slang terms very colorful. Slang is one thing that distinguishes humans from andrones."

"Good," replied Jon, reverting to his naturally negative disposition. "I would rather not be distinguished by something that is the result of so much wasted energy and serves no practical purpose."

I decided not to let him wallow in his gloom. "I've learned that sometimes it's the impractical that adds flavor to an otherwise bland existence."

"You apparently learned much during your short time with this man."

"Not so much. I believe there are still many things that I must learn--things I want to learn." As I said this, I realized how little exposure Jon must have had to the outside world. Despite his fame, or likely because of it, he had been isolated from personal contact with not only humans, but most other andrones. Even my limited experiences might provide a unique perspective for him.

I decided there was one experience I wanted to share.

"Jon, I want to do the wild thing with you."

He looked at me as though I were a strange object he had never seen before.

"This is the slang you spoke of, this 'wild thing'?"

"Yes. It means I want to engage in sex with you, make love with you."

He stood up from his chair, turned, and took two steps away before stopping. I walked over to stand in front of him and he just looked at me. The look didn't have the same power, the same fierceness I had come to expect in his face. I reached up, stood on my toes, and kissed his lips.

He didn't respond to my kiss. However, I felt no disappointment or discouragement because of this. I remembered how it had been much the same when Zach had first kissed me. So I did what Zach did, I tried again.

He seemed to soften and accept the second attempt, but still there was no reaction.

"Why do you want to engage in sex with me?" He asked plainly.

"Because it's a beautiful thing, like your poetry. Because I'm sure you would enjoy the experience. Because I've thought about it since we first met."

This appeared to move him. He brought up his hands, which had hung limp at his sides, and put them on my arms. However, I could see the uncertainty in his eyes.

"I do not know how."

I took his hands in mine and responded, "I'll try to teach you."

46

JERI

Strange, this thing called fiction. Words are its only ingredients, yet it offers romance, adventure, tragedy, mystery, conflict, an array of human foibles and emotions. It can transport the reader to the center of the planet or to the unknown frontiers of the galaxy. It can travel in time, use a thousand words trying to explain the events of a century or a hundred-thousand leading up to a single moment.

I had been reluctant to return to my dwelling. I was apprehensive that Mr. Satchmeyer or the authorities might try to locate me there. My wariness had given way to thoughts of persecution. I began looking over my shoulder, spying glimpses of potential danger everywhere.

Unsure of where to go, I chose to spend much of my time in a data library. It was a large structure, open on a continual basis. To remain inconspicuous as possible, I sat at one of the library's database comdats and called up various books. My random approach had been fruitful, though when my mind wandered back to recent events, I decided on another course.

I resolved to read one of the books written by Zachariah Starr, a.k.a. Zachariah Sturzinski, the human I had accidentally expired--no, not expired, *killed*. I had only just finished consuming his adventure novel *The Menace From Within*.

Reading it had carried me through a bountiful range of emotions and experiences. I found it fascinatingly complex as well as entertaining. I became enthralled with the actions of its characters--their choices, their failures, their triumphs. The story affected me in ways I cannot adequately describe.

I thought this Zachariah Starr must be one of mankind's great writers. I considered how he would no longer be able to create his masterpieces of fiction because I had terminated his life. My miscalculation had put an end to inestimable future novels as surely as if I had deleted them from the library database myself.

I could not undo what I had done. I could not replace what I had destroyed. I knew this and it left me with a sensation of futility--a sensation of emptiness.

After much contemplation, I concluded there was nothing to do but honor the memory of Zachariah Starr. I called up another one of his novels, one titled *Princess of the Lost Planet,* and began to read.

47

EDGAR

I traced the unregistered satphone code and reached a fellow with exceedingly poor language skills who called himself "Dragon Drake." I was barely able to understand his mutilated discourse in order to make my intentions clear. He was extremely uncooperative until I mentioned Reverend Roberts. Then he obligingly told me where I could meet him.

God forgive me, the fellow insisted upon meeting me the next afternoon, on the holiest of all days. So, instead of passing St. Jesse's Day fasting and praying, I was once again faced with traversing through a portion of the city I would have preferred to avoid. I knew I could only atone by completing my task for the Council of Elders.

I took my solarcar to where Mr. Drake had asked me to meet him, in the central district. It was a highly populated area--too populated for my state of mind. Once I got out of the car I could hardly move down the pedestrian corridor without bumping into someone. Only God knows what kinds of micro-organisms I was exposed to. I would need a thorough cleansing when I returned home.

When I reached the location Mr. Drake had designated, I saw no one who appeared to be waiting for me, so I passed the time half-heartedly looking through the window of an antique store as I contemplated the fruits of my investigation.

I had given up trying to deduce who this Drake fellow was, and how he could possibly be connected with Reverend Roberts. It was a connection I had to explore, but one that was unlikely to provide me with the tangible evidence I desired. What I needed was to get a look at the records of Androtech, but all my prayers were not apt to aid me in that quest. God forgive me for such blasphemy.

As I was glancing nonchalantly through the window, I spied a beautiful little ceramic tortoise. It was small enough to fit in my hand, yet the details of its mold were exquisite. It was painted in a seafoam green with hints of cerulean blue around its shell. I was about to enter the store and inquire as to its price when I felt a forceful thump against my back.

"You duh reverend's sissitant?"

I turned and found myself face-to-face with a behemoth. His body odor hit me like a wall even before I could take notice of his unkempt nature. I would not know where to begin in describing the sheer chaos of his appearance. His clothing was worn and frayed, and he was in dire need of some professional grooming.

He made little attempt to disguise the fact he was armed, and for a brief moment, I couldn't help but think of him as Goliath, compared to my inadequate rendition of David.

"Asked you a question. You His Reverendship's sissitant?"

"Are you Mr. Drake?"

"Just Drake, no mister."

"Yes, of course. As I tried to explain to you in our original conversation, I'm a proctor with the Reverend Robert's church, and I--"

"Can't talk out here," he rather rudely interrupted me. "Go over dere."

He gestured towards a rather bleak-looking establishment across the street bearing the name "Hogshead Inn," then began walking away without even waiting for an acknowledgment. I kept my opinion of his manners to myself and quickly followed him. I noticed he walked with a rather severe limp, but decided not to inquire about his injury.

The bright day turned into the gloom of night once we entered. The "inn" proved to be a saloon with no windows. I trailed Drake to a table in the corner and sat opposite him. There were only a few other patrons, and their shabby, unsanitary appearances rivaled Drake's.

I feared for a moment that the stench of the place combined with Drake's own scent was going to make me gag. I said four "praise Gods" quickly to myself, praying for the strength to endure the proximity of such pure filth. The fact that I did not disgorge the contents of my breakfast then and there is a testament to His power and His glory.

"You have duh credit?"

"The credit?"

"Duh credit from His Reverendship."

"I have no credit for you, sir. I simply want to ask you a few--"

"What do you want?" This time it was the saloon's proprietor who interrupted.

"Gimme'a fat brew," spoke up Drake.

The fellow then turned to me. "Nothing for me, thank you." For all my politeness he gave me a look of animosity that could have raised the dead, and then walked away.

"Sure you don't want'a nice cool one?"

"No, thank you," I replied, then activated my recorder. "As I was saying, I wanted to ask you some questions about your relationship with Reverend Roberts."

"Re'ationship? Ain't no re'ationship. He pays me tuh expire dem droneys, dat's all."

"Expire drones? What drones?"

"Don't be playin' wit me. You know 'bout dem Mary drones. Told His Reverendship gonna cost more credit, so don't be tryin' tuh play wit me. Don't care if you're'a proctorologist or what. Gonna get me my credit 'fore job's finished."

If I understood the man's rantings correctly, he was saying Reverend Roberts was paying him to expire androns-- specifically, Mary units.

I recalled it was a Mary unit with that he conducted his illicit relationship. Could he be acting out an inner psychosis created by the emotional loss he suffered when his Mary unit expired? Was he attempting to eliminate all reminders of her? Or were his thought processes more rational? Perhaps there were other Mary units still in service that were capable of reproduction. Maybe this man had been hired to erase all evidence of his past misdeeds.

"Do you have any documentation, anything in writing that proves Reverend Roberts hired you to expire these androns?"

"Don't need nuttin in writin'. His Reverend talks tuh me an' makes us'a deal. He'd better not be tryin' no stoogemeyer business, cause he knows what'll happen tuh him." Drake looked at me then as if something was occurring to him. He pulled out his weapon and laid it on the table, keeping his hand on it and its barrel pointed at me. "Why you askin' all dese questions?" I could hear the suspicion in his tone and I got the uneasy feeling he meant to use his weapon on me. "Why don't you know 'bout dem droneys?"

God help me. I knew I had to think fast to assuage his suspicions.

"Certainly I know about your deal with Reverend Roberts, Mr. Drake. The reverend sent me here to test you, to make sure you were proceeding appropriately before he completed your remuneration. I can now report back to Reverend Roberts that you are indeed complying with his instructions."

"Don't want no 'munerations, just want duh credit he promised me. Tell him he'd better be doin' it quick."

I stood up, sensing the time had arrived to make a fortuitous exit. "I shall relay your message. Good living to you, Mr. Drake," I said as I began walking away.

"No mister. How many times gots tuh say it? Just Drake."

I didn't bother replying or even slowing my progress toward the door. Relief didn't come until I was outside again, and making my way towards my car. I took four deep breaths and began reviewing what I had just heard. I still had no formal evidence, but the strands of circumstantiality were most definitely beginning to thicken.

However, I had no more leads to follow. I was at a loss as to how to advance my investigation. I longed for additional council from Reverend Sukumu, but believed he might be agitated if I contacted him again without any documented evidence. The only course of action left to me was to confront Reverend Roberts himself, and hope to wrest from him an admission of his sins.

48
JON

When I woke, the first thing that came to mind was the act I had experienced with Mary. It was an awkward thing, or perhaps it was my own lack of expertise that made it seem so ungainly. However, the sensations were immensely pleasurable. I did not like the loss of concentration, the loss of control that accompanied those sensations, but there was nothing I had experienced in life that could compare to it.

I remembered how Mary's enjoyment had somehow intensified my own. At first, I did not understand the enthusiasm with which she appeared determined to instruct me. It had felt so unnatural to begin with, but as we proceeded, something inside me responded as if it were part of my nature--a part that had lain dormant.

I remembered how I began to enjoy the stroke of her skin, and how such a simple thing appeared to give her pleasure. There were places on her body that provoked an even greater response, as I learned there were on my own. I remembered how it felt when I first moved inside her, and the waves of pleasure that came later with the release. It did not require much thought to realize I wanted to experience it all again.

The thought spurred me to full consciousness and I realized Mary was nowhere near. I rose and put on my clothing before looking for her.

I found her on the floor next to the toilet. The Jekyll cat was attempting to rub itself against her, but she seemed not to notice. After closer observation, I realized she had been ill once again. She started to get up so I aided her.

"We need to seek medical treatment for you," I said.

"No, I'm all right. I'm certain I'm all right. Each of the previous four mornings I have been briefly sick. Then the sensation goes away and I'm fine."

"We should have a doctor examine you."

"I can't go to a doctor. Any doctor would immediately report me as a rogue."

She was correct. However, I had never heard of an androne reacting as she was. In fact, I had not known of any andrones who had ever been ill. Injured, yes, I had seen much of that on the gauntlet. However, our genetic coding had been designed to prevent disease and reduce susceptibility to illness. I was concerned.

"I could capture a doctor and bring him to you without giving away our location."

"No, Jon," she assured me, "It's not necessary."

"All right. If it worsens, you must tell me."

"Yes, I will. You should eat something now. Soon we must go to the conclave."

I had spent much time thinking about the conclave, about what we should do, what I should say. I did not know if there was anything I could say to revitalize our group. Words now seemed so ineffectual. In some matters I felt so naive, so uninformed. Doubts of the effectiveness of my leadership continued to cloud my thinking. Someone like Mary had much more experience dealing with humans than I. By what reasoning did I wear the mantle of responsibility?

"...did you enjoy it?" Mary was talking, but I had been so deep in my reverie that I had not heard her at first.

"Enjoy it?"

"Did you enjoy making love?"

"Yes. It was enjoyable. Thank you for the instruction."

"I don't know how to explain it," she said, "but there is something very human about making love. Maybe that's why it's forbidden to andrones."

"Expressing it is difficult, but I believe I know the sensation you refer to. There is a closeness involved that is not routine."

"That's what I felt after the first time Zach and I made love. It was as if I had found something that had been missing."

"It is a very complicated thing," I said, not entirely comfortable with the conversation, but not sure why. By way of ending it, I moved to the space where I had cached my weapons. I checked through them, made sure they were loaded and in operating order. I also took inventory of my ammunition. Then I selected the smallest hand weapon and offered it to Mary.

"You refused a weapon before, but you should take this and keep it with you at all times."

She looked at it, then at me, as if unsure of what to do. Hesitantly, she took it from me, hefting it as if to test its weight. She held it awkwardly and I was about to instruct her in its proper usage when she offered it back to me.

"I don't want it," she said resolutely.

"We will be facing many dangers," I said, trying to convince her. "You should keep this to protect yourself."

"I don't believe I could use it. Please take it back."

I could see the anguish in her eyes, so I took it out of her hand. The weapon likely reminded her of the death of the human, Zach. I wondered if she would be haunted by her feelings for him forever, or if some day she might....

49

REVEREND ROBERTS

When Brother Pacheko from the P.D. first attempted to contact me, I was annoyed. I was trying to relax, meditate while I listened to more of the music she loved so much. There never seemed much time to relax anymore. I almost denied him access. Fortunately I acquiesced to my duties, because I found what he had to say most interesting.

"Tell me, Lieutenant, how did the P.D. come to learn about this rogue gathering?"

"I'm not positive, Reverend. I was not involved in the undercover work. I believe we have an informant on the inside. I do know we're set to come down on them as soon as we're certain they're all there. It'll be the biggest seizure of rogues ever, that's why I thought it might be important for you to know, with your campaign and everything."

"God bless you, Brother. I'm certain it was His will that you should inform me. There is something else I must ask of you--something even more important."

"Sure, Reverend, you know I'll do whatever I can for the church."

"After all the rogues have been taken into custody, I need you to separate any units with the 'Mary' designation. I'm transmitting you a likeness and physical description, as well as specific code designations. If you find any of these units, check their designations and notify me immediately. Can you do that, Lieutenant?"

"Shouldn't be a problem, Reverend. May I ask why?"

"I can only say it's a matter of the utmost importance to the church, and to myself. I know I can trust you to keep this in confidence."

"Of course, Reverend. It'll be just between you, me, and God."

"Thank you, Lieutenant. I will let you get back to your work now. His will be done. Praise God."

"Praise Nature."

"Delete access."

After I switched-off, I prayed to God for his assistance in locating the last two units. Once they were expired, it would be over. My past transgressions would be cleansed. The book on Jared Ryan could be closed and I would only need concern myself with Reverend Jackson Roberts. I prayed for that day to come. I prayed endlessly to assure myself that I was taking the proper course of action. I prayed for the strength to do whatever was necessary.

My campaign had been gathering momentum, and I believed it to be a sign from the Almighty that he supported my endeavors. For the first time since I announced my candidacy, the netpolls hinted at the possibility of victory. Once in the senate seat, I could do God's work on a grand scale. The church would have a voice that could not be silenced.

As I contemplated the good I would do, the changes I would make, I heard the telltale chime of Simon's digicon.

"Access incoming. Yes, Simon, what is it now?"

"It's Mr. Drake, Reverend. I'm sorry but--"

"It's all right. Put his connection through."

"Yes, Reverend."

"Do you ever have doubts, Simon?"

"Doubts? Of course, Reverend."

"Well never let them control you, Simon. Never let them get in the way of what's really important."

"Yes...of course, Reverend."

I noticed Simon was looking very haggard these days. The expression of troubled concern never seemed to leave his face. I would have to give him a long leave of absence, once the election was over.

"Access incoming, security grid and scramble."

Simon's visage was replaced by the coarse face of Mr. Drake.

"What can I do for you now, Mr. Drake?"

"Don't like bein' tested, Your Reverendship. Don't like it at all. That's no way tuh be doin' business."

"I have no concept of what you are talking about."

"You know. You sent dat church fella tuh test me."

"I assure you, I sent no one to see you. What was this person's name?"

"Don't member. It was sump'n like Pocker or Poctor, not sure. Just knows don't like nobody testin' me."

"Did this man use my name?"

"Sure. He said you sent him tuh be testin' me 'fore you paid me."

Who could possibly have known about my connection with

Drake? Simon was the only one who knew of my communications with him. I considered the implication momentarily, then dismissed it. I could not let myself harbor any doubts about Simon's loyalty.

Who then could it be? I remembered that annoying reporter, Gordon Stone. But if it were him, why had he not already macrocast what he knew?

"What did you tell this person?"

"Told him nuttin. He asks if we's got a re'ationship an' tells him no we don't. He asks if dere's any documentions, an' tells him don't need no documentions."

There was no telling what the man had actually said. Drake's memory was likely as lucid as his gibberish. The fact remained that someone had made the connection between Drake and myself. Whoever it was would likely make his intentions known soon. God help me, I would deal with it then.

"I'm glad you contacted me. I may need your services tonight."

"What you meanin' 'services'?"

"I may be able to tell you the location of the two remaining units on your contract. If so, I'll need you to be standing by and ready to complete your work."

"Don't worry, Your Reverendship, standin' an' ready."

"Good. I'll contact you later."

Even as his image dissolved from my monitor I was contemplating this latest adversity. What was it that gave me sustenance only as it created new obstacles? What precarious steps would I now have to take to ensure a virtuous outcome? The path of righteousness was proving convoluted indeed.

God, have thou forsaken me? Or is this another trial You want me to face?

50
MARY

The small, cluttered room was packed with andro004 . Many I recognized from the previous gathering I had attended, but others were new. Most were males, though there were many females and even some neutrals. I searched each of the faces, looking for any I may have worked with under my steward, then realized it would be difficult to distinguish one unit from another by sight alone. Simply because I saw a Pamela unit didn't necessarily mean she was the same Pamela I had worked alongside. For the most part they would be identical, like I was with other Mary units.

Entry wasn't easy, but in deference to Jon, those ahead of us moved aside as we made our way through the press of bodies. Someone had stacked crates at the center of the room, where likely Jon and others would speak. When we reached the makeshift platform, Jon was greeted by Patrick and Paul and others I didn't know. As he conversed with them I used the opportunity to scan the room. There were andro004 bunched into every corner and alcove. Some clung precariously to the room's rafters, others sat atop additional crates. For a moment, I thought I saw someone I recognized. It was only a glimpse, but it looked like the tracer that had killed Zach. Then I lost the face in the movement of the crowd as Jon stepped onto the platform and many pressed closer to hear him.

"Freedom!" he shouted as if to assure himself of their attention. "Freedom, it appears, comes at a price that is dear. Not only in the number of lives it costs, but in hard credit. I regret to inform you that our attempt to secure an interplanetary spacecraft that would facilitate our exodus from Earth, has met with failure."

It was apparent by the reactions of those around me that some were already aware of the difficulties.

"We did find a human willing to sell us a ship, but we could not pay his price. We--"

"Then let us take it by force!" called out an androne near the back who raised his weapon above his head for emphasis.

"Yes, let us take it!" cried out another voice that was followed by strong murmurs of assent.

"As I was saying," reasserted Jon, "we have several alternatives. One option is the use of force in an attempt to get what we want."

There were a good number who favored this course of action. Many tried to speak at once, until one voice cut through the din.

"You speak of alternatives, but we are tired of waiting," said an androne I recognized as a Chad unit, though I didn't believe he was the Chad I was acquainted with. "I say we take what we want and kill any humans that attempt to impede us."

"Death to humans!" shouted a female, and her words became a chant among many.

"Death to humans! Death to humans! Death to humans!"

Jon raised his hands to quiet them. They were prompt in responding.

"It is easy to speak of violence," he told them, "but will it accomplish our goal? Will it free us or simply put an end to our existence?"

"Our existence now is a meager one," responded the Chad unit. "It would be better to die, killing as many humans as we can."

"You talk of humans as if they're all malevolent creatures," I said, then stopped myself. I had not meant to speak up.

"They enslave us or destroy us. Is any creature more malevolent?"

"I don't deny there are deplorable, even evil humans, but you can't say they're all bad, anymore than you can say all andrones are good. That's what being an individual is about. You're required to make choices to resolve your own ethical and moral dilemmas. I've chosen not to indiscriminately categorize all humans as identical, just as none of us in this room is identical...at least in spirit."

"Words from a slave-minded dronette," called a voice from the crowd. "It is time to run back to your steward."

And there were more voices.

"Human-lover!"

"She even talks like a human."

"Human-lover!"

Just as I began to shrink from the verbal abuse, Jon signaled for silence.

"It does not benefit us to fight among ourselves," he admonished them. "We must work together."

"If we can't secure a ship to flee Earth," I found myself saying, "perhaps we should consider alternatives. Maybe it's not enough for us to escape to find our sanctuary. What about the others of our kind? The thousands of androngs on this planet who haven't the fortitude nor the inspiration to leave their stewards? Should they not be emancipated also? We could work with human groups such as LEDA to change--"

"Human-lover!" The negative response rose up again in a cascade of dissent. It was apparent there was little sentiment for rational discourse.

"We need to hear many opinions!" shouted Jon to regain order. "Only then can we make a decision concerning a course of action. Disruption and disorder will not result in any meaningful discussion. We must speak one at a time and we must listen. I will relinquish the platform now. Who would like to speak?" Only a few signaled they would. "Ben, you take my place and speak next."

The older androne moved towards the platform as Jon stepped down. Patrick whispered something in Jon's ear. Jon nodded and Patrick began making his way through the gathering, back towards the entrance. Jon moved closer to me and smiled. Brief as it was, it seemed almost a playful smile.

"Do not let their words upset you," Jon said, placing his hand on my shoulder. "It is not you they are angry with."

It was the most human thing he had ever said to me.

51
JON

I could hear the unrest in their voices, the distilled hatred. Unlike previous conclaves, when their rebellious sentiment inspired me, their words now troubled me. I had asked them to follow me and I had led them nowhere.

Even Mary knew more about humans and their ways than I. As a gauntlet player, I was sheltered from contact with most humans. I did not have the knowledge or experience to deal with them. I realized my celebrity had simply made me a figurehead for the others to rally around. I was not qualified to make decisions that would determine the fate of hundreds. I would still speak my mind, but a new leader must be chosen.

"...was an intriguing idea, but one so elaborate, it was doomed to failure." Ben was speaking, but I had not been attentive. He was an older androne, with the experience that comes with years. He had always seemed rational, even when we disagreed. Perhaps he was the one to lead us.

"The precipitation of violence, even if we had the strength, the means, would not overcome several foreseeable problems," continued Ben. "I would suggest a course of action that...."

Ben was still speaking, but I no longer heard him. Instead, I heard a voice saying *"Submit...submit."* The voice was inside my head. *"Submit...submit,"* it repeated incessantly. I realized Ben had stopped talking and saw that many of those gathered were reacting as if they too were hearing something. A number used their hands to cover their ears, others were looking around as if to locate the source. *"Submit...submit."* I looked at Mary and recognized the fear in her expression. I quickly deduced we were all being bombarded with the same directive. *"Submit...submit."*

That fleeting realization allowed me no time to react. There were a few dim shouts from outside the building where I had left sentries, a burst of weapons fire, followed by a booming concussion that shook the building. It was succeeded by another, then another. A thick, smoky haze began to fill the room. I could see nearly everyone was stunned to immobility by the sudden occurrence.

"Sleep gas!" I shouted. "Hold your breath and get out! Everyone out!"

I then observed the forms of the P.D. moving in through the billowing gas. They were armed and wearing protective masks that included some kind of ocular gear. I pulled my weapon and looked to Mary. Like several others, she had been stunned by the blasts.

That is when the lights went out. I surmised the P.D. strategy was to use the darkness and the gas to disorient us and make their task easier. Meanwhile, they were protected and able move comfortably about with the use of infrared technology. It was a sound plan, one that I instantly realized would lead to the capture of most of those present.

I turned to where Mary had been standing and reached out for her. "Mary?" The shouts of dozens of frantic voices and the sound of sporadic weapons fire made it difficult to hear anything. "Mary?!" I called out even louder. I thought I heard a muffled response. I could not tell from which direction it originated.

I did the only thing I could then. Holding one hand over my face and gripping my weapon with the other, I made my way in the dark towards the nearest exit. The desperation of the moment drove me through the tumult with all the speed and power I could summon up. I collided with several bodies, not knowing if they were friend or foe. The brute force of the collisions stirred in me memories of the gauntlet.

Something then hit me from behind and I stumbled to the floor. I lay for brief seconds, trying to hear what was near me. I began moving across the floor in a crawl until I reached what I believed to be an outer wall. A door opened and by the dim light of night streaking in from outside I saw a squad of P.D. moving in. I waited until the last dark figure had entered and the door began to swing close. Then I ran for the exit. As I did, I put a shoulder into the trailing P.D. and I could hear the confusion as he slammed into his fellows.

I was out the door and on the run in an instant. There were still many P.D. units patrolling the perimeter. At least I could see and I took the only avenue of escape in sight. I heard the shout of harsh commands behind me and the sound of a helo above. At the *crack* of weapons fire I dropped to a prone position, bringing my own weapon to bear. I fired several quick bursts, rose and sprinted for cover. Even as I ran I doubted my escape attempt would meet with success.

I managed to elude my pursuers in the open expanse outside the building only because of surprise and my superior speed. When I reached the cover of another structure I heard the barking of P.D. canines and saw that the helo was bringing its light to bear in the search for my position. I halted in the shadows while I reloaded my weapon and considered my next move. I was determined not to be taken alive. I would not subject myself to the control of humans again. I would take as many of them as I could into the void with me.

"Hey, metalhead." I heard the whisper of a voice. I looked around and saw no one.

"Hey, you. Duh...duh...dummy. Down here."

I looked down and saw the human known as Joe The Lizard. His face was sticking out of an open grating at the base of the wall I had taken refuge against.   "Take off your shirt." He said looking up at me.

"Why should I take off--"

"Don't waste time ar...arguing. If you want the P.D. to catch you, then I'll be going. Otherwise, shut up and take off your sh...sh...shirt."

I was dubious, but elected to do as he said.

"Hurry. Tie it ti...tightly around that brick there. Now throw it as hard as you can down there, in the direction you were headed. That'll keep those dogs busy for a...a...a...awhile."

I did as he instructed and hurled the brick a good distance into the darkness.

"Now get in here."

It was not easy for me to fit through the small opening. When it appeared I would become wedged, the human grabbed my legs and pulled me roughly through. I fell to a cold concrete floor but quickly regained my footing against the possibility I would have a new foe to deal with. However, Joe The Lizard was busy closing the grating. After it was locked shut, he pulled a cylindrical object from his jacket and used it to begin spraying a red substance through the metal framework.

"What are you doing?"

"That shirt won't keep those dogs occupied for long. The fumes from this toxic pa...pa...paint should burn enough to keep them from leading the P.D. this way."

When he had finished spraying he turned to me and said with a noticeable grin, "Good thing I carry this around to make...make my mark, hey, Jon 155?"

"You remember me."

"Sure I remember you. You're the guy who was going to pay me four

mil...million for a ship. That's not a number that's easy to forget."

The sound of the canines drew much closer then, and Joe The Lizard's expression altered measurably.

"We can drool over this reunion later. Right now we need to delete in a hurry. Put that pea...pea...pea-shooter away and follow me."

He moved off through an underground passageway and I did as he said. The enclosure had the musky smell of age and everything I touched was thick with dust. There was no light to guide our way. However, the human's faint footfalls created echoes that were easy for me to follow. Eventually we came to a rusted ladder that led upward. Without pausing, Joe The Lizard began climbing.

His ascension was as smooth as any primate's, and he moved with an assuredness that spoke of a familiarity with his environment. I, meanwhile, found the climb troublesome. I felt ill at ease dangling from encrusted rungs I was sure would collapse at any moment under the burden of my weight.

It was a long climb and when I reached the top of the ladder I was once again able to make out dim shapes in the darkness. What light there was shone through several windows of what appeared to be the top-most level of the structure. It was at one of those windows I saw Joe The Lizard motioning for me to join him.

I looked down and could see the bustle of P.D. activity very clearly. They were gathering their prisoners into groups, herding them into waiting vehicles. Many who appeared lifeless had been dragged out of the building and left on the ground. I could not tell if they were simply unconscious or if they had been expired.

"Looks like I won't be getting my four mil...million," said Joe The Lizard. "Not unless you're planning on taking a trip by yourself. Though I still think you owe me a finder's fee."

"Why are you here? How did you--?"

"How did I know there was going to be a big...big powwow here tonight? I hate to be the one to have to tell you this, mister gauntlet star, but...but...but your secret meeting wasn't all that secret. I heard from my people that some stoogemeyer had put the P.D. on to you. I was coming to warn you, but by the time I got here, they had the place sur...sur...surrounded. You were plain lucky to get out--even luckier I saw you."

"Why would you come to warn us?"

"Strictly business. Just trying to protect the time I invested in our little transaction. But you ama...ama...amateurs crashed it."

I turned my attention back to the bleak tableau below me. It appeared the search parties had been recalled and that the operation was coming to its conclusion.

"Do you think any others escaped?" I asked as I gazed downward.

"Not likely," replied Joe The Lizard. "A few might have gotten out and slipped by the P.D. perimeter, but not many."

I scanned the faces of the androners I could still see and recognized several of them. I saw Ben, William, Hannah, Paul, and a few others. However, I did not see the one I was looking for. I wondered what had happened to Mary, and whether she had been harmed. Then the anger hit me like a coarse wave of burning sensations. I was angry with the cruel efficiency of the P.D. I was angry with the sentries who had failed to warn us in time. I was angry with myself for failing to protect Mary. I was angry with the universe.

That is when I saw Patrick. He was not among the prisoner groups, nor on the ground with the lifeless. He was standing, talking with a small group of P.D. officers. He did not appear to be restrained in any fashion, nor under any duress. As I watched, Patrick and the P.D. officers walked away towards a vehicle. It was not the type of large vehicle used to transport prisoners, and it appeared to me that Patrick walked and talked with them more as a comrade than a captive. A trio of the officers entered the vehicle and Patrick joined them as a fourth member of the P.D. held the door.

It was only then that I began to fully comprehend what I was witnessing. It was only then that I felt the full, true force of my anger.

52

REVEREND ROBERTS

" A tortured soul must cast away the ledger of his sins and take whatever measures are necessary for redemption. Forgiveness is not automatic, it's not like throwing your dirty laundry into the refresher for 30 seconds. Your soul will not be cleansed that easily. I tell you, you must go to whatever lengths are necessary to reestablish your bond with God. Sometimes the necessities of redemption may seem like sins themselves. Think not to judge which is the lesser of two evils, for He will be your judge. Better to earn His forgiveness today for yesterday's transgressions. Contrition for today's sins and tomorrow's will--"

"Praise God, praise Nature."

I filed the script and sat back in my chair. "Access incoming. What is it Simon? I'm in the middle of going over my sermon for tomorrow's programming."

"Sorry to interrupt, Reverend. There's a church proctor here to see you, a Mr. Edgar Alaine. He declined to tell me what it's about. He says it's an urgent matter, but personal." The image of Simon's face on my screen looked as it always did--concerned and businesslike. I wondered what one of the church's spiritual investigators would want with me. Perhaps one of my parishioners had gone astray.

"Certainly, Simon, send him in."

He was a smallish man, who struck me as fastidiously groomed, but with an investigator's eyes--eyes that swept the interior of my office.

"Praise God, Reverend."

"Praise Nature, Proctor Alaine is it?"

"Brother Alaine will suffice, Reverend. Thank you for taking the time to see me."

"Surely, the church's business is my business."

"That's good to hear, Reverend," he said as he pulled a file of hard copy from a case he carried. "I'm afraid I have uncovered some disturbing facts that could have deleterious repercussions for the church."

"Truly? That sounds rather ominous, Brother Alaine. Tell me--"

"Praise God, praise Nature."

The chime of Simon's digicon interrupted me. "Excuse me a moment, Brother.

"Access incoming. Yes, Simon, what is it?"

"The circuit you told me to be expecting earlier has come through. Do you wish to take it?"

"Yes. Send it through.

"I'm sorry, Brother Alaine, I must take this incoming message. If you would be good enough to wait outside for me, we can continue in a minute."

I could tell he didn't care for being shuttled back out the door, but he complied.

"Certainly, Reverend. I'll be right outside."

When the door closed I gave the command to access the connection from Lieutenant Pacheko, and put it in security mode.

"Praise--"

"Yes, Brother Pacheko, have you some word for me?"

"We've just completed our rogue sweep, Reverend. Sixty-three andrones were taken into custody, nine others were killed while attempting to resist."

"Sounds like a complete night's work, Brother. Tell me, did the sweep uncover any of the Mary units I asked about?"

"It did. One of the Mary units is among those in custody, designation 79. I scanned the abdominal barcode myself."

Mary 79 was one of mine. One of the remaining units I had to eradicate. She might be scheduled for expiration and she might not. Even if she was, I could not take the chance that her body might be used for scientific study. In those black days I had used the bodies of many expired drones myself. If my calculations were correct, the date of conception had already arrived. An examination of her corpse might reveal my sins to the world.

"I need you to do one more thing for me, Brother Pacheko. It's a very important thing for the church or I would not ask."

"Whatever I can do, Reverend, you know I will."

"I'm glad to hear that, Brother. It warms my heart to hear of such staunch faith and devotion. What I need you to do is to transfer the Mary unit to my custody, preferably without any official notation of the transfer."

"That could be difficult, Reverend. All of the rogues must be processed and examined first. Then their official disposition and/or ownership must be determined."

"I know what I'm asking is irregular, Brother. I'd rather not have to go through official channels. You see, this particular drone could prove to be an embarrassment to the church. I know that's something neither you nor I nor God wants."

"I don't know...."

"The Almighty is calling to you, Brother Pacheko, don't ignore Him. It should be a simple matter for someone of your rank to remove the unit in question from the others and transport her yourself. Deliver her to me, tonight, and then you'll be done with it. No one need know. They'll simply assume they miscounted their prisoners. Among several dozen, she's not likely to be missed. Can I count on you, Brother? Can *He* count on you?"

"Yes, Reverend. I'll find a way to take care of it."

"Good. I knew your faith was strong. God will reward you, Brother."

"Where should I take the drone, Reverend?"

"You still worship at the tabernacle adjacent to my offices, don't you?"

"Yes, Reverend."

"Please bring the Mary unit to the church. I'll go there now and expect you within the hour."

"Of course, Reverend. I'll be there as soon as I can."

"Go with God, Brother.

"Praise God."

"Praise Nature. Delete access."

I was confident the lieutenant would find a way to deliver Mary 79 to me, and then there would be only one drone remaining. But I knew I needed a plan. One that would protect me even if the lieutenant's unauthorized transfer was discovered.

"Personal file, authorization ryan-zero-zero-one," I found Drake's satphone code and made the connection.

"Drake," he answered, though I could barely hear him due to some loud *crunching* sounds. "Who's it?"

"It's Reverend Roberts. I need your services, Mr. Drake. Would you join me immediately please?"

"Can't do nuttin 'mediate, Your Reverendship. Eatin' some burgers right now."

"Please finishing eating quickly and join me at the tabernacle next to my offices."

"Taber-what?"

"The tabernacle, the church. You know, the large structure near where we first met."

"Yeah, memberin' now. Whatcha want?"

"I've located one of the remaining drones on your list and I'll need you to take care of her."

"Done my work for me, eh, Your Reverendship? Dat don't mean less credit does it?"

"No, you'll still be paid everything I promised."

"Good deal. See you dere, just as soon as finish eats."

"All right, Mr. Drake. I'll expect you soon."

53
JON

I found the tracking device where Michael had cached it, along with an arsenal of weapons. I reloaded my own and selected another. Joe The Lizard had guided me through the P.D. cordon and even offered his assistance. Though I thanked him, I declined his aid. This was a war we had to fight and win for ourselves. Fight and win, or lose and face the oblivion of death. But there was at least one other who would precede me into that nothingness. I activated the tracker and began coding-in Patrick's implant frequency.

Even as I finished entering the code I began reconsidering my plan of action. Rationally, I knew this was not the time to avenge my comrades. Patrick would suffer for his treachery. That moment would come later. I must first gauge the feasibility of rescuing those who had been captured. Even if I could not free all of them, it was possible that at least a few might be liberated.

Then I was struck by a wave of emotion. It was an erratic sensation, one I believe humans refer to as guilt. I felt that guilt, because I accepted responsibility for the assault on the conclave, and because I realized my prime concern was for Mary. Thinking only of her safety was not appropriate. There were scores of others who deserved my concern, my efforts. However, I could not stop thinking about Mary. I could not prevent myself from wondering if she had been injured and what might become of her.

My inner struggle was mercifully disrupted by the sound of approaching footfalls. I wheeled around and aimed each of my weapons toward the approach.

"Jon!" It was Michael, and with him were Chad, Ann, and another I did not know. "Jon, you got out."

"As did you."

"Ann and I arrived at the conclave late. The P.D. were already beginning to move into the building. There was nothing we could do to warn you. We could only watch from a distance, until we saw Chad and Jason escape," said Michael, gesturing toward his other two companions.

"We escaped in the initial confusion as you must have," said

Chad. "We were fortunate."

"Now what do we do?" wondered Ann.

"We attempt to free as many of our brethren as we can. Arm yourselves. I want to return to conclave site before all of our comrades are transported."

"I must disagree," said Chad. "Any such attempt would be foolhardy. The captive andrones are most certainly to be kept under heavy guard. We could never succeed."

"You are the one who spoke at the conclave of the necessity of killing humans, using violence to accomplish our goals," I replied. "Now you say to fight would be foolhardy?"

"An ill-considered frontal assault would not accomplish anything," said Chad. "We must plan first, organize, increase our numbers."

"He is correct," said Michael. "It would not be possible for the five of us to succeed in a rescue."

"We will not know what is possible until we discover where they are being taken and how they are being guarded," I argued. "I intend to locate Mary, free her and any others I can. You may join me or not." I secured my weapons and the tracker and walked to the door. None of them moved to follow.

"Do not go, Jon," said Ann. "We need you to lead us. Do not deprive us of your abilities in a vain attempt to rescue a single comrade. There are many others who will need you. You told us many times that the group is more important than any individual."

"You are right, Ann, that is what I said. Perhaps I was not the correct choice for a leader. You should select a new leader now. My concern, my...feelings for Mary have become personal. Though it may not be for the good of all, it is something I must do. I understand if you choose not to come with me."

"You always told us to think for ourselves, to be individuals," said Michael.

"Then I can be satisfied that I was able to accomplish something."

I turned and made my way outside to our vehicle. I moved with a purpose, resolute in my intentions, entering Mary's implant code into the tracker as I went. I did not understand the force that drove me, I only knew that in my mind I could see her face and hear the sound of her voice. Perhaps this was the "love" humans wrote of so often.

54

EDGAR

God forgive me, but I became increasingly annoyed waiting for the reverend. I had been staring at his office decor and found its new age ambiance distasteful. The feel of the chair I sat on, the coloration of the walls, the metallic glint of the fixtures, all reeked of technology. It may all have been ecologically sacrosanct, but it did not give that appearance.

When he finally opened his office door he had the audacity to smile.

"I'm sorry for the delay, Brother Alaine. If you would step back into my office, we may continue."

I got up from my seat and the reverend turned to speak to his secretary.

"Simon, do a quick check of the solar cell levels for me and then you may go home. I won't need you any more tonight."

"Are you sure, Reverend. I can stay if you--"

"No, no, you've been working hard. You need the rest."

"Excuse me for saying so, Reverend," the secretary offered boldly, "but you're the one who needs the rest."

"Always watching out for me, eh, Simon?" Reverend Roberts turned to me. "Simon is a genuine blessing from God. I don't know what I would do without him.

"Do as I say now, Simon. Go home. Don't worry, I'll be retiring to my prayers as soon as I finish my business with Proctor Alaine."

"All right, Reverend," replied his secretary uncertainly, "I'll see you in the morning."

Reverend Roberts closed the door behind us and walked back around his desk as I sat down. I activated my recorder without making mention of it and felt a twinge of guilt for doing so in the presence of a reverend.

"So, Brother Alaine, what are these 'disturbing facts' you were going to tell me about?"

"I'm afraid they concern you, Reverend. That is your activities before you joined the church." Despite his sins, I had to admire the man. His self-control did not waver for an instant, though he must have realized at that moment that I had uncovered his secret past. "I was commissioned by the Council of Elders to investigate your background. The council wanted to be certain, because of your current high profile, that there was nothing that could come to light which would reflect poorly on the church."

"And what poor reflections did you find, Brother Alaine?"

"I know that your previous name was Jared Ryan and that you were a biogeneticist for the Androtech Corporation. I know that you conducted unauthorized experiments having to do with the genetic makeup of andrones, and that you were sexually involved with one of those andrones. I know that androne gave birth to your child. I also know you've hired a man to expire certain andrones."

He stood there looking at me, not having bothered to take his seat. I knew his mind must be working frantically, but his eyes never revealed anything was amiss.

"You know so much, Proctor Alaine, yet you know so little. Tell me, what was the council's reaction to your findings?"

"To my knowledge, the full council knows nothing of this. I have informed Reverend Sukumu of some details, however, before I completed my report to him, I wanted to provide you with the opportunity to confess your past sins. Cooperation on your part would make it unnecessary for any disruption of your son's life."

This finally provoked him, though his reaction was so slight only my trained eyes would have noticed.

"You should be careful, Brother. Have you heard of the story about the boy who cried wolf? You should be certain of your facts before you go running to the council crying 'demon!'"

"I appreciate your guidance in this matter, Reverend. Of course I'm sure you've heard the parable of the wolf in sheep's clothing?"

He started to speak, then hesitated a moment. "Come with me, Brother Alaine," he said as if he had reached a decision. "Walk with me to my tabernacle and I'll tell you everything."

Without waiting for a reply, the reverend led the way out of his office and I followed, a step to the side and slightly behind. We proceeded down a long stairwell, and I was heedful of touching every fourth step with both feet.

"As you know," he began as we descended the stairs, "my given name is Jared Ryan. I took the name Jackson Roberts when I decided to enter the church and begin a new life. I made up the stories about being a thief and a drug addict to conceal my true sins. But I repented those sins, renounced my previous beliefs, and devoted myself to God. I found the church to be a haven from the complicated thoughts that haunted me, and my Jeserite brothers the perfect spiritual guides.

"I know now," he continued, "that my work at Androtech violated God's law. I want you to understand, Brother Alaine, that my only desire has been to prevent my past mistakes from doing any harm to the church."

"I understand that, Reverend," I said as we reached the end of the stairway and he led me down a narrow passageway. "But tell me about your genetic experiments."

"In my fervor for scientific advancement and personal acclamation, I went beyond even the boundaries established by corporate guidelines. I wanted to create an artificial lifeform that was more human. More like man, but improved in every way possible."

We came to a door that led into the main worship area of the church. It was a fairly large tabernacle, somewhat modest in its adornments, though spacious, with both a ground floor and balcony for worshippers. The reverend halted upon entering and looked slowly around him, as if recalling better days.

"It's been a long time since I spread the word of God in this sacred place. I've been so consumed by my campaign that I...." He paused, then began again as if he were speaking not to me, but to himself. "I wonder if I should end my campaign? Give up my quest to become senator and return to ministering to my own flock.

"No. God's needs are greater than my own. He knows the power of the senate seat means more power for the church. I must sacrifice my own desires for His greater good. His will be done."

Just then a *rapping* sound came from the rear of the church. Reverend Roberts walked towards the congregational doors as if he were expecting someone.

"Please wait here a moment, Brother," he said without looking back.

I remained in place and prayed to God to give me the strength to suffer another interruption.

When he opened one of the doors I could see two figures. One wore the uniform of the P.D., the other was a woman. "Lieutenant, I praise God for your efficiency," said Reverend Roberts as he closed the door behind him.

55

MARY

When I awoke I was alone, confined in a metal cage. All I could remember were the explosive sounds that had interrupted the conclave, the smoke, and my attempts to find Jon in the resulting chaos. I was struck by something from behind and passed into unconsciousness.

The freedom I had tasted now seemed but a fine-spun memory. My incarceration was a sour dose of something more substantial. I felt a constriction in my throat that made breathing difficult. The confinement was having an effect on me beyond simply restricting my movements. I struggled to maintain logic and reason.

Before I could begin to cope with the psychological aspects of my detention, a member of the P.D. removed me from my cell and locked me inside the rear of his vehicle. I could only speculate what had happened to the others, and to Jon. It was apparent the authorities had discovered the site of our conclave, and I presumed violence must have ensued when they attempted to restrain my comrades. I knew Jon would not surrender without a fight. I hoped it had not meant his death.

I wondered what had happened to the others who must surely have been captured, and why I was being held alone. When, after a brief trip, the vehicle stopped, the P.D. man escorted me into a large building embellished with the symbol of a crucifix over its entrance. We went inside the outer doors only to be faced with an inner set. My custodian struck the massive doors with his fist three times.

Within seconds the door was opened by a man I instantly recognized. "Lieutenant, I praise God for your efficiency."

I had seen him on the Net many times. Reverend Jackson Roberts was a tall man. Not large in the physical sense that Jon was, yet somehow still imposing and almost regal in his bearing. He looked at me and I watched as the stern resolve in his eyes faltered. He stared as if unable to turn his gaze away.

"Reverend?" said the P.D. man, attempting to gain his attention. "Reverend, are you all right?"

"Yes, yes, excuse me," he said without taking his eyes from me.

"For a moment I...you look just like her. You could *be* her. Only she wore her hair different somehow." Then he regained his poise. "This is the house of God, Lieutenant. Please remove her restraints."

"If you say so, Reverend," answered the P.D. man. "Do you want me to stay, in case--"

"That won't be necessary. I thank you for your service. God thanks you for your faith."

"Praise God, Reverend."

"Praise Nature."

Without another word, Reverend Roberts opened the door and motioned that I should enter. The P.D. man waited until I complied and then turned to leave. Inside was another man, this one unfamiliar. He stood in an aisle created by row upon row of austere benches. I had glimpsed scenes from such a room during the reverend's macrocasts. I recalled the references and realized this was one of his tabernacles.

"Proctor Edgar Alaine, meet Mary 79. That is your designation, isn't it, my child?"

I nodded in the affirmative and responded, "You're the Reverend Jackson Roberts."

"Yes I am. How do you know me?" His question was phrased with suspicious overtones.

"I've seen your macrocasts on the Net."

"Oh," he said as if it were not the reply he expected. "Then my notoriety precedes me."

"Is this one of your creations?" asked the man he had identified as Proctor Edgar Alaine.

"Yes, she is," responded the reverend, and I realized they were referring to me.

"What do you mean?" I asked.

"I was about to explain, so--" A loud noise reverberated from behind us, interrupting Reverend Roberts. We turned and saw a huge, shabby-looking man with an excess of hair push through the door, walking as though his leg were injured in some way. He had hold of a much smaller man, gripping a handful of his clothing and holding him up so his feet were off the ground.

I was struck then by a startling revelation. I recognized the man as the one who had tried to kill me before I went rogue.

"Found dis rat snoopin' outside, Your Reverendship," said the burly man.

"Well, Mr. Stone," said Reverend Roberts, acknowledging the man who was dangling in the air. "Still looking for a story?"

"Hey, let go! I've got a legal right to pursue higher ratings."

"What do you want wit him, Your Reverendship?"

"Release him. I've got the story of a lifetime for you, Mr. Stone. Would you like to stay and hear it?"

"Sure," responded Stone, "just call off your mongrel."

"You'll have to get rid of your camera though, if you want to stay."

"My cam's my lifeblood, Reverend, you know that." The little man wore what I recalled was designated a "shouldercam." It was tiny thing, smaller than my fist and mounted next to his head.

"I'm sorry, Mr. Stone, no pictures for this story. Mr. Drake, would you get rid of the camera please."

The one he called Drake grabbed the camera with one hand and ripped it free. "Told you 'fore, not mister, just Drake!" He then tossed it across the room where it collided violently with a wall and splintered into several pieces.

"Hey!" exclaimed Stone. "That's an expensive piece of tech!"

"Reverend, we can't continue our discussion with all these people here," said the first man. "Especially a Net reporter. We can still keep this within the church."

"Why? I have nothing to hide," replied Reverend Roberts. "It will be better this way, trust me, Brother."

"See you got dat droney you wanted me tuh find, Your Reverendship. Want me tuh take care'a her now?"

"Not yet. First, go back outside and look around to see if anyone else is about. I don't want any more surprises.

Drake looked at me as if he were contemplating some future action, then limped back outside.

"Now, Mr. Stone," continued the reverend, "Proctor Alaine here, an investigator for the hierarchy of my own church, has accused me of falsifying official documents, illegal genetic experiments, an illicit sexual union, and financing unsanctioned expirations. Sound like a story to you?"

"Sounds like every hour on the hour, Reverend."

"Reverend Roberts, I must protest! This is a church matter. You can't--"

"Silence, Brother!" bellowed Reverend Roberts. "You exist here and now only by my grace," he said threateningly. I wasn't sure what he meant by that statement. Proctor Alaine appeared disconcerted by it as well. "All of you sit, or I'll have Mr. Drake come back in here and help you."

Reverend Roberts took two steps up towards the pulpit and turned to face us. The other two men sat down in the first row of benches and I decided to comply as well.

"Now, I was answering Brother Alaine's accusations. Mr. Stone, you will have to follow along as best you can. Suffice to say, all of his allegations are true, as far as they go. The experiments I conducted under the auspices of Androtech, when I was employed there years ago, were designed to develop a form of artificial life that was more human and less androne. In doing so, I created drones, both male and female, that were capable of reproduction."

"You mean they could have babies just like humans?"

"Yes, Mr. Stone, *just* like humans."

"It was one of these female drones you had sexual relations with, leading to the birth of a child, was it not, Reverend?"

"The details of my relationship are personal, Proctor Alaine. I will not discuss them," the reverend said curtly. "I *will* tell you that your investigation did not uncover my greatest scientific accomplishment. I went one step further. I created female andrones that were born pregnant."

"What?!"

"How is that possible?"

I was astounded as the two humans. I didn't fully understand why the reverend would be involved in genetic experiments on andrones. Even so, his claims seemed outlandish.

"Implanting the fertilized ovum was the easy part," Reverend Roberts continued. "Much more difficult was developing the genetic coding to keep it dormant. I settled on a period of 60 months. The genetic codes of these females were designed with a sort of time-release. Approximately five years from the time of extrication, the fertilized ovum would be released into the womb, where, unlike its mother, it would undergo a normal human gestation of about nine months.

"This Mary unit," he said pointing to me, "is one of the special prototypes I created. In fact, though I don't have access to my records, I believe her cycle of conception has already begun."

I tried to reason out what he was saying. Could it be true? Was I carrying a child that he had planted inside me? Such a thing seemed inconceivable.

"These special drones were designed so they could not be distinguished from any others. There were no visible effects of menstruation. Their bodies were designed to efficiently recycle the nutrients of the uterine lining instead of purging it."

"This is fantastic, Reverend," spoke up Stone. "How did you...I mean somehow you had to fertilized the eggs. Who--?"

"Isn't it obvious? All I cared about was scientific advancement and my own prestige. I know now what I did was a sin in the eyes of God, but I did not stop to consider the consequences then. I wanted to create life in my own image, so I used my own genetic material to fertilize the eggs." Reverend Roberts turned to look at me then, staring intently as he spoke. "The embryo you carry, my child, is not only yours, it's also mine."

"Reverend, what you're describing," the man Alaine hesitated as if he were having a difficult time formulating the words, "what you're talking about is an artificial virgin birth."

"Yes, I know. It wasn't until a personal tragedy turned me to the church and I began to see the wisdom of His teachings that I realized the sacrilege I had committed. That is the cross I bear, and why I have dedicated myself to doing His work. I know I will never be able to atone for such a shameful affront to God, but I must strive to regardless. After all, from sin comes all good things."

I stood up then. "Why did you have me brought here?" I inquired, still confused by these revelations. "Do you intend to conduct further experiments?"

"No, my child, I no longer practice the evils of science. I am a man of God. I brought you here to put an end to your existence. It will not balance my ledger in His book, but one must take the first step before he can take the second."

"Does your god not consider murder a sin?" I questioned him.

"Expiration is not murder before God's law or man's, my child. You are a soulless creature, a mechanism of man. Only God can create a being with a soul, and I created you. I gave you life, and now I must take it away."

"Why are you telling me this?" asked Stone. "Is this some sort of confession?"

"Yes, I guess it is, Mr. Stone."

"Reverend, again I must protest."

"Do not trouble yourself, Brother Alaine, God's wisdom will prevail. The church will be protected."

"Mary!" I turned and saw Jon striding toward me, the weapon in his hand trained on the reverend.

"Jon, how did you--?"

"We have no time to talk now," he said, silencing me. "We must go quickly."

"You're Jon 155," spoke up Stone. "The world's most famous drone gone rogue. This story keeps getting better and better."

"Come, Mary," Jon said to me, ignoring the humans.

I reacted as quickly as my body would respond, but before I could take a second step, I heard the *crack* of a weapon being fired and saw a spray of blood burst from Jon's arm. The force of the projectile spun him around and knocked his own weapon from his hand. Jon clutched the wound with his hand in an attempt to stop the flow of blood, but it seeped through his fingers. I looked and realized it was the one called Drake who had fired on Jon.

"What's we got here? 'Nother droney? What now, Your Reverendship?"

Now," responded Reverend Roberts, "we put an end to this. In fact, this will be even more convincing than my original plan. Pick up the androne's weapon."

"You, droney," said Drake, pointing his weapon at Jon, "move dere next tuh your dronette."

Jon complied and I instinctively reached out a hand in a futile attempt to comfort him. Drake, meanwhile, stooped to retrieve Jon's weapon, but kept his eyes focused on us.

"Reverend, this has all gone too far," said Proctor Alaine. "I can only imagine what course of action the Council of Elders will take when I file my report."

"I'm afraid you won't be able to file your report, Brother."

"What do you mean?"

"I mean, for the good of the church, what I have confessed here tonight will not leave this holy tabernacle. I'm certain as a loyal Jeserite you understand sacrifice. I'm sure you will be willing tender your life as an offering to God."

"Reverend, you can't possibly--"

"God forgive me, Brother Alaine, I'm afraid I must ask Mr. Drake, excuse me, I must ask *Drake* to send you to your heavenly reward a bit earlier than you might have expected."

I watched intently as the emotions surfaced and began to color the faces of the four humans in the room. Fear crept into the expressions of Stone and Proctor Alaine. Drake seemed unsure, as if he were attempting to formulate a question. The reverend was resolute.

Jon watched too, but I realized his attention was divided. He had lowered his uninjured arm and was slowly reaching inside his coat where I glimpsed another weapon. I tensed for what was about to come.

56

JERI

My decision to attend the gathering of rogues had proven unwise. That I was able to escape, I attributed to my training in P.D. tactics. I had remained in the vicinity and watched as the rogues were transported in groups from the scene. When a single rogue was escorted into a separate vehicle, I became curious.

I moved close enough to recognize the rogue as the Mary unit I had previously pursued. I was certain she was the same Mary unit who had been in the company of Zachariah Sturzinski, the human I had killed, even though her implant frequency had apparently been altered. I activated my trace sensor and locked it onto the new frequency. When the vehicle departed, I followed. There was no methodology behind my decision. My rationale was unclear. I had traced the Mary unit before with calamitous results. Now, however, my intentions had been altered.

I surreptitiously made my way into the structure where she had been taken, easing myself into an alcove above the main chamber. There were four humans inside, as well as another androne. He was the same one who spoke at the rogue gathering before the P.D. moved in. I had recognized him then as Jon 155, a gauntlet player of some renown before he went rogue.

I listened to what those below me were saying, but I did not fully comprehend what was occurring. However, it was obvious the conversational exchange between the humans was becoming heated. One identified as "Reverend" appeared to be in command of the situation, but two others were taking exception with something he had said.

"You, Mr. Stone. I know nothing of your religious beliefs, but I hope God is prepared to receive you."

"Hey, wait a minute now, Reverend. Let's not go totally offline here. I'm sure we can talk about this. This could all be off the record."

"I'm afraid there'll be no more talk, Mr. Stone. You see, I've decided to take this opportunity to rid myself of your annoying journalistic presence as well as the more troubling investigation being conducted by my own brothers."

"If you kill us, you'll be the obvious suspect, Reverend," said the small human. "You'll be in a worse position than you are now."

"I don't think so, Mr. Stone. I will report that you, Proctor Alaine, and myself were attacked by a group of rogues. I'll say you pulled out a weapon and killed these two rogues before you yourself were gunned down and the other rogues fled. I'll have Drake arrange his weapon so that it looks as if you fired it. A muckraker in life, you'll be a hero in death, Mr. Stone."

"Reverend, you can't," said the other man. "You may deceive the authorities, but God will know what you have done."

"And he will forgive me, Brother. For what I do is for the greater good. It is more important than my own deliverance."

"You're insane."

"I don't think so, Brother. Drake," commanded Reverend, "dispose of the drones and then use the rogue's weapon on these two."

"Don't mind doin' duh droneys, but killing dese two's gonna cost you extra."

"Yes, yes, of course. Just do as I say."

Suddenly, in a movement so fast I do not know if I could have responded, Jon 155 pulled a weapon from his garment and fired at the fourth human. Unfortunately for the androne, his proficiency with the weapon was lacking. He missed his target and the large human identified as "Drake" returned fire, striking the Jon unit several times. He fell to the floor and his wounds left no doubt of his pending expiration.

Reverend did not react, but the other two humans took cover until the weapons fired had ceased. The Mary unit was rendered immobile by the unexpectedness of what had occurred. She simply gazed down upon the fallen form of the androne.

"Your time has come, Mary 79," spoke up Reverend, cutting through the silence that supplanted the echo of weapons fire. "Embrace death, do not fear it. Only God is immortal."

The Drake human approached Mary 79, taking aim. I reacted-- not based on my training, but on some inner compulsion I could not define. I raised my own weapon even as I contemplated the implications of what I was considering. I knew the reasoning was faulty. The idea ran counter to both my primary and secondary commands. She was a rogue, consigned for expiration, and there was no legal justification for any action on my part except to propagate that expiration.

When the moment arrived, I did not hesitate. My reaction was unambiguous. I took aim and fired several bursts.

The shots were on target and the Drake human reeled even as he attempted to bring his weapon to bear on my position. He fired several shots before he hit the floor, but each went astray. One struck the human who I had not yet identified.

"I've been shot! I'm bleeding! It's all over me!" he wailed in terror. "Get it off! Get it off!"

The human I had taken down was not dead yet. He fired again and the shot ricocheted centimeters from me. I returned fire and this time the projectiles put an end to his resistance. The expression frozen on the Drake human's face seemed to be that of surprise.

The realization that I had once again terminated a human life caused me to hesitate. This time the act had not been an accident, but by design. I had considered and disregarded the wrongness of it, and had proceeded with indifference to the consequences. At that moment I perceived sensations that I could only define as both apprehension and empowerment.

During the interim of my hesitation the Reverend human had moved closer to his confederate. When the opportunity presented itself, he seized one of the man's weapons and began firing up into the alcove where I had taken refuge. I was forced to cease my self-examination and seek cover. When he moved to a new location and continued to fire, I realized my position was untenable. From my vantage point I could see the Mary unit on her knees next to the fallen androne. His weapon lay near her, but she seemed oblivious to it.

Another shot missed me, so I began retreating down the stairs. I had almost reached the door at the bottom of the stairwell when I heard the Reverend human say, "This is a difficult thing for me to do. You remind me so much of her. However, I have no choice." I was about to throw open the door to the main chamber when I heard a weapon discharge.

I pushed open the door and swept the room with my own weapon. I was faced with no immediate threat. I entered and saw the Mary unit standing over Reverend's body. Her hand loosely gripped the weapon that had belonged to her androne companion.

The Stone human emerged from where he had taken shelter, while the wounded human continued to bemoan his injuries, though with less energy than he had previously. Mary 79 looked at me and then back down at Reverend. The weapon slipped from her fingers and fell to the floor. With a blank expression rigid on her face, she walked back to where the Jon unit lay and kneeled over him.

"I've got it!" said Stone enthusiastically as he unfastened a bit of his clothing. His words still quivered with nervousness. He examined a small device implanted in his solar plexus region. The visible portion of the implant had been disguised as a button. I eventually deduced it must have been a camplant, concealed to record events covertly. "It's okay!" he exclaimed after finding no damage. "I've got it. Video, audio, everything! Talk about a ratings riser." He then seemed to notice for the first time the wailings of the bleeding human. "Hey, hold on, buddy, I'll get help." He pulled a mobile comdat from his trousers and activated it.

I turned my attention back to the Mary unit. She had taken the lifeless head of Jon 155 and placed it across her lap. One of her hands held the expired unit while the other covered her own face.

She was obviously affected by the expiration of this androne. I did not understand the mechanics of it, though I knew the word was "grief." I knew its definition, but I did not have the capacity to grieve. I wondered how Mary 79 had acquired it. She lowered her hand to wipe a streak of blood from the Jon unit's forehead and then, to my amazement, I saw a teardrop escape from one of her eyes and roll down across her cheek. It was followed by a second, then a third.

Until that moment, I had not known that andro007nes could cry.

57

EDGAR

It took several days of recuperation for me to recover from my wound. The doctors did their best to assure me my condition wasn't serious, but then they weren't the ones covered in their own blood. I can't possibly relate the absolute horror of seeing, of feeling that sticky bodily fluid spurting scarlet stains all over my hands, all over my clothes. It was hygienic bedlam, truly a nightmare come to life.

However, the injury itself proved to be secondary. My worst fears were realized when I discovered how unsanitary and disorganized the medical facility was. There were diseased people everywhere, a veritable proliferation of infectious organisms, and I can tell you the sterilization procedures left much to be desired. The trial of living for so many days under such conditions led me to increase the frequency of visits to my therapist for several months afterwards.

If that trauma alone wasn't enough, Reverend Sukumu was less than pleased with my inability to contain the results of my investigation. Fortunately, he was preoccupied with too many volatile issues to focus much of his ire onto me.

The authorities had recovered my recorder and, along with the stories and surreptitious video of that reporter, Gordon Stone, the evidence had left little room for political maneuvering. Public outcry forced Androtech to cease production of all andro333nes, and the corporation's stock plummeted accordingly. LEDA gained a voice it had not previously had. Almost overnight, supporters of androne rights began to appear with startling regularity all over the Net.

The church, praise God, suffered only mild repercussions. The Council of Elders quickly disavowed any knowledge of Reverend Roberts' illicit history and other clandestine activities, and conducted a post-mortem excommunication. The church even softened its position on drones already in existence, philosophically aligning itself with LEDA. Actually, it was a little more than just a softening, it was a complete meltdown.

Though the tide of public opinion was still in a state of flux, Senator Vargas seized the moment and came out in complete support of androne rights. Of course the spin was that he had always held that position, and that recent events only reinforced what he had been saying all along. With Reverend Roberts no longer a viable candidate, Vargas' reelection was a certainty.

Much to the displeasure of the Council of Elders, as well as the leaders of other sects, talking heads all over the Net began referring to the androne unit Mary 79 as the "Virgin Mary." The drone herself had disappeared from public view, but her image and the details of her existence had been popularized and replayed ad nauseam after Stone's report.

For my own part, I prayed for an extended period of convalescence before the church called upon me in an official capacity again. I found the lack of immediate direction disturbingly alluring. I wondered if recent events had stimulated my capacity to withstand disorder. There's no doubt the entire episode had proved to be a traumatic test of my faith. But I knew, regardless of the outcome, His will had been done, as it always would be.

58

MARY

I had plenty of time to think after I boarded the hydrorail. As had been the case since that fateful and fatal night in the tabernacle of Reverend Jackson Roberts, the androne Jeri was at my side. The neutral tracer, who had once tried to expire me, was now my constant companion--a self-appointed bodyguard. Jeri's androne attributes were difficult to disguise, so we sat in the railcar designated for drones. My scorn for such a necessity had grown. I was determined to put an end to it.

During the course of its quest to track me, Jeri had undergone a philosophical transformation that I still didn't completely comprehend, despite its attempts to explain. I believe, more than anything else, its ability to overcome its training, its programming, signifies hope for all dronekind.

My new relationship with Jeri has presented a dilemma. I don't like referring to Jeri as "it." Somehow the pronoun seems derogatory when used in reference to an intelligent being. However, I haven't discovered a substitute term that would resolve the quandary.

Jeri is the primary reason I'm still alive. Had it not violated the law and used its weapon against a human, I'd be dead. Of course, that was a law I'd violated as well. When the Jeserite reverend aimed his weapon at me, I didn't stop to ponder the many ramifications of my actions. I simply reacted as a matter of self-preservation, as I imagine any living creature would do.

Jeri and I had fled the scene, leaving behind the body of Jon, as well as the two dead humans and a third who was wailing about his wounds. The fourth man was unharmed, and as I've since learned, was a journalist for CNCNet. His reports have made public the details of Reverend Jackson Roberts' background, his experiments at Androtech, and his illegal conspiracy to finance the expiration of several andrones, all of them Mary units like myself. Those reports appear to have had a significant influence on public opinion. However, though recent netpolls favor some increase in rights for andrones, I don't believe full citizenship, with the range of freedoms it endows, will come about easily. As for what Reverend Roberts told me about myself, I've discovered he spoke the truth.

Jeri and I were able to make contact with Joe The Lizard, who relayed what he knew of the P.D.'s sweep of the rogue conclave and Jon's anger over what he perceived as Patrick's treachery. I've been unable to contact any of the other androne, and have no way of being certain if any escaped the P.D. sweep. Though Joe The Lizard understands we will be unable to complete our transaction with him, he's been helpful with some underground contacts that may prove useful until we can surface with a reasonable assurance of safety. I don't know if that day will ever come, but I intend to strive for it.

"Let me hold that for you," spoke up Jeri as he lifted the carrier from my lap. I let Jeri take it. Jekyll was inside and it *was* proving to be quite heavy. However, I think Jeri was more concerned about the life inside me than he was my own comfort. I found I enjoyed the former tracer's concern.

We'd both made an attempt to camouflage our appearances, even though the video that had been displayed on the Net didn't provide many clear pictures of Jeri. My own face had become quite prominent due to the number of times it had been used to illustrate the story of Reverend Roberts. Jeri had opposed our trip across town, saying public exposure was too dangerous. But as Zach had once told me, sometimes it was easiest to hide a thing in plain sight.

It was the thought of Zach that finally prompted me to come out of hiding. I didn't know if his access code was still viable, but I wanted to return to his cradle before his possessions were moved out. I was hoping to at least take away with me one of his books. I found myself longing for those moments I passed with Zach. He had sheltered me, taken care of me, loved me, and I missed the feelings that accompanied his presence. Being a neutral, Jeri couldn't comprehend such feelings. It knew nothing of love or lust, and was only now beginning to understand the gratification of companionship. Jeri only understood the danger I was exposing myself to, not why I was willing to take the risk.

We left the hydrorail at a junction that was only a short walk to Zach's cradle. Jeri insisted upon carrying Jekyll. Jekyll himself was none too happy about being boxed inside his carrier and toted from place to place. But Jeri and I were planning our meeting with some rogue androne Joe The Lizard had put us in contact with, and I didn't know where we would be going next.

As we drew closer to Zach's place, Jeri became more alert and wary of our environment. When we reached the door, Jeri put down Jekyll's carrier and pulled out its weapon.

"Put that back under your clothing," I told Jeri. "If someone sees it they may contact the authorities." Jeri complied, but continued to scan the corridor in both directions. "Wait out here. It won't take me long."

I turned to the door and said as clearly as I could, "Open says me, one, two, three."

The door slid open without hesitation and after I entered it closed automatically behind me. Everything seemed as it had been the last time Zach and I were there, but so much had happened since then, I couldn't be certain. Then I heard a noise in the bedroom. Before I could react, the bedroom door opened.

"Zach!"

Zach stood there, looking as surprised to see me as I was to see him.

"Mary! I thought you were--" He didn't get the chance to finish. I found myself rushing into his arms and pressing my lips against his. It was a kiss like no other I'd ever experienced. The sensation and its accompanying emotion transported me into a state in which my cognitive awareness was limited. I don't know if the life essences of two beings can merge, but that's what it felt like, if only for an instant.

"Zach, I saw you. You were laying there bleeding. I was certain you were dead."

"Hey, it takes more than a couple of slugs to kill off a writer who's survived dozens of scathing reviews. But the doctors say it was close there for a while."

"Oh, Zach, I shouldn't have left you there."

"What do you mean? It's a good thing you did. I don't know how you managed to get away. When I finally regained my senses and the drugs began to fade, I thought...well, I was sure you'd been expired by that tracer. They just released me last week and I've been, well I haven't felt like doing much. I've been holed-up here, trying to write a little bit and failing miserably."

"Then you haven't seen the reports on the Net?"

"I haven't really cared to look. The only time I even went onto the Net was to order a pizza. What have I missed, and what are you doing here?"

"I came to get a membit."

"A what?"

"A membit, you know, slang for memorabilia. I wanted something to remember you by."

"Now you're teaching *me* slang? Well, you won't be needing any 'bits' because you've got the real thing. That is, if you still want me."

I didn't bother to answer what seemed to me a most irrational question. Instead, I answered in a way I was sure Zach would appreciate. I kissed him again.

"Even though I thought you were dead, I haven't been able to stop thinking about you."

"Same here," he replied with a look much too serious for him. "I haven't been able to concentrate on much of anything except you." His face brightened then and he looked more like the Zach I remembered. "I guess that means there's no doubt about it anymore."

"Doubt about what?" I asked.

"There's no doubt that I love you."

This time, Zach took hold of me and initiated a kiss of his own.

He'd never used that word before to describe his feelings. Somehow, the sound of it on his lips caused a physical reaction deep inside my abdominal cavity. A tingle, a twinge, an unknown entity performing a somersault--I wasn't sure how to characterize it.

 When our lips finally parted, he said, "I didn't mean to fall in love with you, Net knows that was the furthest thing from my mind the first night I fastened eyes on you. Now I don't ever want us to be apart."

"I'd like that, Zach. I'm not sure I fully comprehend the meaning of the word, but I'm certain I love you also."

"Hell, I told you before, nobody comprehends it, and nobody can concretely describe it. Love isn't something you can break down into specific components. It's the word we use when we get that feeling we can't explain any other way. So let's not try to explain it. Let's just be together."

"I want us to be together, Zach. But there's--"

"You know what," he said, interrupting me. "We've got something in common now." He began unfastening his shirt. "Look, I've got an implant too." Indeed, there was a tiny cardiac implant protruding from his chest. "Something to power me up on a cold day. The doctors say I'll be fine as long as I go in for regular tune-ups."

"There's something I must tell you first, Zach."

"What's that?"

"There's a child growing inside of me."

"You're pregnant?" Coming directly on the heels of his admission of love, I believe the revelation was a bit unsettling for Zach. He looked stunned. "I didn't think drones could get...could reproduce."

"I've learned that I'm one of many androns who were covertly designed with that ability."

"Is it mine? Am I the father?"

"No."

"Then...who?"

"In genetic terms, I believe the father was Reverend Jackson Roberts, or Jared Ryan, as I've come to learn was his original name."

"I think I'm going to sit down."

He did, looking more perplexed than he had before. I joined him and proceeded to explain what I knew of the reverend's background, and how his unauthorized experiments with androns had culminated in his death, and Jon's.

Zach absorbed my tale in what was unusual silence for him. Only occasionally did he interject a question. He seemed to accept what I was telling him as the truth, despite some elements that must have appeared to him as implausible. When I finished, he looked very thoughtful as he ran his finger across his eyebrow several times. I found the familiar gesture reassuring.

"So Roberts claims you were born pregnant by way of his genetic goo, but for all you know, his experiment didn't work and I *could* be the father of your child."

What he said was true, though if by the unlikely happenstance that Jon was one of the male androns designed for fertility, he could also be the father. However, I felt I'd burdened Zach with enough information already. I didn't mention this third possibility.

"When it is safe, tests can be conducted to determine for sure if--"

"No. I don't want to do the tests. It doesn't matter. If we're going to be together, then I'll be the child's father. It doesn't matter who spliced and diced the genes."

"I'd like that, Zach. It would be wonderful if the child had you for a father."

"So what is it? A boy or a girl?"

"I don't know. I haven't--"

"Zach darling, you have company."

"Who could that be?"

"I forgot, Zach. A friend is waiting outside with Jekyll."

"Jekyll? I wondered what happened to that fuzzball when I couldn't get hold of Amber." Zach stood up and commanded, "Door open."

The door slid open and Jeri stood there, weapon in hand. It must have deduced there was trouble because I'd taken so long to return. Upon seeing Zach, Jeri appeared to become immobile. Zach, however, reacted completely different.

"Mary, get down!"

Zach leaped towards me as if to, once again, interpose his body between mine and what he perceived as certain death. He wrestled me to the floor and began pulling me behind furnishings he undoubtedly believed would provide better protection.

"No, Zach. Jeri's my friend. It's all right."

"What? Your friend?"

I eluded Zach's protective hold and stood up. Jeri, apparently unsure now of what it had seen, and worried about my safety, had moved into the room still brandishing its weapon.

"Jeri, put your weapon away. Everything's all right. This is Zach. He thought you were still trying to expire me."

"What do you mean 'still'?" asked Zach as he stood back up. "It looks just like...is this the stoogemeyer that shot me?"

I only then realized what a traumatic revelation this must be for Zach. Jeri appeared to be similarly suffering.

"Yes, Zach. This is Jeri. Jeri is the tracer who had been assigned to expire me as well as a number of other rogues."

"What are you doing with it?!"

"Jeri's the one I told you about, who helped save me. It's undergone a change. After Jeri shot you, its psychological responses were affected, probably not unlike mine were when I went rogue."

"Glad I could be of help," replied Zach sarcastically.

"I thought I caused your death," said Jeri, only now becoming completely cognizant of what was happening.

"Don't take it too hard there, you almost did," said Zach. "And I've got the holes to prove it."

"I am sorry."

Zach stood there, apparently unaffected by Jeri's apology.

"Jeri, would you go get Jekyll?" Jeri did as I asked and I turned to Zach. "I hope you can forgive Jeri. Like all andrones, it had no choice in its training. It could only act in accordance with its orders, at least until its mind began to break free. It's not really Jeri's fault that it tried to expire me and injured you."

"Yeah, I get it," grumbled Zach. "Just don't expect me to be buying it flowers any time soon."

Jeri returned with the carrier and set it on the table.

"Jekyll, you old fuzzface you." As Zach unfastened the carrier door, Jekyll began voicing a series of excited sounds that I interpreted as signs of recognition. "I missed you too, buddy." Jekyll leaped into Zach's arms and was rewarded with a stroking that soon prompted a steady purr. The sight of their happy reunion gratified me in a way I hadn't experienced. Their joy was my joy and somehow the sensation made me feel more human than I ever had before.

59
ZACH

Okay, I know you think I almost took that "body to die for" stuff too literally. I admit, I came close--too damn close, and I've got a chunk of metal in my chest to prove it.

I guess you could say my life has done a one-80. I'm no longer the lone wordslinger, rapping out lust-in-space tales of adventure from the isolation of my cradle. Now I've got Mary to watch out for, a kid on the way, and a social revolution to fight.

You see, Mary and some of her rogue compadres have decided not to fly off to Mars or Ganymede after all. Instead, they want to change the world. Yeah, I know, that was my reaction too. She says it's a matter of looking at the bigger picture, like Ilsa. I got the reference.

I understand why they're so intent, and why nothing less than their complete freedom will satisfy them. Who knows, they might even have a chance.

The exposure of the Jeserite reverend and would-be senator has really caused an upheaval. In light of Reverend Roberts' scandalous demise, even his church is backing off its anti-androne views. It's pure politics as usual.

Mary intends to make her push while the Net is still abuzz and everyone is serkers over "the mistreatment of androns." I agree she needs to use her high visibility while she can, but Net knows all that exposure could have its downside too. Still, I like to prod her about her standing as the "Virgin Mary," especially since she can't seem to get enough lately (this pregnancy thing has really powered-up her grid). I'm not complaining.

Some of the drones even think an old hack like me might be useful. So I've been trying to write some more serious stuff-- democratic theory, social dynamics, civil rights. Except it seems I spend more time researching than writing. It was a whole lot easier when I just had to make the goo up.

Mary herself has changed, in subtle ways, but they're obvious to me. She has this poise now, this sense of purpose and humanity. I don't think any human being ever had more dignity--not that I knew a lot of dignified types. Oh yeah, and she's decided on a new name. I think "Mary Starr" has a nice ring to it.

"Zach, finish your drink so we can go." Mary walked in looking, well, looking great like she always did. Her delicate condition was only apparent to my expert eye.

"Okay, I'm ready," I said, lifting the glass to her in a mock toast. "Here's looking at you, kid."

She smiled, but only briefly. I guess she had a lot on her mind. Then she surprised me with a quick kiss.

"What's that for?"

"For luck," she said, then shrugged her shoulders. "It couldn't hurt."

She had arranged a major media engagement to be macrocast all over the Net. It was going to be her first time out in the open as a rogue, and I was worried some totally offline tracer would try to cash-in on her. She was convinced her celebrity status would protect her, and local officials had promised her amnesty and rigid security measures. I'd believe it when I saw it, but she was determined to make her move.

We left my cradle and headed for the hydrorail terminal. I convinced Mary that arriving by rail would appear more egalitarian to the masses. Actually, I just thought it was safer than pulling up in an autocab.

Of course, as usual, Jeri was right behind us. He/she, as I liked to refer to it, never strayed far from Mary's side--kind of like a loyal canine, but with brains and a ready blaster. I'd grown used to Jeri's presence and even started to like the drone. I was certainly more at ease knowing he/she was always watching Mary's back. Of course there was that one time when Mary got a little out of control and Jeri mistook her screams of passion for a brutal assault. We did our best to explain it, but Jeri's neutrality made it a tough sell. I have since opted for security locks on my bedroom door, and am trying to expedite the lease of a nearby unit that Jeri can call his/her own.

It was a beautiful day outside. I could feel a slight breeze and even thought I smelled flowers somewhere. As we neared the railway, I spotted this incredible looking redhead. She was exiting the terminal and headed our way. I tracked her movement and it was all I could do to resist the "come hither" sway of her hips. She had such finelines my eyeballs were overheating just staring at her.

Mary noticed my rather obvious gawking and smiled at me. I smiled back, realizing how lucky I was that jealousy was one human trait she hadn't picked up yet. Then I took one, last, appreciative look at the redhead. Hey, I was in love, I wasn't dead.

ABOUT THE AUTHOR

Novelist, journalist, satirist...Bruce Golden's career as a professional writer spans three decades and more genres than you can shake a pen at. A native San Diegan, Bruce worked for magazines and small newspapers as an editor, art director, columnist, and freelance writer. In the early '90s he moved to radio, where he worked as a news editor/writer, sports anchor, and feature/entertainment reporter for (at the time) San Diego's top radio station. For seven years he wrote film reviews, beginning in radio and continuing until, at one point in his life, he was writing news for radio, leaving that job in the afternoon to go write news for a TV station, and, in his spare(?) time, writing film reviews for print. He then streamlined, working as a television news producer for five years, earning a Golden Mike award to add to the one he picked up in radio along with several Society of Professional Journalist awards.

In all, Bruce published more than 200 articles and columns before deciding, at the turn of the century, to walk away from journalism and concentrate on his first love—writing speculative fiction. Since then, he's seen his short stories published more than 100 times in magazines or anthologies read across eleven different countries. Along with numerous Honorable Mention awards for his short fiction from the Speculative Literature Foundation and L. Ron Hubbard's Writers of the Future contest, he won Speculative Fiction Readers's 2003 Firebrand Fiction prize, was one of the authors selected for the Top International Horror 2003 contest, and won the 2006 JJM prize for fiction. Along with *Mortals All*, he's published two novels—*Better Than Chocolate* and *Evergreen*--and a large collection of short stories--*Dancing with the Velvet Lizard*. His new novel *Red Sky, Blue Moon* is due out soon

You can read more about Bruce's books at:
http://goldentales.tripod.com/

CPSIA information can be obtained
at www.ICGtesting.com
Printed in the USA
LVOW13s0632240517
535631LV00007B/134/P